Stone Barrington finds intrigue abroad in this sensational thriller from *New York Times* bestselling author Stuart Woods.

Stone Barrington is no stranger to schemes and deceptions of all stripes—as an attorney for premier white-shoe law firm Woodman & Weld, he's seen more than his share.

But when he travels to Europe under highly unusual circumstances, Stone finds himself at the center of a mystery that is most peculiar, even by his standards. Two unexpected invitations may be the first clues in an intricate puzzle that will lead Stone deep into the rarefied world of European ultrawealth and privilege, where billionaires rub elbows with spies, insider knowledge is traded at a premium, and murder is never too high a price to pay for a desired end. . . .

"Slick . . . Barrington [is] smooth as silk, whether making a multimillion-dollar deal, bedding attractive women, or acting heroically."—*Publishers Weekly*

PRAISE FOR THE NOVELS OF STUART WOODS

Collateral Damage

"A fast-paced thriller from beginning to end."
—*Midwest Book Review*

"Woods's blend of exciting action, sophisticated gadgetry, and last-minute heroics doesn't disappoint."
—*Publishers Weekly*

"Woods's fans won't want to miss this action-packed thriller." —*Booklist*

continued . . .

BOOKS BY STUART WOODS

FICTION

Collateral Damage[†]

Severe Clear[†]

Unnatural Acts[†]

D.C. Dead[†]

Son of Stone[†]

Bel-Air Dead[†]

Strategic Moves[†]

Santa Fe Edge[§]

Lucid Intervals[†]

Kisser[†]

Hothouse Orchid[*]

Loitering with
Intent[†]

Mounting Fears[†]

Hot Mahogany[†]

Santa Fe Dead[§]

Beverly Hills Dead

Shoot Him If He
Runs[†]

Fresh Disasters[†]

Short Straw[§]

Dark Harbor[†]

Iron Orchid[*]

Two Dollar Bill[†]

The Prince of Beverly
Hills

Reckless Abandon[†]

Capital Crimes[‡]

Dirty Work[†]

Blood Orchid[*]

The Short Forever[†]

Orchid Blues[*]

Cold Paradise[†]

L.A. Dead[†]

The Run[‡]

Worst Fears
Realized[†]

Orchid Beach[*]

Swimming to
Catalina[†]

Dead in the Water[†]

Dirt[†]

Choke

Imperfect Strangers

Heat

Dead Eyes

L.A. Times

Santa Fe Rules[§]

New York Dead[†]

Palindrome

Grass Roots[‡]

White Cargo

Deep Lie[‡]

Under the Lake

Run Before the
Wind[‡]

Chiefs[‡]

TRAVEL

A Romantic's Guide to the Country Inns of Britain and Ireland (1979)

MEMOIR

Blue Water, Green Skipper

[*]A Holly Barker Novel   [†]A Stone Barrington Novel
[‡]A Will Lee Novel   [§]An Ed Eagle Novel

UNINTENDED CONSEQUENCES

A STONE BARRINGTON NOVEL

Stuart Woods

A SIGNET BOOK

SIGNET
Published by the Penguin Group
Penguin Group (USA) LLC, 375 Hudson Street,
New York, New York 10014

USA | Canada | UK | Ireland | Australia | New Zealand | India | South Africa | China
penguin.com
A Penguin Random House Company

Published by Signet, an imprint of New American Library, a division of
Penguin Group (USA). Previously published in a G. P. Putnam's Sons edition.

First Signet Printing, December 2013

ISBN 978-0-451-41439-7

Printed in the United States of America
10 9 8 7 6 5 4 3 2 1

1

Stone Barrington dreamed terrible dreams, then he jerked awake and immediately forgot them, as he always did. He was in a small room, dimly lit by a very large digital clock, which glowed red, making the room pink. The time read 9:46.

He lifted his head from the foam rubber pillow and looked about. Walls, ceiling, steel table with two chairs, steel shutter lowered over the only window. His bladder was near bursting, and he got out of bed and wobbled over to a closed door, behind it a small bathroom. He relieved himself noisily, then turned to his left to examine himself in the small mirror over the sink. Too dark. He groped for the light switch and found it, wincing in the bright light. He could have described the image in the mirror only as haggard. He splashed cold water on his face, then looked again: just the same. On the counter next to the sink were a plastic-wrapped toothbrush, a tiny tube of toothpaste, a tiny can of shaving cream, and a disposable razor. He tried the toothbrush first, and scrubbed away the fur that coated his teeth.

The beard was hard to deal with, and he wished for electric clippers. Still, he got it scraped off, cutting himself only twice. He tried the shower next, and it worked well. He used the tiny bottle of shampoo on the soap dish next to the tiny bar of soap. He used the only towel to dry himself and noticed a flesh-colored bandage on the inside of his left elbow. He ripped it off and found two tiny wounds in the vein. Then he toweled his hair dry and brushed it back with his fingers. He got into the cheap terry robe hanging on the bathroom door, noticing that the bedroom or cell, as it might be, was now lit by weak sunlight, and a dry cleaner's plastic sleeve and a shopping bag now hung on a hook on the door. He thought he smelled food somewhere, and his stomach growled.

He walked over to the door and noticed a button on the wall next to it, with a plastic sign reading "Ring for attendant."

Attendant? Had he been involuntarily admitted to a mental hospital? He aimed a finger at the button, but a voice stopped him.

"That won't be necessary," a man said.

Stone wheeled around and found a young man dressed in green hospital scrubs seated at the table, two plastic trays heaped with eggs and bacon before him.

"Would you like some breakfast, Mr. Barrington?" the man asked, indicating the other chair.

"Thank you, yes," Stone said, taking a seat and attacking the food, which was still fairly warm. He washed eggs down with orange juice made from concentrate. "At the risk of employing a cliché," he said, "where am I?"

The man took a mouthful of eggs, chewed for a moment, and swallowed, washing it down with coffee from a foam cup. "Where do you think you are?" he asked.

"This appears to be a hospital room, and you appear to be a doctor," Stone said, peering at the plastic name tag pinned to the man's scrubs. "Dr. Keeler."

"Only your second guess was good," Keeler said, "and you cheated."

"Funny farm? Addiction treatment center?"

"Are you insane or an addict?" the doctor asked.

"Neither. I thought perhaps you thought I was one or the other, maybe both. Somebody seems to have injected me with something in my left arm." He took a sip of the awful orange juice.

"You are in the American Embassy, in Paris," the doctor replied.

Stone choked on his orange juice.

"France, not Texas."

"Thank you for making the distinction," Stone said, coughing.

"How do you feel?" the doctor asked when Stone had recovered normal breathing.

"Fuzzy around the edges," Stone replied.

"I'm not surprised. What's the last thing you remember before waking up?"

Stone thought about that. "I was at a party in my home," he said finally, "celebrating the marriage of some friends. I remember the police commissioner gave them both medals."

"Why?"

"They were both police officers who had recently behaved in a courageous manner."

"What was the date of the party?"

"Ah, the fourteenth."

"That was four days ago," he said.

Stone gulped. "I've lost four days?"

"It would appear so. You ingested or were injected with a drug called hypnotol. You may remember that it was a popular sleeping medication about eight years ago, until several people died from taking it, and some others who had taken too much suffered memory loss—usually temporary, sometimes permanent. Based on your bloodwork, I would describe the dosage you received as too much."

"Who injected me? I assume that's why I had tape on my arm."

"No, that's from drawing blood and administering an IV. If you didn't take the drug yourself, then someone probably gave you something to drink that had been doctored. The right dosage would have made you into a sort of walking, talking zombie."

"And destroyed my memory of the last four days?"

"Presumably."

"Including traveling from New York to Paris?"

"A reasonable assumption."

"How did I get to the American Embassy?"

"A kindly taxi driver picked you up at the airport but couldn't understand what you were saying, and when you passed out, he went through your wallet." He got up, went to the door, and returned with the shopping bag that had been hanging there. He reached into the bag and came up with a zippered plastic sack containing what Stone recognized as the normal contents of his pockets, including his passport and wallet, and emptied it onto the table. Keeler opened the wallet, removed a card, and handed it to Stone. It read "Holly Barker, Assistant Director of Intelligence."

"That got the attention of a marine guard at the front gate." He handed Stone a CIA ID with his picture on it. "So did this."

"Ah," Stone said.

"We've been unable to reach Ms. Barker," Keeler said. "She is away from her office at some sort of retreat."

"Retreat? That doesn't sound like Holly."

"In any case, once we had made you as comfortable as we could here and sent your blood for analysis, someone typed your name into a computer and came up with a very interesting CIA file that identified you as a consultant to the Agency, hence the ID card."

"That is correct," Stone said.

"And you are also an attorney with the New York law firm of Woodman & Weld?"

"Correct."

"Do you have any idea why you came to Paris? Had you been planning a trip?"

"No, I had not, and I have no idea why I came here."

"You had a first-class, round-trip ticket on Air France," Keeler said, "with two baggage claim stubs but no baggage. We're checking into that now."

"Thank you. Why do you have a room like this in an embassy?"

"It's actually in that part of the building dedicated to the intelligence services. Sometimes we have . . . guests."

"I see."

"The clothes you were wearing have been cleaned and pressed. Why don't you get into them, and I'll introduce you to some other people here?" He got up and left the room.

Stone got dressed.

2

Dr. Keeler returned to the little room. "Come with me," he said. Stone got into his blazer and followed.

They walked down a corridor, then into a large room divided into cubicles where men and women were at work. There seemed to be an unusually large number of monitors on their desks. They passed half a dozen glassed-in offices, then stopped at a closed door. Keeler rapped on it, then looked up at the ceiling, where a camera peered back at him. The door made a clicking noise and Keeler opened it.

They stepped into a large, comfortably furnished office where a man in his mid-forties with thick, graying hair spilling into his eyes was talking with a man and a woman. Stone reflexively appreciated that the woman was in her mid-thirties and quite beautiful.

"Mr. Barrington," Keeler said, "this is Whit Douglas, our station chief. The lady is Rose Ann Faber, our chief of analysis, and the other gentleman is Richard LaRose, who does God-knows-what around here."

Stone shook their hands, and the group moved to a seating area with a sofa and some comfortable chairs.

"How are you feeling, Mr. Barrington?" Douglas asked.

"It's Stone, please, and I'm feeling reasonably well, I guess, sort of jet-lagged."

"It's the drug," Keeler said. "Your state of consciousness for the past few days would have prevented jet lag."

"Have I really been unconscious for four days?"

"No," the doctor said, "as I mentioned before, you were walking and talking for part of the time. You probably weren't drugged until the day before yesterday."

"Why do you say that?" Stone asked.

"You would have had to be reasonably sober in order to make the decision to travel to Paris, not to mention getting through security and onto an airplane."

"But I can't remember getting on the airplane."

"The drug has obliterated four days of your memory," the doctor explained, "which may or may not return. The obliteration need not occur at the time of receiving the drug—it can work backwards and erase earlier memory, too. There have been cases where people have lost several weeks."

"We hope your memory returns," Whit Douglas said, "because we want to know how a consultant to the Agency happened to get ahold of a giant Mickey Finn, and we want to know why."

"So do I," Stone replied.

"Do you remember talking to anyone on the airplane?"

"I don't remember *being* on the airplane," Stone said. "If my memory returns, when will that start happening?"

"At any time," Keeler said. "You could start getting flashbacks immediately or in a couple of days. If you don't get anything back in that time, you're probably faced with the permanent loss of those four days."

There was a rap at the door. Douglas pressed a button on the coffee table and let in a young man, who walked across the room, Stone's airline ticket in his hand. "Mr. Barrington, we've found your luggage. It was in the tank at De Gaulle."

"Tank?"

"A pressure chamber that limits the effect of an explosion. The airlines get nervous these days when there's unclaimed baggage. Would you like the bags sent to your hotel?"

Stone thought about it. "I don't know if I have a hotel."

"Where did you stay the last time you were in Paris?" Douglas asked.

"At the Bristol, but I didn't like the location, so I don't think I would have booked in there."

"Can we book a room for you somewhere?"

"Okay, how about the Plaza Athénée?"

Douglas nodded to the young man, and he left.

Stone dug out his iPhone. "I should call my secretary," he said. "Maybe she can help with the memory." His phone was dead.

"Use the one on my desk," Douglas said. "Give the operator the number."

Stone did as he was told, and Joan, his secretary, picked up the phone.

"Woodman & Weld," she said. "Mr. Barrington's office."

"Hi, it's Stone."

"Well, where the hell have you been? Your hotel said you never checked in, Dino's on his honeymoon, and Holly has vanished."

"What hotel is that?"

"The Plaza Athénée. That's where you said you were staying."

"I had to make a detour," Stone said. "Listen, I need your help. Describe to me what I did between Dino's engagement party and right now."

Joan thought this over for a moment. "You want *me* to tell *you* what you were doing?"

"Exactly. Pretend I don't know." Stone pressed the speaker button so the others could hear.

"All right, you got to your desk late the day after the party, then you had lunch with Bill Eggers and had a meeting at the firm, then you got back here around five, and I went home."

"How about the next day?"

"The same, pretty much. With Dino gone and Holly moved out, you didn't have anybody to play with."

"And the day after that?"

"You got a call from somebody in the middle of the afternoon, then said you were going to Paris for a few days. An envelope arrived by messenger with a first-class, round-trip ticket on Air France, and a note saying a car would pick you up at seven that evening. There was no return address on the envelope. You were due into Paris at nine the next morning."

"Did I see anybody in my office?"

"No."

"Did anybody call that you didn't know?"

"No, but I was in the ladies' when the afternoon call came, and you picked up."

"Can you think of anything else? What did I do in the evenings?"

"Like I said, you didn't have anybody to play with, so I guess you dined at home alone."

"Thanks, we'll talk again later." Stone hung up and went back to the sofa. "Not much help, huh?"

"Rose Ann," Douglas said, "find out who called Stone's office in the afternoon day before yesterday."

Stone gave her his business card, and she went to the phone on Douglas's desk, then returned. "They'll have it in a few minutes," she said.

The phone rang, and Douglas picked it up and listened, then hung up. "You're booked into the Plaza Athénée. They were expecting you yesterday. We got you an upgrade."

"Thank you," Stone said. "There's something missing."

"What?"

"My briefcase. I always travel with a briefcase."

Douglas got up. "Oh, I forgot." He walked behind his desk, came back with Stone's briefcase, and handed it to him. "We couldn't open it. Three zeros didn't work."

"The CIA couldn't get into a briefcase?" Stone

said. "What's the world coming to?" He unlocked the briefcase and opened it. "Euros," he said, holding up a thick envelope containing a stack of notes secured by a rubber band.

"That reminds me," Douglas said. "We gave the cabdriver a hundred."

Stone extracted a hundred-euro note from the stack, handed it to him, then put the rest into his inside pocket with his passport. "Nothing unusual in the case," he said. "My iPad and charger, some stationery, no business papers." He closed the briefcase.

"Well, we won't keep you," Douglas said, rising.

Stone got to his feet and shook hands with everybody.

"We'd like to know if and what you start remembering," Douglas said, handing him a card. "That's my direct line and cell number. Doc, will you walk him to our side entrance? There's a car and driver waiting for you there, Stone."

"Thank you, Whit, and I thank all of you for taking me in."

Keeler led him on a short walk to an exterior door and opened it for him. "The car's through there," he said, waving Stone through the door and pointing at the walkway to a wrought-iron gate. "Right down the garden path. Call me if there's anything I can do for you."

3

The driver delivered Stone into the hands of a doorman at the Plaza Athénée who directed him to the front desk, where a man in a dark suit greeted him. "Good morning, Mr. Barrington," he said. "We were concerned about you when you didn't turn up yesterday."

"I'm sorry about that," Stone said. "I was unavoidably detained, and I couldn't call."

The man nodded and handed Stone an *International Herald Tribune*. "Would you like a paper delivered every day?"

"Yes, thank you."

"And how long will you be with us?"

"I'm not sure. I'll have to let you know."

"That will be fine. Your suite is ready."

Stone followed the bellman, who carried his briefcase, to the elevator, then to the top floor. The suite was larger than he needed and filled with sunlight. There were French doors leading to a terrace.

The bellman handed him his briefcase. "You have no other luggage, sir?"

"It's being sent from the airport," Stone said.

"We'll see that it's delivered immediately upon arrival."

The doorbell rang, and Stone opened the door. Another bellman stood there with his two cases on a luggage cart. Stone directed him to the dressing room.

"Would you like anything pressed?" the man asked as he set down the bags.

"Let me see." Stone opened the two large cases and found that everything had been removed, then stuffed in haphazardly. "Please have everything pressed but the underwear and socks," Stone said, removing suits. He noted that he was traveling with a dinner jacket, something he did only if some event at his destination would require it.

"We'll have everything back as soon as possible," the man said. Stone tipped both bellmen and closed the door behind them, then he got his charger from his briefcase and plugged in his iPhone. He sat down and had a look through the *Trib*; all the news was fresh to him. He called the front desk and asked if they had any old *Trib*s and was told no. He had just sat down again when his phone buzzed. He went to the desk, picked up the phone, and sat down. He didn't recognize the calling number.

"Hello?"

"Stone? It's Holly."

"Oh, hello. I was told you were at a retreat and couldn't be reached."

"I'm at a conference of department heads, at our training facility, the Farm," she said. "They made us turn in our cell phones, but somebody brought me a message from Whit Douglas in Paris, and he told me what had happened to you."

"Good, that saves me from having to explain it again," Stone said. "I'm afraid I don't know any more than he told you."

"No memories have returned?"

"Not yet. Can you help?"

"No. When I left you that morning I went straight to my apartment and left my luggage, then went to my office and was summoned to Fort Peary, in Virginia."

"Wait a minute, you moved your things into your apartment? Did we have a fight or something?"

"No, but it was intimated to me from the top that Langley would feel more comfortable if I weren't shacking up with you."

"That was very narrow-minded of them."

"Well, we're getting a lot of attention from the press since the thwarted bombing, and they didn't want photographs of me arriving at or leaving your house at odd hours."

"What's happened in that regard since I last saw you?"

"Well, all hell broke loose in the press," Holly said. "I only escaped the reporters because I ran back to the office immediately after Viv and I dealt with the perps, so she got all the attention, which was just fine with me and with Langley, too. They don't like our names appearing in the press under such circumstances. They're giving me the Intelligence Star medal, but then I have to give it right back. The Agency calls these decorations 'jockstrap medals' because we never get to wear them."

"Congratulations."

"How are you feeling after your ordeal?"

"I don't remember an ordeal, so I guess I feel okay."

"When are you coming home?"

"I don't know. Before I do, I'd like to at least know why I'm here."

"We'd like to know that, too. We don't like people associated with the Agency being drugged. I don't know how you escaped being interrogated by somebody, or even tortured."

"Now, there's a pleasant thought—that some-body might want to torture me."

"Well, maybe not, since they didn't. This whole thing is baffling."

"Tell me about it," Stone said wryly.

"Listen, I've got to get to my first meeting of the day. Oh, by the way, the president has made the appointment of Lance Cabot to succeed Kate Lee. Hearings start tomorrow."

"I'll look for them on TV."

"Don't bother. They'll be public only long enough for the press to get some shots. Every-thing else will be in closed sessions."

"Okay, I won't bother."

"You're sure you don't remember anything yet?"

"Not yet. Oh, when I opened my luggage I found a tuxedo, which I thought was odd, since I don't travel with one unless I know I'll need it."

"I guess you must have missed the party, then. Gotta run. I'll be back in the office in a couple of days if you need to reach me."

They said good-bye and hung up. Stone sat at the desk, staring into his briefcase. He didn't know what to do; he had no business to conduct in Paris; he had no social events to attend; he didn't know anybody in Paris, except the people he'd met at the embassy earlier. He was hungry, though, so he ordered a sandwich from room service, then he phoned Woodman & Weld's managing partner, Bill Eggers, with whom he was supposed to have met three or four days ago. Maybe Bill could shed some light on why he was in Paris.

"Mr. Eggers's office," the secretary said.

"Hi, it's Stone. Is he in yet?"

"No, and he won't be."

"Can I reach him on his cell?"

"I'm afraid not. He's fishing or shooting moose or something in the wilds of northern Maine and can't be reached."

"I'm in Paris. Ask him to call me when he returns."

"That won't be until the end of next week."

"Never mind, then." Stone hung up.

He was eating forty-five minutes later when he heard the doorbell, and an envelope was slid under his door. He put down the sandwich, opened the door—nobody there—then closed it and picked up the envelope. His name was written on it in beautiful calligraphy, but there was no return address. He opened it and extracted a card.

Dinner is at eight o'clock this evening, black tie. A car will call for you at your hotel at seven forty-five. The same calligraphy, but it was unsigned. The paper appeared to be expensive.

Stone went back to his sandwich, but the phone rang, and he had to get up again. "Hello?"

"Stone, it's Amanda Hurley. How are you?"

"Very well, thank you." Who the hell was Amanda Hurley?

"From the plane, remember?"

"Of course."

"Are we still on for dinner tomorrow night?"

"Certainly."

"I've booked a table for us at Lasserre, on Avenue Franklin Roosevelt. Do you know it?"

"I went there once some years ago."

"Is that all right, then?"

"Yes, fine."

"I've got to go somewhere for drinks first, so I'll meet you there at eight thirty."

"Good."

"The table is in your name. See you then." She hung up.

Stone went back to his sandwich, reflecting that he was now attending a dinner party at an unknown place with unknown people, then having dinner with a woman he couldn't remember.

His calendar was filling up.

4

Stone tied his black bow tie and began filling his pockets with the detritus that travels with every man: wallet, cash, keys, cell phone, linen handkerchief, comb—the works. He stopped when he picked up the envelope containing the stack of euros from his briefcase, took them out and counted them. Apart from the €100 used to pay for his taxi ride from the airport, it was mostly €200 and €500 notes. It came to €20,000, less the €100 for the cabdriver. He was shocked; he would never travel with that much cash; what were credit cards for? He locked the stack in the safe in his closet and got into his jacket.

Ten minutes later he was standing in front of the

hotel when a black Maybach, the Mercedes-built limousine, glided to a halt. The doorman tapped on the passenger-side window. "For Mr. Barrington?" He got his answer, then opened the rear door for Stone.

"Good evening, Mr. Barrington," the driver said.

"Good evening." He didn't ask where they were going or who his host might be; after all, he was supposed to know. The car moved silently down the street, and he made himself comfortable in the large, reclining seat.

Nearly half an hour later the car was in the Bois de Boulogne, the forested park on the outskirts of Paris, more than twice the size of New York's Central Park. They passed a couple of women standing next to parked cars.

"Damsels in distress?" Stone asked the driver.

"Hardly, sir, they are prostitutes, what you call in America 'hookers.' The authorities keep trying to root them out, but they always spring up again, like weeds."

"Ah," Stone said, not knowing what else to say.

Shortly, they turned into a drive lined with flower beds on each side, and a couple of hundred yards later drew to a halt before a large, handsome, and well-lit house. A servant, dressed as an eighteenth-century footman, opened Stone's door and showed him into the house.

A butler greeted him. "Mr. Barrington, I presume?"

"Yes," Stone replied.

"One moment, please." The butler let himself through a set of double doors, leaving Stone alone for a moment.

A stack of mail rested on a hall table, and Stone took the opportunity to glance at it. Everything was addressed to M. Marcel duBois.

The butler returned. "This way, please, Mr. Barrington." He led the way down the hall to another set of doors and preceded Stone into the room. "Mr. Stone Barrington," he announced to the group of a dozen or so people arrayed about a large, two-story, richly paneled library.

A handsome, white-haired man of sixty-something broke away from the pack and came toward Stone, his hand extended.

"Ah, Stone," the man said, grasping his hand warmly. "So good to have you in my home."

"Thank you for having me, M'sieur duBois," Stone said.

"Please, it's Marcel. We are all on a first-name basis here."

"Thank you, Marcel."

DuBois clapped his hands for silence. "Everyone," he said, "this is M'sieur Stone Barrington, who is visiting from New York." DuBois led him around to various groups, introducing him. It was an international group—French, Italian, British, and one or two accents Stone couldn't place, and he couldn't register all the names, except one. She had nearly white-blond hair and was a very tall woman in her high heels, taller than Stone, who was six-two. Her name was Helga Becker, and he was determined to remember that. She was wearing a strapless black dress, and Stone tried to pry his eyes from her décolletage.

"It is a pleasure to meet you, Stone," Helga said. "I've heard so much about you." German, he figured, from her name and accent.

"I'm very pleased to meet you, Helga," he replied, "and I hope you've not heard too much."

She laughed, a low sound, and flashed perfect teeth. "Not nearly enough," she said.

Stone now noticed that all the women were dressed in black, though not all in the same style. Somehow they and the men, who were in black as well, gave the elegant surroundings even more elegance. "Did you and all the other women collaborate on your evening wear?" he asked.

"Ha. No, our invitations specified black. Every woman has a black dress, after all."

"Do women not see that as an infringement by their host on their right to choose their own colors?"

"With any other host, perhaps, but not with Marcel. He is in every other way too kind. You are a New Yorker, Marcel said. What is your business there?"

"I am an attorney-at-law," Stone said. "Pretty boring."

"That depends on how you practice the law," she said. "I shall not judge you too harshly until I know you better."

"I'll look forward to your judgment," Stone said.

"Have you seen the car yet?"

Stone nearly asked her what car but caught himself. "Not yet."

"I have a feeling we may have a look at the Blaise before the evening is over."

A tiny bell rang in Stone's head. He had read about this car but not seen any pictures. It was the creation of a wealthy Frenchman who had racing teams, and that must be his host.

Stone chatted idly with other guests but contrived to stay near Helga. She seemed comfortable with that.

"Are you here alone?" Stone asked her when he got the chance.

"No, I am with you," Helga replied. "I believe that Marcel has . . . how do you say? 'Fixed us up.'"

"How very kind of Marcel," Stone said.

She gave him her most dazzling smile. "Yes," she said, "how very kind of him."

A man taller than both Helga and Stone, Mediterranean-looking, with black, slicked-back hair, approached them. "*Buona sera*," he said. "Good evening."

Italian, Stone assumed, and he watched as the man expertly began to divert Helga's attention from Stone to him. Helga did not respond as he perhaps would have liked and pointedly included Stone in their conversation. Soon, he wandered in search of more amenable prey.

"Italians!" Helga said with a snort. "Unstoppable!"

"And yet," Stone said, "you stopped him."

"Discouraged, perhaps," she replied. "I think you will be better company."

"I'll do my best," Stone replied.

Then from behind him the butler announced half a dozen other people, and for Stone, one name stood out, one he had heard earlier in the day.

"M'sieur Richard LaRose," the butler said.

5

LaRose's eyes passed slowly over the crowd, not pausing to recognize Stone. His appearance was distinctly different from the other men in the room: his tuxedo was not custom-made, but perhaps rented, draped on his thin frame as if on a hanger; his shirt collar was half an inch too big, his bow tie a clip-on, and his haircut of barber-college quality. Still, he seemed oddly at ease in the group, chatting easily with whoever came to hand.

Stone took LaRose's lack of attention to him as deliberate and did not go out of his way to greet the man. He thought he must surely be here in his professional capacity.

Finally, LaRose was handed off by an uninterested knot of people to Stone and Helga. Stone introduced them both; LaRose spoke a few words to Helga in a language he did not recognize, then returned to English.

"Your Swedish is very good, Mr. LaRose," Helga said.

"Thank you. I spent some time in our embassy there."

"Are you a diplomat?"

"I am the commercial attaché at our Paris embassy," he replied, glancing at Stone as if to see if he caught his drift.

"What does that mean?" Stone asked, as if he were really interested.

"It means that I work to promote commerce between the United States and the country in which I am serving," LaRose replied smoothly.

Helga looked across the room and spotted a woman waving at her. "Please excuse me for a moment," she said. "I'll be right back."

"Richard," Stone said quietly, "if you're going to mix with this crowd, ostensibly on embassy business, you should find yourself a good tailor at once."

"You have a point," LaRose said. "I was unprepared for the invitation and had to rent this suit. Can you recommend a tailor?"

"Charvet is very good, if your employer is paying."

"They've offered me a clothing allowance, but I haven't taken advantage of it."

"Tomorrow would be a good time," Stone said. "European tailors work at a deliberate pace. Charvet makes shirts and ties as well."

"The people with whom I mixed at my previous postings were not so demanding," he said. "What clothing should I have made? It's a serious question."

"Half a dozen suits, a dozen shirts, not all of them white, and, by all means, a tuxedo. Then a navy blazer and a couple of tweed jackets for less formal occasions." He looked down. "And shoes, though they need not be custom-made. Try Berluti."

LaRose was taking notes on a jotter. "I'm grateful to you," he said. "My only other avenue of advice would be the ambassador, but he's too far above my pay grade."

"And find somebody who has a good haircut and ask him where he got it."

"Good idea," LaRose said, making a note. "I've been cutting it myself."

"What are you doing here, Richard, if I may ask?"

"It's Rick, and I'm here on business."

The butler's voice rang out. "Ladies and gentlemen, my lords and ladies, dinner is served."

The group began streaming out the doors and across the hallway to the dining room, where a long table had been elegantly set. Stone estimated twenty-four chairs. He found his place card near the center, next to his host, and a moment later, Helga took his other side. "I'm sorry to have stuck you with that rather strange gentleman," she said. "There was someone I just had to speak to. Who was that man?"

"Richard LaRose, commercial attaché at our embassy. He was more interesting than you might have thought."

"He was dressed rather oddly."

"His luggage was lost, and he had to make do."

"Ah," she said, nodding. "His Swedish was commendable, though. I don't think he could have learned it simply by working in the American Embassy in Stockholm."

"I imagine he went to a rather good language school," Stone said.

"I suppose the State Department has such a school," Helga said. "That hadn't occurred to me."

It hadn't occurred to Stone that Helga was Swedish, not German.

"Are you from Stockholm?"

She shook her head. "From a small town north of there, on the Baltic."

"Do you live permanently in Paris?"

"My legal residence is in Monaco, for tax reasons, but I keep a flat here in a hotel."

"What do you do, Helga?"

"I was married for a living for some years. Now I'm divorced for a living."

Stone smiled. "Congratulations."

She shrugged, emphasizing her cleavage. "The work suits me."

The waiter poured Stone some white wine, and he caught sight of the label: Le Montrachet, with ten years in the bottle. He sipped it, rolled it on his tongue.

"Do you like the wine?" Marcel duBois asked.

"As we say in New York, 'What's not to like?' Le Montrachet would be my favorite white, if I had it often enough to remember."

"The secret to drinking good wine is to buy it on release, or in futures, then lay it down until it's ready to drink. You can save hundreds of dollars a bottle by doing that."

"Very good advice," Stone replied. "I have a cellar in my house, but I'm a bit slapdash about stocking it on any regular basis."

"Then you are condemned to drink wines of the second and third rank," duBois said. "Find yourself a good wine merchant in New York and place some standing orders with him."

"Perhaps you're right. I'll mend my ways."

DuBois laughed. "I hope so for your sake."

"Marcel, I'd like to thank you for seating me with Helga. She's absolutely spectacular."

"There was a time when I would have thought it dangerous to introduce you to her, but now she's happily and profitably divorced, so she's no longer a threat to your net worth, though perhaps to your liquidity."

Stone laughed. "Was she really so predatory?"

"She arrived in Stockholm from some rural village and knocked the town on its ass, as you Americans would say. She attracted the industrialist son of a very big industrialist father, who had the grace to die in his sixties and leave the boy a very large fortune, comfortably tucked away in various tax havens. When she'd had enough of him and requested a divorce, he was reportedly so grateful to her for establishing his reputation as a ladies' man that he wrote her a very large check as a farewell gift—rumor has it for forty million euros, which hardly dented his fortune."

"An enterprising woman," Stone said. There was a tap on his shoulder, and Stone turned to find Helga looking at him curiously.

"Are you two talking about me?"

"Only in the most admiring terms," Stone replied.

A waiter heaped a large portion of beluga caviar on their plates, ending their conversation. Stone observed that the table was much quieter while the diners contemplated their good fortune.

6

They were served three more courses after the caviar, and Stone had to restrain himself. Then, just when he thought the dining was over, footmen with large trays of cheeses appeared. He accepted a chunk of Pont l'Évêque and found it to be *à point*. A decanter of port was passed from his right; he poured himself a glass and passed the decanter on to his host. He sniffed and sipped. "Mmmm," he said to duBois, "what is it?"

"A Quinta do Noval, 1972," duBois replied. "It has been waiting patiently in my cellars for forty years just to please you."

"I'm much easier to please than this," Stone said. "I'm more in the line of overwhelmed."

"You have a good palate," duBois said. "Look

at others around the table—most of them haven't even noticed that they have been given something wonderful."

"If I begin to buy vintage ports now," Stone said, "I'll be a very old man when they're ready."

"Fortunately, I bought well when port was out of fashion," duBois said, "and I bought enough to keep me for all of my life." He raised his glass. "I hope to drink the last bottle of this on my deathbed."

Stone smiled. "I hope God gives you that favor."

"Would you like to experience something else beautiful?" duBois asked. "You may bring your port with you." He stood and rapped a knife against a wineglass. "My friends, please bring your glass with you and adjourn with me to my forecourt. I have more beauty to offer you."

Stone gave Helga his arm and followed duBois through some French doors and out of the house. On the way, he brushed past Rick LaRose. "See if you can find out why I'm at this party," he whispered to the man.

Then there before him, gorgeously lit, Stone saw perhaps the most beautiful automobile he had ever seen. It was somewhat larger than a Porsche or Ferrari, but smaller than the usual sports sedan, like the Panamera or the Maserati. It was a gleaming black, and as Stone and Helga approached an open door, he looked inside and saw an interior of soft, glowing leather, so perfectly cut and stitched that it might have been the inside of an Hermès handbag. There was much oohing and aahing among the guests.

DuBois reached past them, flipped a lever, and pulled the front passenger seat forward. "Helga, I would be grateful if you would assist me in making a point. Please climb in."

A footman took her port glass. Helga put a foot inside, turned, and was swallowed by the seat. DuBois allowed the front seat to slide back into place. "Are you quite comfortable?" he asked.

"*Very* comfortable," she replied. "I even have plenty of legroom."

"So you see, my friends, that the rear seat of the Blaise can accommodate even so statuesque a person as the lovely Helga. Stone, take the driver's seat, please."

Stone gave the footman his glass, walked around the car, and lowered himself into the bucket seat, even as duBois got in on the passenger side.

"Wait a moment," duBois said. "The seat will accommodate itself to you."

Stone felt the seat move in all sorts of ways for perhaps two seconds. He put his hands on the wheel. "Perfect," he said.

"Press the start button, here," duBois said, pointing. "The key is in my pocket."

Stone pressed the button and the engine came alive; he had not even heard the starter button. The headlights came on as well.

"Now," duBois said, "drive to the end of my road and turn right."

Stone did so.

"Now just follow your nose and drive," duBois said. "At this time of night there will be little traffic."

Stone goosed the accelerator, and the car pressed him into his seat as it leaped forward, making a noise like a distant Ferrari. Stone took a very sharp curve without touching the brakes, then gained more speed. For a moment he was at 180 kph, with effortless acceleration. "It's so quiet and smooth," he said.

"The windows and windscreen are double-glazed," duBois replied, "and we have paid close attention to noise abatement. What you are experiencing is active noise cancellation, as if you were wearing a noise-canceling headset. Except the whole interior of the car is like a headset." DuBois touched the instrument panel and symphonic music flooded the cabin. "The electronics also have the effect of enhancing the music."

"I can hear nothing from outside the car," Stone said, "except the muted sound of the engine."

DuBois pressed another button on the dash,

and suddenly the vehicle sounded like a race car, and there was road noise from the tires. "If you want the pleasure of hearing the car perform, there you are," duBois said. He pressed the button again, and serenity was restored.

"What's under the bonnet?" Stone asked.

"A twin-turbocharged V12, producing six hundred and fifty horsepower," duBois said. "Top speed, two hundred ten miles per hour—zero to sixty in two-point-nine seconds."

"I've never felt anything quite like this," Stone said.

"Neither has anyone else. It has taken me six years to bring it from a clean sheet of paper to production."

"What sort of price will you put on it?"

"In New York, with various taxes and dealer fees included, the MSRP would be about three hundred and fifty thousand," duBois said. "However, if you would like one I will give it to you for, say, two hundred twenty-five thousand? I would like it to be seen being driven in New York."

"And when would you be able to deliver one?"

"This is the first production model, which I have reserved for myself, so that I can test-drive it every day. We have thirty completed cars at the factory now, waiting to be shipped to various dealers in Europe and the States. One of them has your name on it, if you like. They are all metallic black and equipped exactly like this one. There are no options, so you have no other decisions to make."

"I'll send you a check tomorrow," Stone said. "I have just enough room in my garage for it."

"Turn right here, and we'll go back to the house," duBois said. "I have abandoned my guests, and I imagine some of them would like to have a turn in the car. Your car will be delivered to your home in a week to ten days," he said to Stone. "The cars for the U.S. are being flown over."

Stone pulled back into duBois's driveway and stopped before the gathered guests. He got out and called to the crowd. "You won't believe this!" he said to the group.

DuBois assisted Helga from the car, and Stone took her arm. His driver from earlier in the evening appeared.

"Mr. Barrington, I will drive you back to your hotel whenever you wish," he said.

"Thank you. Helga, may I give you a lift?"

"Yes, thank you, but I'd like to visit the powder room first."

"I'll be waiting." She went back into the house.

Rick LaRose approached. "I've brought your name up a few times, and all that I could learn is that duBois considers you a very special guest."

"He just sold me one of his cars," Stone said.

"Then you are a very special guest indeed," Rick replied, "because he has declined even to take orders for the car before it reaches showrooms. Billionaires all over the world will be clamoring for it. Tell me, have you recollected anything of the past few days?"

"Not a thing," Stone replied, "and I'm wondering what I could possibly have done for Marcel duBois to make him so grateful to me."

7

Stone and Helga stepped into the Maybach, the doors were closed by footmen, and the car moved away, its only noise being the crunch of gravel under the tires.

"Where would you like to go?" Stone asked.

"The Plaza Athénée Hotel, please," she replied. "I have an apartment there."

"What a coincidence," Stone said, wondering if it actually was.

"You are at the hotel, too?"

"I am."

"How convenient," she said, placing a hand on his thigh.

Stone could not but agree. "How long have you known Marcel?"

"Since my divorce—about two years."

"Was this evening typical of his style of entertaining?"

"Except for the presence of the Blaise, yes, entirely typical. Marcel once told me that as a young man starting out, he always desired the best he could afford, and now that he can afford anything he likes, the results are remarkable. Can you afford whatever you like?"

Stone laughed. "Yes, but my desires are more achievable than Marcel's."

"That is probably wise. One should not try to compete with Marcel—not in any way."

"That's good advice."

"I was astonished that Marcel offered you the car this evening, and flabbergasted that he gave you that price. That can only mean that he places a very high value on your acquaintance. Why is that, do you suppose?"

"Helga," Stone said, "I have been trying to figure that out all evening. I don't even know why I was at the dinner."

She looked at him oddly. "Have you and Marcel known each other long?"

"For less than a week," Stone replied.

"I am surprised that Marcel went out of his way to put us together," she said. "He indicated to me that he had a very high opinion of you, and that impressed me."

The car came to a halt in front of their hotel.

"He has a high opinion of you, too," Stone replied. "And if he wants so much for us to be together, it would be churlish of us to disappoint him."

"Come with me," Helga said, alighting from the car. She led him to an elevator he had not seen, one with only one button, which she pressed. The doors opened not into a hallway, but directly into a private vestibule, furnished with only an antique table and a very large floral display. She led him into a handsome drawing room, furnished with pieces clearly not from the hotel's inventory, then into a bedroom, also beautifully decorated.

She stopped, turned to him, and touched her lips to his.

It was the first time, he reflected, that a woman had ever had to bend down to kiss him. As if reading his mind, she reached down and shed her shoes. That brought them exactly nose to nose. "There, is that better?" she asked.

"It's perfect," Stone said, kissing her again. She pushed his jacket off his shoulders; he caught it and tossed it onto a chair, then she pulled his bow tie loose and unbuttoned his collar.

"Do you think you can finish doing this while I step out for a moment?" she asked.

"I think I remember how," Stone replied, working on his buttons. He watched her walk from the room, reaching behind her for a zipper, while he draped his dinner suit carefully over the chair and stood, waiting for her.

The lights dimmed, but not too much, and she came back into the room naked. Nothing like her since Anita Ekberg, Stone thought. They kissed again, and while he rubbed her nipples with the backs of his fingers, she reached down and took him in her hand.

"Ah, so you are glad to see me?" she said.

"It would appear so," he replied.

They fell into bed, and the next hour would count among Stone's fondest memories. Whatever two people could do, they did, holding nothing back.

Stone awoke alone in bed, completely disoriented. Not until she came into the room did his sense of things flood back. She was wearing a beautiful dressing gown, and she tossed a terry robe onto the bed for him. "Let's not shock the room service waiter," she said, leaning over and kissing him. "He'll be here in a moment."

Stone repaired to the bathroom for a quick shower and the use of a hotel toothbrush. He brushed his wet hair back and got into the robe, and when he arrived back in the bedroom, the waiter had come and gone, leaving a large tray table laden with breakfast. He sat down, and Helga served him eggs Benedict and champagne, a Krug '90. He couldn't bring himself to mix it with his orange juice.

"What does your day hold?" Helga asked.

"I have a dinner engagement," he replied. "And I hope to get some work done."

"How long will you be in Paris?"

"I don't know, but probably not more than a few days."

"Will you have dinner with me tomorrow evening?"

"Of course."

"Tour d'Argent at eight o'clock?"

"Perfect."

They finished breakfast, then returned to bed for another hour. Finally, Stone got into his tuxedo, kissed her, and returned to his suite.

It was after ten, and when he opened the door he found another envelope, addressed in the same calligraphy as before. It contained a brief note from Marcel:

Stone, it was a great pleasure to have you as my guest last evening. Enclosed are the pertinent documents for your car. My customs agent in New York will clear the car at JFK airport and deliver it to your home. It is my hope that you will enjoy it for many years to come.

Stone found an invoice among the papers. He wrote a check for $225,000, then e-mailed Joan to move the cash to his checking account. Then he wrote a note of thanks to Marcel for his hospitality and for the privilege of buying the car. He phoned down for a bellman and sealed the check in an envelope addressed to Marcel's offices, as per the invoice. "Please have this delivered by messenger," he said to the man, slipping him twenty euros along with the envelope.

Stone shaved and dressed in a tweed jacket and open-collared shirt, then left the hotel and walked for a while. It was a crisp autumn day with clear skies, a perfect time to be in Paris. The trees along the sidewalks were beginning to change their colors.

A car pulled up beside him, and a window rolled down. "Good morning," Rick LaRose said. "Hop in."

Stone got into the car. "Good morning."

"I trust your evening continued to go well after the dinner," LaRose said.

"It did indeed."

"I have an appointment at Charvet. Will you come with me? I'll need advice."

"Sure," Stone said. "Then I'll buy you lunch."

8

LaRose was being measured by the tailor while Stone flipped through fabric swatches. At Rick's insistence, he chose six suit patterns, two tweeds for jackets, cavalry twills for odd trousers, cashmere for a blue blazer, and a lightweight Italian worsted for a tuxedo. Then he turned to shirt swatches, picking Sea Island cotton for the whites, and Egyptian cotton for the stripes and checks. A dozen neckties. Then, their business done at Charvet, they stopped into Berluti for shoes, then went back to Rick's car.

"Saint-Germain-des-Prés," Stone said. "Do you know it?"

"Yes, I think," Rick replied, slipping the car into gear.

"How long have you been in Paris, Rick?" Stone asked.

"Not quite a month."

"And before that?"

"Postings in Africa and the Middle East."

"That would explain your need for better apparel."

"It would, and I managed to combine the clothing allowances for three postings with some poker winnings, just managing to cover the Charvet bill. The shoes came out of my pay."

"The clothes should last you for many years, if you don't wear them for black bag jobs."

"What do you know about black bag jobs?" Rick asked. "You're a corporate lawyer."

"Surely you read my file more closely than that."

"All right, you were a cop, but you didn't do black bag jobs, did you?"

"No, I caught people who did."

"Sometimes I think I'd rather hold that end of the stick," Rick said.

"There, grab that parking spot," Stone said, pointing.

Rick swung into it, then they got out and walked fifty yards down the boulevard to Brasserie Lipp.

"What is this place?" Rick asked.

"Alsatian food and a slick clientele," Stone

replied. He was surprised that the headwaiter recognized him after a three-year absence and gave them a favored table on the ground floor instead of sending them upstairs with the tourists. Stone introduced Rick to the headwaiter, explaining that he was an American diplomat. The man gave Rick his card, and they sat down, Stone with his back to the wall at Rick's insistence.

"For many years I hung out at a restaurant called Elaine's in New York."

"I've heard of it."

"Lipp is the closest thing Paris has to Elaine's. You'll want to try the choucroute, and beer is good with it."

"Order for me," Rick said.

"Is 'commercial attaché' your usual handle when you're out and about?" Stone asked.

"It is if I'm to be with businesspeople. If I'm with the artsier types, then I'm the cultural attaché. Whatever works."

"That could be the Agency's motto," Stone observed.

"And a good one at that." Rick's eyes flicked to the mirror above Stone's head. He was sitting with his back to the room.

"See someone you know?"

"Someone I'd like not to see me. The man in the pin-striped suit."

Stone glanced across the room. "Who is he?"

"Opposition."

Stone offered his sunglasses. "Will these help?"

"Thanks," Rick said, slipping them on. "You don't want him to see me with you—that might cause unwanted attention to be paid to you."

"You've been here less than a month, and already you know the opposition and they know you?"

"I read the files on all of them as soon as I hit Paris," Rick said, "and I expect they've had a look at my file, too. It's par for the course. It's also interesting that that guy is frequenting this particular place—the headwaiter seemed to know him. I'll put that in my report."

"You write a lot of reports, do you?"

"It's a big part of what I do."

"Try and keep me out of them, will you?"

"Are you kidding? You float in over our transom in a drug-induced coma, and you don't want anybody to notice?"

Stone shrugged. "I guess that was naive of me."

"It was."

The choucroutes arrived—a bed of sauerkraut covered with slices of pork and veal.

"Very, very good," Rick said after a couple of bites.

"Don't eat it all, you'll sleep through the afternoon."

"Good advice."

"Rick, can you run a name through your computers for me?"

"Does it relate to this trip?"

"Yes. The name is Amanda Hurley."

"Who is she?"

"I've no idea. She called the hotel and said we met on the airplane and invited me to dinner. I can't even give you a description, except of her accent, which was mid-Atlantic."

Rick produced a smartphone and typed for thirty seconds, then put it away. "Soon," he said.

"How'd you get into this racket?" Stone asked.

"I had a misspent youth," Rick said. "I left home at sixteen and got into all sorts of trouble, did a little local time, nothing felonious. A guy came to see me, said his name was Jim. I got the impression that a detective who had busted me a couple of times had said something to him about me. He asked me if I spoke Spanish—asked me in Spanish—so I conversed with him in that language. He knew that I'd just barely gotten through high school and asked where I'd picked up the tongue. I told him on the street, and he seemed impressed."

"He was Agency?"

"He must have bailed me out, because when I hit the street he was waiting for me. He bought me some clothes—even then I dressed unsuitably—and took me to dinner at a big-time steak house, where the conversation ranged over everything I had ever done—crimes, sports, hobbies, whatever—then it turned to what I was going to do with my life."

"How old were you at the time?"

"Nineteen, going on forty-five."

"Did he make you an offer?"

"He asked me if I'd give him a few weeks of my time, and I didn't have anything better to do, so I said sure. I figured I owed him. He asked me if there was anything in my rented room that I couldn't walk away from, and I thought about it and told him no."

"What happened then?"

"When we left the restaurant there was a car and driver waiting for us. We were driven to JFK, and Jim gave me some cash and a ticket, said I'd be met at the other end. Next morning I found myself in Monterey, California, at a language school, learning Russian. I aced that, and after a couple of weeks they tried me with Arabic. Turns out I had a gift. I was there for fourteen months and left conversant in half a dozen languages, including Swedish and French.

"During my time there, people came to see me, people with only first names. I filled out a lot of forms, wrote my biography, and was given three polygraph exams. On my last day, when I had no idea where I'd go next, I was offered a trainee's position with the Agency. I flew to D.C., where somebody met me and delivered me to Fort Peary, Virginia."

"The Farm."

"That's the place. I learned enough new skills there to make a very fine living as a burglar, a safe-cracker, a con man, or an assassin, and then I found myself in Africa, never mind where. I loved it. Four years of that, then two Middle Eastern postings, where my Arabic was an advantage, then I think they decided I was getting a little too wild and woolly, so they sent me here to get me civilized. One of the things they'd been after me about was clothes, so I appreciate your guidance this morning. I think I could learn a lot from you."

"I'm at your disposal while I'm in Paris," Stone said. "In the daytime, anyway."

Rick fished his smartphone from his pocket and read an e-mail. "Your Amanda Hurley is interesting," he said, then his eyes flicked at the mirror behind Stone. "What's that passage to my left?"

Stone looked at it. "Men's room," he said.

"My man just went in there, and I don't want

to be here when he gets back. Thanks for a terrific lunch." He got up and started out.

"Hey, wait a minute," Stone called after him. "What about Ms. Hurley?"

"Later," Rick said, and he was gone.

9

Stone arrived at Lasserre at eight sharp, was taken up in an elevator to the dining room and seated at a table for two. The other chair was empty. He looked around and admired the room, as he had on his earlier visit some years before.

It was essentially square with a sunken center, and the seating was arranged so that everyone could see everyone else. The decor was simply beautiful, and overhead was a frescoed ceiling. As he watched, it slid open to reveal a rose arbor and the night sky. That happened periodically, he recalled; it let out hot air and, in the old days, French cigarette smoke. A pianist played old tunes.

A waiter was taking his drink order when he looked up to see the maître d' leading in an attractive woman. Stone stood to receive her. "Good evening, Amanda," he said as the maître d' seated her. "Would you like a drink?"

"Champagne *fraise des bois*, please," she replied.

"Two," Stone said, and they were left alone with the menus and each other. She was a slender, attractive woman with chestnut hair and beautiful skin. She wore an Armani dress—black, since that seemed to be about all Armani sold.

"How nice to see you again," she said.

"Indeed. How have you occupied yourself since you arrived in Paris?"

"Museums and galleries, mostly."

"Is art your business?"

"I have degrees in art history," she said, "and I work as the curator for a couple of corporate collections in New York. I come to Paris to refresh my eye and to buy for my clients."

"Sounds like interesting work."

"I learned on the airplane that you are a lawyer, but then you passed out—and after only one drink. Does alcohol disagree with you?"

"Alcohol and I normally get along very nicely, thank you, and don't take it personally—I assure you, it wasn't the company. I suppose I must have been very tired."

"What kind of law?"

"Over the years, a bit of everything. Currently, mostly corporate work."

"Is it enough to keep the mind alive?"

"Quite enough."

"Actually, I know a good deal about you," she said.

"How?"

"I read the book."

"Book?"

"*Golden Couple*," she said, "by someone called Kelli Keane."

Stone took a quick breath. "God, is that out?"

"Didn't you know? I picked it up in the airport bookstore."

"I knew it was coming—the pub date must have slipped my mind." Now he had at least one reason for leaving New York for Paris: so no one could find him.

"My condolences on the death of your wife."

"Thank you."

"Did you duck out of town because of the book's publication?"

"That may have had something to do with it."

"It got a very good write-up in *The New York Times Book Review*—*Wall Street Journal*, too."

"Well, that means that everybody I know has read or is reading it."

"And a great many other people, too—looks like it's going to be a bestseller."

"Ah, fame."

"Are you upset about this?"

"Not exactly—after all, I cooperated with the author. I wanted to be certain she had her facts straight."

"If it matters, she treated you sympathetically."

"I suppose that's better than getting slammed."

"At all times. Did you have a publicist representing you?"

"No."

"How many times did you speak with her?"

"Four or five, I suppose, an hour or two at a time."

"You were lucky to get out with your skin. One should always have representation in such situations."

"Sounds like you've had some experience."

"Not personally. I've seen friends go through it. They didn't always fare as well as you, especially the ones without professional help."

"I hope that by the time I get home people will have forgotten about it."

"I wouldn't count on that."

They ordered, and Stone redirected the conversation away from him. "Give me your concise bio," he said.

"All right. Born in a small town in Georgia called Delano—you've never heard of it."

He had, but he let it pass.

"Moved to Atlanta as a child, did well in school, scholarship to Harvard, where I stretched the experience to three degrees. I loved it there. Got an entry-level job at the Metropolitan Museum of Art, left there for Sotheby's, worked as a freelance adviser to people with a lot of money and no taste, got a corporate client, then another, and here I am."

"Ever married?"

"Once, foolishly. The divorce was more fun."

"Where do you live?"

"At Park and Sixty-third. I bought a little co-op with a big commission on an important sale. I do quite well, actually."

"Congratulations."

"Tell me, since your wife's death have you been attracting flies?"

"Flies?" He was baffled.

"Young things with ambitions to marrying money without benefit of prenup."

"Oh, those. No, not really."

"Things will change in that regard because of the book."

"I'll have to get some bug spray."

"Yes, you will."

"What else did we talk about on the airplane before I dozed off?"

"Not all that much. You asked me to dinner and told me where you were staying. I was just across the aisle, and after you slipped into the land of Nod, I read the book. I was first off the airplane, so I didn't see you again."

"Question: who served me the drink?"

She looked at him oddly. "A stewardess, I guess. Excuse me, flight attendant. I don't know why they'd rather be called that."

"Neither do I. Did the, ah, flight attendant pay special attention to me?"

"You're an attractive man, Stone. What do you think?"

"Was there anything about her that caught your attention?"

"Like what?"

"Like anything unusual?"

She cocked her head and gazed at him. "Are you asking me if she put something in your glass besides bourbon?"

"I suppose I am." He returned her level gaze. "The second choice seems to be you."

Her mouth fell open. "Do you really think you were drugged?"

"I'm certain of it."

"And you think *I* drugged you?"

"From your own account, it had to be the attendant or you. Or was there another alternative?"

She furrowed her brow. "There was that woman."

"What woman?"

"She came down the aisle, looking a little drunk, a glass in her hand. She seemed to spill her drink on your arm and apologized profusely. You were dabbing at your shirtsleeve with a handkerchief, and she was bending over you."

"Describe her."

Amanda closed her eyes. "Fiftyish, but she'd had work done, so she could have been sixty, fashionably dressed: Chanel pantsuit, hair so good it might have been a wig, bright red lipstick." She opened her eyes. "That's all I remember."

"That was very good," Stone said. "I apologize, I don't really think you drugged me."

"But somebody did?"

"I have no recollection of even being on the airplane, I don't know why I'm in Paris, and I don't remember meeting you."

"Then why . . . ?"

"Because I thought you might tell me something. And you have. I'm grateful to you."

"Then I'm no longer under suspicion?"

"You're off the hook."

She clinked her glass against his. "Then let's start over."

10

By the time they were on dessert, most of the previous tension between them had passed, and they were chatting amiably.

"Tell me," Stone said, "why did you buy the book?"

"I'd read something about it on Page Six of the *Post*." She held up a hand as if to ward him off. "Yes, I confess, I'm a regular reader. I didn't know I would be sitting across the aisle from one of the subjects, not until I opened the book and saw the photographs."

"There are photographs?"

"Quite a few, including some taken at the Virginia house where . . ."

"Where Arrington was murdered."

"Yes. It's a very beautiful house. Do you still own it?"

"No. After a feature about the house appeared in *Architectural Digest*, it began attracting interest. I accepted an offer on behalf of my son's trust a few months later."

"Your son's story was the one part of the book that wasn't very clear."

"It's best that way. I don't want him bothered."

"Where is he now?"

"At the Yale School of Drama. He'll be graduating this winter."

"Winter?"

"He's on an accelerated course, ahead of most of his class. He and two friends are on a parallel track, and they'll graduate with him."

"Is one of them his girlfriend, the pianist?"

"Yes, she's studying composition. The other is his friend Ben Bacchetti, who's majoring in theater production and business."

"Do they all have plans together?"

"They do. They want to make films together— Peter writing and directing, Ben producing, and Hattie scoring."

"Sounds like quite a team. Do you think they'll get anything produced?"

Stone smiled. "You'll recall from the book that Peter's stepfather was the actor Vance Calder. As a result, Peter's trust is the largest stockholder in Centurion Studios."

She laughed. "Well, I guess they'll get produced."

"Yes, and they'll make their artistic home at Centurion."

Stone paid the bill and they left the restaurant. "Is it too cold out, or would you like to walk a bit?" he asked.

"Let's do that."

They wandered down the Avenue Franklin Delano Roosevelt, took a right, and strolled aimlessly into a neighborhood of small shops and houses.

"Tell me," Stone said, "is there anything mysterious about your life?"

"Mysterious?"

"Enigmatic, surreptitious, cloaked."

"That's an odd question," she said. "Why did you ask it?"

"Why didn't you answer it?"

"I asked you first."

"All right: a man in a car has been following us with his headlights off since we left Lasserre. Don't look back, check the reflection in the shop-window coming up."

She did so. "And you think he's following me?"

"Tell me what you think."

"I don't know what to think."

"Do you have any reason to fear for your safety?"

"Not until just a moment ago. I see the car now."

"Anyone you know?"

"I can't see the driver—glare on the windscreen."

"Do you think we should run for it?"

"I've a better idea: my hotel, the San Régis, is a few yards ahead. You can drop me there and take your chances with the assassin, if that's what he is."

"You would deny me shelter from an assassin?"

"I would deny you my bed, at least for the moment. I have a prejudice against first-date performances. You can wait in the lobby until he moves on."

They reached the hotel. "Good night," he said. "I hope to live to see you again."

She laughed. "Somehow, I think you'll manage." She pecked him on the cheek and went inside.

Stone left the hotel and walked back in the direction he had come. The car sat idling, its lights off. Stone grasped the front passenger door handle, opened the door, and got in. "You're a very clumsy surveillant," he said to Rick LaRose. "Your trainers at the Farm would be ashamed of you."

"Promise not to tell them," Rick replied, putting the car in gear and driving away.

"Why are you following me?"

"What makes you think I'm following *you*?" Rick asked.

"Is there something about Ms. Hurley that I don't know?"

"A great deal," Rick replied. "Almost everything, in fact."

"Tell me."

"Tell me what she told you."

"Small-town girl, Harvard, the Met, Sotheby's, art world, curator."

"That's all true, as far as it goes."

"What did she leave out?"

"The part about her recruitment in college, her extensive training, her clandestine service in the art worlds of London and Paris."

"Recruitment by whom?"

"Us."

"Oh."

"Yes, oh. If she didn't mention that, then she certainly didn't mention the suspicions that arose about her—that she was fucking a member of the opposition and might have been turned."

"Was she booted out of the Agency?"

"You might say she resigned under a cloud after failing two polygraphs. Charges were never brought, either administrative or criminal. She is, however, on the watch list of every airport security team and major intelligence service in the world, and she will never again go anywhere or do anything that a lot of people won't know about."

"Is she dangerous?"

"Only to your reputation."

"Is she *in* danger?"

"Only from you."

"Why from me?"

"Because we're not the only ones keeping track of you. Twice I've spotted a tail. And you will have made them interested in her."

"By whom am I being tailed? Apart from you, I mean."

"We were never able to make an ID. But I expect we'll have other opportunities."

"Am I a threat to someone?"

"That remains to be seen." The car came to a halt outside the Plaza Athénée. "Good night, sleep tight," Rick said.

Stone got out of the car. "Should I look over my shoulder?" he asked through the open window.

"Never look over your shoulder. Look at the reflections in the shopwindows. Elementary tradecraft."

He drove away.

11

Stone had finished his breakfast and was working on the *International Herald Tribune* crossword, which is to say the *New York Times* crossword, when the phone rang.

"Hello?"

"I'm relieved to find that you are still alive," Amanda Hurley said.

"So am I."

"Did you have any further trouble?"

"The car was gone when I left the hotel."

"Good. Thank you for a lovely dinner. I haven't been to Lasserre in years, and it's good to find that it hasn't changed. Everything else has."

"I am in complete agreement with both your points."

"Do you enjoy art?"

"I do."

"If you'd like to see some, I'll buy you lunch and we'll visit some galleries."

"Sounds good."

"Do you know Brasserie Lipp?"

"I do."

"There at one o'clock?"

"You're on."

"Bye." She hung up. His cell phone began ringing.

"Hello?"

"It's Holly." Something was strange in her voice.

"Hi. Is something wrong?"

"I just read a cable from our station in St. Marks." This was a Caribbean island where she and Stone had spent some time a few years back.

"Yes?"

"There was a crash at the St. Barts airport late yesterday afternoon. Our station head's name was on the passenger list. No survivors."

"I'm sorry to hear that."

"You knew him. You met him when we were in St. Marks."

"I remember. I recall that there's a very short runway at St. Barts."

"There's more," she said. "The names of Mr. and Mrs. D. Bacchetti were also on the passenger list."

Stone froze, unable to speak.

"They were in St. Barts on their honeymoon, weren't they?"

"Yes," Stone said. "Do you have any way of confirming this?"

"I've dispatched someone from our station in St. Marks to St. Barts to make an identification of our man, and I've asked him to confirm the other names, too."

"Will you let me know?" Stone asked.

"Of course I will. I'm not going to believe any of this until our officer has investigated thoroughly."

"Thank you for calling," Stone said. They both hung up.

This was impossible, Stone thought; this couldn't be happening. He thought about what he should do, and he knew that Dino's son, Ben, would have to be told. But not yet. Not until the confirmation came in. He called the concierge.

"Concierge desk."

"This is Mr. Barrington."

"Yes, Mr. Barrington. How may I serve you?"

"I need a seat on the next flight to St. Barts, in the Caribbean."

"Of course. There is a flight in the early afternoon. May I call you back?"

"Yes, please."

Stone was experiencing tiny flashbacks of his

friendship with Dino—their time together as partners on the NYPD, their travel together, their hundreds of nights at Elaine's. It couldn't end like this.

The phone rang. "Yes?"

"Mr. Barrington, it's the concierge. The daily Air France flight to St. Martin is fully booked, and there is a considerable waiting list. I took the liberty of booking you on tomorrow's flight. It departs de Gaulle at two p.m. and arrives in St. Martin at five p.m. You have to take a short flight from there to St. Barts, and I have you a tentative reservation on the first flight the day after tomorrow."

"Tentative?"

"Apparently, the regular flight to St. Barts crashed yesterday, and the service has been temporarily disrupted because of a shortage of aircraft to cover all their flights. Their spare airplane is out of service."

"You'd better get me a hotel room in St. Martin, then."

"I have already taken the liberty of doing that. Will you be returning to Paris?"

Stone thought for a second. "I don't know yet." He still didn't know *why* he was in Paris, and he wanted to know.

He went and stood in the shower for a long time.

12

Stone got dressed and sat on the edge of his bed for a few minutes, trying to think of every way this news could be wrong. He knew Dino and Viv were in St. Barts; their names were on the passenger manifest. But why? They should have arrived in St. Barts days ago. Could they have gone to another island for some reason, then returned? He could not get his mind off what he was going to have to say to Ben Bacchetti.

He called Amanda Hurley's hotel to break their luncheon date: no answer at her room, and he didn't have her cell number. There was a strange buzzing noise, and he suddenly realized that his cell phone was dancing across the glass desktop. He ran for it; had to be Holly, maybe with good news.

"Hello?" He was short of breath.

"Stone?" A man's voice.

"Yes?" Why didn't he hurry up and talk?

"It's Dino."

"What?"

"It's Dino. What's the matter, do we have a bad connection?"

His brain thrashed through the gears of recognizing the voice. "Dino?"

"I told you twice."

That was Dino. "Are you all right?"

"Yes."

"And Viv?"

"Just fine. Did somebody call you?"

"Holly called, said you were on the passenger manifest of the airplane that crashed yesterday."

"I heard about that. It was a Mr. and Mrs. David Bacchetti, of Denver, Colorado, no relation that I know of."

"There are two Bacchettis?"

"There are lots of them, but mostly in Italy."

"Then you're alive?"

"Do I sound dead?"

"No more than usual."

"Somebody called our hotel and told me to call you. Are you in New York?"

"I'm in Paris."

"Why the fuck are you in Paris?"

"I have no idea."

"That doesn't make any sense, and it's too early in the day for you to be drunk. I mean, isn't it?"

"Yes, it is."

"Then what are you talking about?"

"I was hoping you could tell me what happened after your wedding."

"Stone, I haven't talked with you since the wedding. How would I know why you're in Paris?"

"I lost four days."

"What did you do with them?"

"All I know is that I spent one night on a flight to Paris. The rest is a blank."

"Are you feeling all right, Stone?"

"I am now, but I was drugged when I got to Paris."

"Who would want to drug you in Paris?"

"I mean, on the airplane. Somebody drugged me then. I apparently managed to get through the airport and into a cab under my own steam, then I passed out, and the driver went through my pockets, then took me to the American Embassy, where Holly's people took care of me."

"You need me to come to Paris?"

"Hell, no! I want you to enjoy your honeymoon!"

"Okay, I'll be sure and do that. What are you going to do now?"

"I'm going to try to find out what happened during those four lost days."

"And you think sleeping with a few Parisiennes is going to make that happen?"

"Come on, Dino."

"Well, that's your usual solution to any problem. What's the matter, aren't there enough women in Paris?"

"More than enough."

"Well, eventually one of them will enlighten you."

"Funny you should mention that, it's what I hoped would happen."

"How many have you tried so far?"

"Only two."

"You'd better get your ass in gear, then."

"I'll do that. I'm glad you're not dead, Dino. I already had a plane to St. Barts booked."

"That's sweet of you, kiddo, but what I'm doing here, I don't need any help. Call me if you need me."

"Will do." They hung up. Stone couldn't seem to get enough air in his lungs. He walked around the room taking deep breaths, swinging his arms and mopping his sweaty face on his sleeve. He looked at his watch: a quarter to one.

He went downstairs and asked the concierge to

cancel his travel plans, then he got a cab to Saint-Germain-des-Prés. Before he entered Brasserie Lipp, he leaned against a streetlamp, pressing his forehead against the cool metal, then he took a few more deep breaths and went inside.

13

Amanda was already sitting at a good table. Stone sat down, his back to the room, and patted his forehead with his napkin.

"I saw you outside leaning against the pole," she said. "You looked as though you were screwing up your courage to come in here. Is it me?"

"No, no, nothing like that."

"What was that, then?"

"I just got some good news."

"That's how you react to good news? I'm glad it wasn't bad news."

"I got the bad news earlier and had to sweat it out until I got the good news."

"What was the good news?"

"That the bad news wasn't true."

"What was the bad news?"

"That a friend of mine—no, my best friend in the world—and his new wife were killed in an airplane crash in St. Barts on their honeymoon."

"But the good news fixed that?"

"Yes, the couple killed had the same surname."

"And how did you hear about this?"

"A friend called me from the States."

"So everything is all right now?"

"Yes, everything."

"I gave the maître d' your name, and he didn't put me upstairs with the tourists. I'm impressed. How long since you were here?"

"Yesterday."

"Oh. I should have suggested someplace else."

"This is just fine—in fact, it's my favorite place in Paris."

"And you have a high tolerance for choucroute?"

"I do." Stone flagged down a waiter and ordered the dish for both of them. "And a beer?" he asked Amanda.

"That's good."

The waiter went away and came back with two of the big round glasses with their creamy heads.

Stone took a deep draught.

"Feel better now?"

"Much." Stone glanced up at the mirror and saw the reflection of the man Rick LaRose had described as "opposition" taking the same seat he had the day before.

"See somebody you know?"

"Not know, just familiar."

"The guy with the shaved head and the hooked nose?"

"Yes."

"He's a Russian spy."

"You think he's after Lipp's choucroute recipe?"

She laughed. "Isn't everybody?"

"He was here yesterday, too; that's why he looks familiar."

"Who were you with yesterday?"

"A friend from the embassy."

"The American Embassy?"

"Yes. I passed out in a cab at the airport, and the driver took me to the embassy, where they . . . I don't know what they did. I woke up there."

"Passed out on the floor?"

"No, in a kind of hospital room."

"They have hospital rooms at the American Embassy?"

"Just the one, as far as I know. It wasn't a very nice room."

"How long were you there?"

"I don't know, exactly, maybe twenty-four hours."

"What kind of drug were you given?"

"Something called hypno something or other."

"Hypnotol?"

"That's it."

"Jesus Christ, that stuff can kill you. It was only on the market for about ten minutes before the FDA yanked it. People were dropping like flies."

"How do you know about this?"

"I read something about it in the science section of the *New York Times.*"

Their choucroute came and they attacked it.

"What part of the embassy was your hospital room in?"

"I don't know," Stone lied. He regretted having told her about the embassy.

"When you left, did you leave by the front door?"

"No, there was some sort of side entrance, through a garden."

She put down her fork and looked at him hard, chewing. "You were in spookville," she said.

"Beg pardon?"

"In the CIA offices, one floor down from the main entrance."

"If you say so."

"Why would they put you in a room in spookville?"

"When I passed out in the cab, the driver went through my pockets and found the card of a friend of mine who works for them. He showed it to a marine guard, and they took me there."

"Did they grill you when you woke up?"

"Not the way I'm being grilled now," Stone said with some irritation.

She held up a hand. "Sorry, I'm just trying to figure out what happened to you."

"So am I."

"Was the friend you were here with yesterday a spook?"

"He's the commercial attaché."

"That means he's a spook. How do you know him?"

"I met him at a party in the Bois de Boulogne the other night."

"At the racing club?"

"No, at someone's home."

"If you know someone who owns a house in the Bois, then you're mixing with a high-altitude crowd."

Stone shrugged. "He sold me a car."

Her eyes narrowed. "Wait a minute, you were at Marcel duBois's house?"

"How did you know that?"

"He's been working on this supercar for years, and the papers say it's ready to hit the market, and he lives in the Bois."

"That's the one."

"The Blaise?"

"Yes."

"It's named after his son, Blaise, who was killed in a racing accident several years ago."

"He didn't mention that."

"How do you know Marcel duBois?"

"I don't know."

"He's one of the things you don't remember?"

"Yes. I got a dinner invitation, and I was curious, so I went."

"Who else was there?"

"*Tout le monde,*" Stone replied. "Or at least, that part of it that counts. There were twenty-four at the table."

"Who else did you meet there, besides the commercial attaché?"

"I don't remember a lot of names. There was a Swedish woman named . . ."

"Helga Becker?"

"Are you sure you weren't at this dinner party?"

"Absolutely sure. I'm not on M'sieur duBois's invitation list."

"So who is Helga Becker?"

"A famous divorcée and beauty. I heard she got a hundred thousand euros when she split with some Swedish businessman."

"That much? Where did you hear that?"

"On the grapevine—you know how those things go."

"Who is Marcel duBois anyway?"

"You don't know?"

"If I did, I don't remember."

"But he remembered you."

"Yes, he seemed to."

"Well, if he sold you a Blaise, you're probably the first man in the world to own one. It's not being released until next week. DuBois must owe you for something."

"I was wondering about that," Stone said. "Tell me about him."

"He's said to be the richest man in France, maybe even Europe."

"How'd he make his money?"

"The hard way: he inherited it. Or at least enough to give him a running start in the world. He's into everything. He's the Warren Buffett of France."

"Well, good for him."

"He's almost unknown in the States, but . . ." She looked at him.

Stone's brow was screwed up.

"You remembered something, didn't you?" She leaned forward. "What?"

"Unknown in the States," Stone said. "That

rings a bell, but I can't remember where I've heard that. How could someone that rich be almost unknown in the States?"

"He's a creature of France. He'd be known in certain circles in London or Milan, but I don't think he's ever even been to the States."

"He's been to New York," Stone said. "I know that much."

"How do you know that?"

Stone sighed. "I don't know."

14

They left Brasserie Lipp and began strolling through the back streets of Saint-Germain-des-Prés, checking out gallery windows.

"Amanda, why do you think the bald guy at Lipp is a Russian spy?"

"He's a well-known figure about town, turns up at gallery openings and the like, chatting up people. Much like your friend the commercial attaché, I expect."

"Why would a 'spook,' as you call LaRose, be interested in me?"

"Did he seem to want anything from you?"

"He asked my advice about clothes. I took him to Charvet, where he spent more money than a diplomat should be able to."

"That means he's not a diplomat, he's a spook."

"Why would a spook have tens of thousands of dollars to spend on clothes? And why would he?" Stone asked.

"Maybe he has family money. A lot of the old boys came from that. As to why he would buy a lot of clothes, maybe he wants to fit in better in Paris. A spook would."

"Well, he was wearing a rented tuxedo at duBois's dinner party."

"There you go. He's probably just come in from an assignment in some station where clothes don't make the man, like Africa."

"How is it you know so much about the CIA?" Stone asked.

"If you live abroad long enough, you meet those people, just as you did. After a while, you get to know the drill with them. Who is your friend in the Agency?"

"She's a retired army officer who joined them and seems to have done well."

"How well?"

"She got promoted last year. She works directly for the director, I think."

"So you are very well connected at the Agency."

"I wouldn't say that."

"If you were connected there, you certainly wouldn't."

"Look, I'm an attorney and an investor. Any connections I may have arise from those two things."

"How did you meet your lady friend, the spook?"

"Oh, it was years ago. I went down to Florida to take delivery of an airplane at the factory. I was in a local bank, getting a cashier's check to pay for it, when a couple of people with shotguns walked in and robbed the bank. I saw them shoot a customer, then run. I did what I could for the man until the ambulance arrived, but by that time he was gone.

"He was about to marry a woman who was the local chief of police. A while after that she was in New York for something, and we had dinner."

"That's a bizarre story," Amanda said. "In fact, it smacks of an Agency cover story."

"Oh, come on! It's a highly improbable story that just happens to be true in every respect."

"Do you still have the airplane?"

"I traded it for something bigger and faster."

"What airplane?"

"A Citation Mustang."

"You fly it yourself?"

"I do."

"I'm impressed."

"Why do you know about airplanes?"

"Oh, I got my private license many years ago, but I couldn't afford an airplane."

"How would you know if a story smacked of an Agency cover story?"

"I've heard a few."

"From whom?"

"Various folks."

"Amanda, are you now or have you ever been associated with the CIA?"

That stopped her in her tracks, literally; they had been walking and she just stopped and stared at him.

"Well, come on," Stone said. "Give me a straight answer."

"Let me put it this way," she said. "If I had been, I wouldn't be able to tell you."

"You wouldn't be able to tell me if you were still with them, but if you left, you have no obligation to dissemble when asked that question."

"Why do you think I might be CIA?"

"You know too much about it not to be. And you still haven't answered my question."

"I've given you the only answer I can," she said.

"Ah now, that answers my question in part, but not the part about whether you're still in the Agency's employ."

"All right, I'm not."

"And why should I believe a trained liar?"

She burst out laughing. "I can't win, can I?"

"Hang on," Stone said. He had stopped in front of a gallery window and was staring at a painting inside. "Let's go in," he said. He led her into the shop and asked the woman inside if she could remove the painting from the window. She did so, and he looked closely at it and inquired of the price. A little haggling ensued, and Stone handed her his American Express card and his address.

"I don't get it," Amanda said as they waited for the transaction to be completed.

"Don't get what?"

"You're walking around Paris with an expert, and you don't even ask my advice. Or my opinion, for that matter."

"You might have disagreed with me," he replied, "and my only criterion when buying art is whether I like it enough to want it in my home. But now that I've bought it, what do you think of it?"

She smiled. "If you hadn't bought it I would have bought it myself for one of the collections I curate. You got a good price, too. Where did you learn about art?"

"From my mother, by osmosis. She was a painter."

"Wait a minute, I've got it! Your mother was Matilda Stone?"

"She was."

"Her work is on my permanent to-buy list, whenever it becomes available, not that it does very often."

"In that case, you're very smart. She's on my permanent to-buy list, too. I've picked up two small paintings in the last year. I hope I won't have to start competing with you."

"You may have to," she said.

"Tell you what: I'll give you a generous reward for every picture of hers you lead me to."

"My arrangement with my clients allows me to freelance," she said. "You're on."

Stone signed the bill, and they left the shop. "You know," he said as they strolled down the street, "I can see why you're no longer a spook."

"And why is that?"

"You can't have been very good at it."

"That's a terrible thing to say. Why did you say it?"

"Because the bald guy from Lipp has been following us since we left. He's across the street in a doorway now, pretending to look at a piece of sculpture."

"Well, shit," she said. "On the other hand, why do you think he's following *me*?"

"You're the ex-spook. Why would he follow me?"

"Maybe because he's seen you at Lipp on two consecutive days, in the company of people he believes to be CIA?"

"Well," Stone said, "I'm going to have to start hanging out with a better class of people."

15

Stone got back to the Plaza Athénée and checked his messages: Holly had called. He went upstairs to his suite, and as he opened the door he found the place dark. That surprised him, because the maids always threw open the curtains to his terrace. As his eyes became accustomed to the gloom he started. A man was sitting in one of the comfortable chairs across the room. Stone felt for a light switch and turned it on. Lance Cabot was sitting in the chair, his chin on his chest, apparently dead.

Stone went to the windows and pulled the curtains open.

The corpse moved a little, then opened its eyes. "Hello, Stone," it said.

"Lance, what the hell are you doing here?

Aren't you in the middle of Senate hearings on your appointment as director?"

"The hearings are over," Lance replied, stretching. "We expect a favorable result in a couple of days."

"Why are you in Paris, then? Shouldn't you be getting sworn in or something?"

"Yes, I should, but until I am sworn in I'm still deputy director for operations, and I have to deal with the unbelievable mess you've made in Paris." He stood up and began pacing.

"What the fuck are you talking about?"

"You managed to get yourself drugged on an airplane, and you've thrown my Paris station into a frenzy."

"Well, your first statement is apparently true, but how have I thrown your station into a frenzy?"

"Let's see," Lance said, holding up a finger. "First, you turn up semiconscious at the embassy and cause my medical officer to have to save your life, instead of doing what he's supposed to be doing. Then you've got my station head worrying about your activities in Paris instead of confounding his country's enemies. You're taking up most of the time of one of my best officers, who has apparently adopted you as a role model and has stuck me with a forty-thousand-dollar bill at Charvet. You've interfered with his approach to Marcel duBois, whom I had hoped he could make into an asset for us. You're fucking another very effective operative of ours, who should be paying attention to others, and wasting the time of yet another, who is dawdling at lunch and in galleries with you instead of doing her work. You've also brought her to the attention of a Russian named Majorov, who was previously unaware of her existence, which is the way I like it, and somebody has already taken a shot at her."

"A shot? At Amanda? I left her only twenty minutes ago."

"And she was shot at ten minutes ago, no doubt by Majorov or one of his operatives."

"And all of this is *my* fault?"

"Certainly it is. If you weren't in Paris, none of this would have happened. How the fuck do you happen to know Marcel duBois?"

"I'm not entirely certain of that," Stone said.

"Has the drug wiped out all memory of the man?"

"Well, yes, now that you mention it."

"You don't even remember meeting him in New York?"

"I was drugged," Stone said defensively. "You said so yourself."

"You weren't supposed to be. The woman who dropped the stuff in your drink was supposed to put it in the drink of a man in the row behind you, but she was drunk and screwed up, because Amanda was talking to you and not the target. You were simply an unintended consequence of our plan."

"Is the woman who drugged me one of your operatives, too?"

"Not anymore, she isn't. She's now doing clerical work in a windowless basement office at Langley, waiting for her retirement to kick in. Think carefully: what were you and Marcel duBois doing in New York?"

"I told you, I don't know."

"Have you talked to your managing partner, Bill Eggers, about this? Maybe he knows."

"Eggers is in darkest Maine—moosing or something—and can't be reached."

"Swell. Now you are going to have to be my way to Marcel duBois."

"*Me*? You want me to recruit the richest man in Europe to be your spy?"

"Not a spy, just an asset. Can you imagine how much information duBois could pass to us, given his business contacts on the continent? He could be invaluable."

"Why would he consider an approach from me?"

"He sold you that fucking automobile, didn't he? And at a steeply discounted price, when half the billionaires in the world would pay a high premium to get their hands on one."

"Well, it's a very nice car, and you can't blame me for accepting his offer."

"I'm not blaming you, I'm happy for you. I hope you'll let me drive it sometime. My point is, if he likes you enough to practically give you his greatest prize, then maybe he would respond favorably to an approach from you on our behalf."

"And you came all the way from the States to ask me to do this?"

"I did. That's how important it could be to us. A word from you in his shell-like ear might open a world of high-level business dealings to us. Can't you see how important that could be to us in achieving our ends for our country? Have you no feeling for your homeland? No patriotism?"

"That's pathetic, Lance! Pandering that way to get me to do your bidding. Patriotism, indeed!"

"I'm perfectly serious. You have a golden opportunity to make a difference in Europe for your country, and you're feigning memory loss to get out of it!"

"*Feigning*? I remember nothing!" Stone shouted. "But I would if you hadn't had me drugged with that stuff!"

"I told you, it was an accident! An unintended consequence!"

"That doesn't matter, the effect is the same! I could have died! You said so yourself!"

"Now, now," Lance said placatingly, "let's get

control of our emotions and discuss this like gentlemen."

"Gentlemen? You're no gentleman! You have people drugged on airplanes!"

Lance sank into his chair again, massaging his temples. "Look, this effort can still be saved. We've lucked into an entrée to duBois, the sort of thing that could happen once in a lifetime. What do I have to do to get your help? Do you want me to tell Helga to keep fucking you?"

"Well, that's not the worst offer I've ever had," Stone said, "but quite frankly, I don't think I need any help from you in that regard."

"Perhaps not, but I can see that it never happens again. I can send her back to Stockholm."

"A threat! Now we have threats!"

"Get duBois on our team, and I'll give you a medal."

"A medal? One of your 'jockstrap' medals that nobody can wear in his lifetime?"

"Well, there is that."

"I don't want your fucking medal, I just want to get my memory back."

"Our doctor tells me that shock treatments might help."

"Shock treatments? That's like something out of a bad movie! I haven't heard about shock treatments since *The Snake Pit*."

"Well, there was *One Flew Over the Cuckoo's Nest*, with Jack Nicholson."

"Yeah, and look how that turned out!"

"It was just a thought. I was trying to help."

"Help? Help me get strapped to a table with a rubber thing between my teeth and electrodes on my temples?"

"All right, forget the electroshock treatments. Tell you what I'll do: I'll send somebody up to the North Woods of Maine to find Eggers and give him a satphone. Then you can ask him what you and duBois were doing in New York. He'll know, won't he?"

"Now, *that* is the first sensible thing you've had to say since you broke into my suite."

"I'm a spy. I don't need to break in," Lance pointed out. "I know how to pick locks."

"Is that how you got in here?"

"I also know how to give a hundred-euro note to a bellman."

"All right, get a satphone to Eggers. I'll talk to him, and then we'll talk again."

"I'd buy you dinner, but I hear Helga has dibs."

"Yes, and don't you say another word to Helga," Stone said.

Lance whipped out his cell phone and started issuing orders.

16

S tone was dressing for dinner when his cell phone went off. "Hello?"

"It's Holly. Didn't you get my message?"

"Yes, but I was interrupted and didn't have a chance to call."

"Did you hear from Dino?"

"Yes, and thank you for that. I was very relieved."

"I would have called you myself, but I've been in a marathon meeting with no phone."

"Are you back in New York?"

"Tomorrow. Oh, by the way, Lance is going to be confirmed as director."

"Yeah, he told me."

"You've talked to Lance?"

"Yes, he was in my suite when I got back from lunch—bribed a bellman."

"Stone, it's the drug. You're hallucinating."

"What are you talking about?"

"Lance is down the hall in his office."

"Not anymore he isn't."

"Stone, you've got to see a doctor."

"Look, Holly, I've just had an extremely unpleasant half hour with Lance, and I'm not hallucinating."

"Stone, listen: Lance cannot be in Paris."

"I don't know why the hell not."

"I've told you, he's here."

"Tell you what, put me on hold, walk down to Lance's office, and open the door. Then ask his secretary where he is."

"Hold on."

Stone stood, tapping his foot for two minutes before Holly came back on the line.

"All right, so he's in Paris."

"And I'm not hallucinating?"

"And you're not hallucinating. What did he want?"

"He wants me to . . . Wait a minute, this isn't a secure line, is it?"

"It is on my end. What are you talking on?"

"My iPhone."

"Then don't say anything that you don't want heard."

Stone was silent.

"Hello?"

"Yeah?"

"Are you going to tell me what he said?"

"You just told me not to. Make up your mind."

"Shit."

"Will you excuse me, please? I'll be late for dinner."

"Where and with whom are you having dinner?"

"I can't say. I might be overheard."

"So what?"

"So the last person I was talking to, before Lance, had a shot taken at her. I don't want that to happen to my dinner companion."

"You are infuriating."

"I'm pretty infuriated myself. Turns out Lance is responsible for what happened to me."

"I don't understand."

"Well, I can't explain it to you on this phone."

"Never mind. Good-bye!" She hung up.

The phone on the bedside table rang, and Stone picked it up. "Hello?"

"Stone, it's Marcel duBois. I hope you're well."

Stone relaxed a little. "Yes, Marcel, I'm very well, thank you."

"I wonder if you're free to have lunch with me tomorrow?"

"Of course. I'd be delighted."

Marcel gave him an address. "Ask for me at the front desk," he said. "One o'clock?"

"That's fine." They both hung up.

Stone was five minutes late for dinner and was embarrassed to find Helga waiting for him, already seated at a table by the big windows. He kissed her and sat down, but before he could speak, someone else pulled up a chair. Lance smiled at him sweetly. "Good evening, Stone, Helga."

"Oh, Lance!" Helga said, sounding delighted. "What brings you to Paris?"

"I wish it were you, my dear, but it's Stone."

Helga looked at Stone oddly. "You two know each other?"

"Unfortunately," Stone said.

"Stone," Lance said, "give me your cell phone and your passport."

"Why?" Stone demanded.

"Don't be difficult."

Stone sighed and handed over the two items.

Lance produced another cell phone, then turned on both of them. He made some data entries in each. "Give it a minute," he said. "The two phones are syncing."

"I didn't know you could do that," Stone said.

"You weren't supposed to know. Ah!" He handed Stone the new iPhone, a white one, and slipped Stone's into his pocket, then he removed Stone's passport from its chocolate alligator holder and inserted another passport. "Sign this," he said, pointing to a line on the passport.

Stone signed it.

"Now," Lance said, "what you have is an iPhone that operates exactly as yours did, except that when you are connected to one of our phones, it automatically scrambles the conversation. It is a secure phone. And your new passport is a diplomatic one."

"Why do I need that?"

"Because the way things have been going, it wouldn't surprise me to hear that you've been arrested. That passport is a get-out-of-jail-free card."

"Why would I be arrested?" Stone asked.

"For carrying this." Lance, keeping his hand low, handed Stone something solid in a leather pouch.

"What did you just give me?" Stone asked.

"A small pistol, in a soft holster. Hook it to your belt."

Stone did as he was told. "And why do I need this?"

"I told you, another of our people was shot at today."

"And you think I could be next?"

"Who knows what tomorrow will bring?"

"You can say that again."

"My people have located Bill Eggers, and you will receive a phone call from him on your new phone around noon tomorrow. You should make the most of the call, because it wasn't easy to arrange. It required an airplane on floats."

"All right."

"Now, I want you to arrange to see duBois again, the sooner the better."

"How about one o'clock tomorrow?"

"That would be convenient. Why then?"

"He invited me to lunch."

"Well," Lance said, rising, "my work here is done. Call me at this number after you have spoken to duBois. I would like very much to meet with him." He handed Stone a card.

Stone shrugged. "I'll see what I can do."

"I'm so sorry I can't dine with you both," Lance said.

"Don't be sorry," Stone replied.

Lance gave a little wave and disappeared.

17

Stone turned his attention back to the gorgeous Helga. "I'm so sorry about that," he said. "Lance can be a royal pain in the ass."

"I know," Helga replied. "I'm astonished that you know each other. How is that?"

"It's a long and very boring story."

"And you are working for him?"

"I'm under contract to his organization as a consultant. Now and then, Lance pops up and asks me to do something I'd rather not do."

"Always?"

"I can't remember an occasion when I was happy about what he wanted me to do. I'm sure you must have had that experience."

"Well, yes, I have. It was fun, at first, but . . ." She didn't continue.

"Did he ask you to meet me?"

"No, that was Marcel. I had no idea you were connected in this manner and, I'm sure, neither did Marcel."

"I figured."

"The other one, I knew about."

"LaRose? You'd met before?"

"No, I just spotted him for what he was as soon as he walked in wearing that awful dinner suit and said he was a commercial attaché."

"Not an undue assumption."

A waiter appeared with an ice bucket and a bottle of Krug '78. Stone tasted it, approved more than he could say, and the waiter poured a glass for both of them.

"This is the first time I've had Krug twice in the same week," Stone said, raising his glass.

"This one is on me," she replied, sipping the wine.

"Oh, no, I'm happy to deal with that."

"It was my invitation, it is my dinner. In fact, I've already ordered for us."

"Then I am your grateful guest." Stone glanced out the windows. There, just across the Seine, was Notre Dame, beautifully lit. "There's only one view like this," he said.

"Yes, and it comes with superb food and a romantic atmosphere."

"A wonderful combination."

"What was it that Lance said about you being shot at?" Helga asked.

"Not I—another of Lance's friends. He's just hoping I get shot at."

"Why is that?"

"Lance likes giving orders, and I have a strong antiauthoritarian streak. I hate taking them, so I always make him persuade me. It annoys him."

"I'm impressed that he gave you a diplomatic passport," she said.

"So am I, now that you mention it. I've always wanted one. Now I can park anywhere."

She laughed. "That is to be wished."

"How did you become entangled with Lance?"

"I met him at a dinner party two years ago, and he charmed me into sending him the occasional report."

"How often do you do that?"

"Oh, a few times a year. I don't want to bore him."

"Do you know how Lance persuaded me to help him this time?"

"How?"

"He threatened to send you back to Sweden."

She threw back her head and laughed. "That's wonderful, but don't worry, he can't do that."

"I wish I had known that at the time."

Their first course arrived: a slab of foie gras, sautéed medium rare. Stone tried a slice. "Mmm-mmm," he breathed. "Just wonderful."

"Do you know you can't have foie gras in California anymore?" she asked.

"I knew that," Stone replied. "I'm a partner in a business in Los Angeles, and we're giving it away to our guests."

"What sort of business, a restaurant?"

"A hotel called The Arrington, which has four restaurants."

She leaned forward. "This I have read about, I think. It is in Bel-Air, is it not?"

"It is."

"And how do you come to be a partner?"

"My late wife inherited the land from her late husband, and now my son's trust leases it to the hotel company. I am his trustee, and I serve on the board of directors."

"Oh," she said, looking disappointed, "this ruins my plan."

"What plan is that?"

"I was going to persuade you to move to Paris by supplying you with a lovely apartment and lots of beautiful clothes."

"What a nice thought," Stone said. "Being your kept man might be interesting."

"But you are too rich. I can't afford you."

"We have a saying in America. 'Why buy a cow when milk is so cheap?' You see, you can have me for the price of a dinner at Tour d'Argent."

"You are right," she said. "This is a much better arrangement."

"And I come with my own clothes."

She giggled. "I have just had a wonderful thought."

"Tell me."

"Since we both report to Lance from time to time, let's each write a report about this evening—tell him everything we had to eat and everything we do to each other after dinner!"

"What a wonderful idea! It will annoy him no end!"

Then one of Tour d'Argent's famous ducks was presented to them, beautifully prepared, then eviscerated at the table by a captain and served.

"I can't wait to tell Lance about this," Stone said.

"I can't wait to tell him what we do after dinner," she replied.

18

Stone sat at the desk in Helga's sitting room at the Plaza Athénée, using her computer and printer, naked. Helga's report to Lance was beside him, and he consulted as he wrote. "You're really going to say this?" he asked.

"All of it. It will be good for Lance."

"Okay, I'm with you. Small differences: where you say you kept my attention through the night, I'm saying you kept me *at* attention."

"Perfect."

Stone printed the document, then they both put them into Plaza Athénée envelopes and addressed them to Lance. Helga hung over his shoulders, pinching his nipples. "Oh, no," Stone said, "I'll be late for lunch with Marcel."

"Are you going to his home?"

"No, to his office."

"His city home is the top two floors of his office building. The one in the Bois is his country home—well, one of them."

Stone got into his clothes and kissed Helga enthusiastically.

"Tonight?" she asked.

"Of course. Book us someplace you love, but this time and in the future, it's on me."

"As you wish."

Stone was just closing the door to his suite when his cell phone began to buzz. "Hello?"

"Stone?" The voice sounded very far away.

"Bill?"

"What the fuck is going on? We had this airplane land on the lake last night and had to put up the pilot in the guest house, and now I'm phoning you in the middle of the night, almost."

"Bill, I'm sorry about that, but this is an emergency."

"What sort of emergency?"

"Did you and I meet with a Frenchman named Marcel duBois?"

"What, you don't remember?"

Stone gave the briefest possible explanation of why he didn't remember.

"And how much time did you lose?"

"About four days, starting after Dino's wedding. Bill, why am I in Paris?"

"Because duBois invited you, schmuck."

"Why didn't he invite you?"

"Because he wants The Arrington."

"Wants it? What do you mean?"

"He stayed there for a couple of days when he was meeting with his West Coast dealer for his car, and he was overwhelmed. He wants to buy it—lock, stock, and wine cellar."

"Holy shit. Did he make an offer?"

"He said he'd give you one in writing when you came to Paris. Has he?"

"No, but I've seen him only once, at a dinner party at his house. I'm having lunch with him in less than an hour."

"Well, expect to hear a lot of zeros thrown around."

"Okay. Did I do anything for him while he was in New York?"

"Do anything? What do you mean?"

"I mean favors."

"You mean like getting him laid?"

"No, no. Did I introduce him to anybody of consequence?"

"Well, there was me."

"Besides you?"

"Not that I know of. Listen, the firm wants his business for everything he does in the States, so sell him the fucking hotel, will you?"

"Thanks, but I don't think so. Does Mike Freeman know anything about this?"

"I don't know. Did you tell him about it?"

"I don't know. I'll call him after lunch."

"Great. Now, can I give this pilot his satphone and go back to sleep?"

"Sure, Bill, and thanks for bringing me up to date."

"Oh, Stone?"

"Yes?"

"There was one other thing about our meeting."

"What?"

"I can't remember. I'm drawing a blank."

"Has somebody drugged you, too?"

"No, I'm just having a senior moment, okay?"

"Take your time."

"I'm sorry, I just can't remember what it was. I'll have to call you later."

"How are you going to do that without a satphone?"

"You have a point."

"Tell the pilot you're keeping it and that you'll send it to Lance when you get back to New York."

"Good idea!"

"Go back to sleep, Bill."

"I'll never get back to sleep now."

"Well, go moosing or something." But Eggers had already hung up.

19

Marcel's car was waiting for Stone when he arrived downstairs, and on the way to lunch he thought a lot. The pieces of his four lost days were falling into place, but he knew only what others had told him. He still remembered nothing, and he was beginning to think he never would.

They arrived in front of a traditional building of twelve stories or so on a broad avenue. They drove through a gate and into an inner courtyard, where Stone departed the car and was directed to a door. Behind that sat a uniformed security guard.

"M'sieur Barrington?" the man asked.

"Yes."

"Please travel in this elevator," he said, pointing to one of three.

"Which floor?"

"There is one button only," the guard replied.

Stone pressed the only button, and the car rose for half a minute, and the doors opened into a vestibule. A man in a white jacket and black trousers with highly polished shoes greeted him and led him into a living room that Stone estimated to be fifty feet in length, furnished with sofas and chairs in groups, scattered about the room. Stone thought it must be a perfect room for a very large party. They continued toward the rear of the building into a large, paneled library, where a spiral staircase led up to a second level that carried the circumference of the room. A table was set for two in the center of the room, and Marcel duBois sat at a desk at the end before large windows, speaking German into a telephone. He waved a hand, indicating that Stone should sit on a sofa.

Stone did. While duBois finished his conversation Stone looked at the beautifully bound volumes, perhaps two thousand, he thought, perhaps three, lining the room, and there was still room for a dozen or so large paintings—old masters, mostly.

DuBois hung up, navigated around the desk, and came to Stone's sofa. Stone stood and greeted him, and they sat down.

"Are you well, Stone?"

"I am very well, thank you."

"Have you seen more of the lovely Helga?"

"I have, and with much pleasure. Last night she made me a very good offer to become her kept man—an apartment, clothes, the works."

DuBois threw back his head and laughed. "You must really have impressed her, because that is the exact opposite of her usual operating technique. How did you respond?"

"With an old American aphorism which says 'Why buy a cow when milk is so cheap?' She was buying dinner, and I told her that was reward enough."

DuBois laughed again. "Wonderful, wonderful." He took an envelope from his pocket. "Forgive me if I dispense with business before lunch."

"Of course."

DuBois handed Stone the envelope. "This is my offer for The Arrington."

Stone opened the envelope and removed a single sheet of paper. Typed on it was a number: one billion dollars.

"What do you think?" duBois asked.

"I think it's low," Stone replied. "I know what the land is worth, and I know how much we spent on construction, landscaping, and staffing."

"Forgive me, my offer does not include the land. I would continue to lease it from you on favorable terms."

"Then your offer is a serious one," Stone said, "but I'm not inclined to accept it. Please let me explain."

"Please do."

"This is the first business I have ever been involved in that I and my investors built from the ground up. Therefore, I am very attached to it, and the property includes the house where my son grew up."

"I see," duBois said, looking at the ceiling. "Perhaps I can make the offer more attractive."

"Please don't," Stone said. "Let me suggest another alternative."

"I am all ears," duBois said.

"We would like to build more Arringtons—we thought in the United States. But building some in Europe might be a good idea, too."

"That was my fallback position," duBois said. "As it happens, I inherited a chain of hotels from my father—nothing fancy, meant for commercial travelers and tourists on a budget. There are forty-odd of them, all pedestrian and beginning to decay, but perhaps a dozen of them are built on spacious plots of land in neighborhoods that began gentrifying a decade ago and that are ripe for razing and redevelopment."

"Very interesting," Stone said. "We could provide design and decorating services, in line with the look of the Bel-Air property, and train staff to our standards. And, although I and my investors are not in your class of capitalists, we would also be able to offer investment in the group."

"Shall we get specific, then?" duBois asked.

"Oh, please, no. I do not fancy myself negotiating a business deal with you. I am not equipped for that. If we agree in principle, then I will send representatives to work out a concrete arrangement."

"I agree in principle," duBois said. "How about you?"

"I, too, agree in principle."

"Then," duBois said, rising, "let's talk no more of it and enjoy our lunch." He led Stone to the table, where their first course, a slab of terrine, awaited them. A waiter held Stone's chair and poured the wine.

"You know," duBois said, "I have never done business in America, though I have, of course, dealt with many Americans in Europe. I like their straightforward attitude. They are, or seem to be, guileless. Of course, one must, as you say, dot i's and cross t's as in any business arrangement."

"I hope to see you do a lot of business in the States," Stone said, "and speaking for Woodman & Weld, we would be very pleased to represent you in any venture you might undertake."

"Thank you, Stone. I have already done my due

diligence on your firm, and I would very much like you to represent me."

"Thank you, Marcel."

"I also admire the American fashion of governing, and I just read a very interesting new book by a former CIA officer. I was very impressed with some of the operations the Agency conducted."

Stone had an inspiration. "You're interested in intelligence work, then?" he asked.

"Intelligence is half of business," duBois said, smiling. "I could not survive without it."

"Perhaps you have read in the papers that our director of Central Intelligence is retiring."

"I have, and I understand you are acquainted with Mrs. Lee and the president. Do you know who will succeed Mrs. Lee at the CIA?"

"I do. His name is Lance Cabot, and he has recently been testifying before the Senate Select Committee on Intelligence. I believe he will be confirmed within a matter of days."

"Is he a good man?"

"The best for the job, I think. As it happens, he is in Paris at the moment. Would you like to meet him?"

DuBois's face lit up. "I would like very much to do so."

"It would have to be on short notice. He'll be returning to the States shortly."

"I am available at all times," duBois said.

"Perhaps I can reach him now."

"Please do."

"Excuse me for a moment." Stone rose and walked to a corner of the room and got out his cell phone. He called the number that Lance had programmed into the new phone.

"Yes?" Lance said.

"It's Stone."

"Good day."

"Good day. Would you like to meet Marcel duBois?"

"Yes! When?"

"In an hour?"

"Yes, good!"

Stone gave him the address, hung up, and returned to the table. "He will be here in one hour," he said to duBois.

"Astonishing! You are full of surprises, Stone."

"Merely a happy coincidence," Stone said. And one, he thought, that would get him off the hook with Lance. Now the man could recruit his own asset, and Stone could avoid further entanglements with the Agency.

20

Stone and Marcel were having coffee when Lance was shown into the library. He appeared to have recovered from his jet lag and was beautifully dressed in a dark, chalk-striped suit. Stone made the introductions.

"I am so pleased to welcome you to Paris, Mr. Cabot," Marcel said.

"It's Lance, and thank you."

"I am Marcel. And may I congratulate you on your appointment?"

Lance smiled. "It's a little early for that, so thank you again."

"I'm sure that must be a very great responsibility," Marcel said.

"It is, but I believe I'm prepared for it."

The conversation continued, with Marcel asking pointed questions and, Stone thought, Lance giving him remarkably straight answers.

They had been at it for an hour when Lance's tone became more serious. "Marcel," he said, "one of my Agency's great strengths has always been the friends we have in the world, people like you, who are attuned to the activities of business, the professions, and the arts—who can help us understand the tenor of the times in their part of the world."

"I can see how that might be very helpful to you," Marcel replied. He obviously knew what was coming, and he seemed to relax as Lance went on.

"I would very much like to think of you as our friend and colleague," he said, "and to hear from you directly from time to time."

"Are you inviting me to become a spy for the CIA?" Marcel asked, amusement in his voice.

"Certainly not," Lance replied smoothly, "just a friend and colleague. I'm sure that, in your daily dealings, you hear things that might be of interest to us, indeed things that might be of great help to us as we try to help make the world a better and safer place."

"Oh, is that what you do?" Marcel replied, chuckling. "Make the world a better place?"

"Making the world safer for free men makes it a better place, does it not?"

"I suppose it does."

"I would never ask you to take any position against the interests of your own country or your business affairs."

Stone spoke for the first time. "Marcel has told me that intelligence is half of what he does."

Lance smiled. "The sharing of even a fraction of that intelligence could make a difference for France, Europe, and the United States."

"I believe I understand you," Marcel said. "What sort of arrangement do you envision?"

"Whatever sort you would feel comfortable with. I will give you a secure means of communicating directly with me, and I will have one of our best men, serving locally, available at all times to assist you in any way he can."

"Would that man be Mr. Richard LaRose?" Marcel asked. "The 'commercial attaché?'"

Lance laughed. "That's right, you and Rick have met, haven't you?"

"He was a guest in my home at the suggestion of a friend of mine, Helga Becker. Is she a friend of your Agency's, too?"

"Helga moves in interesting circles. From time to time, she hears something I might like to hear. It's no more than that."

"If you expect Mr. LaRose to continue representing himself as a diplomat, you should take him shopping," Marcel said.

Lance smiled. "That has already been accomplished," he said, "with the assistance of Stone. I had a word with the managing director at Charvet to hurry along Rick's order. Now we must wait only for his hair to grow."

Marcel laughed out loud.

"I assure you, Rick is most accomplished in his work and, once made more presentable, will blend in beautifully. He is, among other things, a brilliant linguist, fluent in the better part of a dozen languages. It's how he originally came to our attention, when he was very young."

"I must say, I was impressed to hear him speaking Swedish with Helga," Marcel said. "It made me nearly overlook the dreadful suit he was wearing."

"Would you like to see the new Rick LaRose?" Lance asked. "He's waiting downstairs in my car."

"By all means," Marcel replied. "Invite him up."

Lance produced an iPhone and pressed a single button, then put it away. Marcel picked up a phone and spoke a few words, then hung up.

No more than a minute had passed when Rick entered the room. Stone was impressed. He wore a dark gray flannel suit, a striped shirt, and a beautiful necktie, and carried a handsome briefcase. His hair wasn't much longer than when Stone had last seen him, but it was much better cut. Stone made the reintroduction and Marcel invited him to sit.

Marcel spoke a couple of sentences of what sounded to Stone like Russian, and Rick replied smoothly in the same language. Marcel repeated in German and Italian, and Rick responded with ease and what sounded like perfect accents.

"How old are you, Rick?" Marcel asked in English.

"I'm thirty-two," Rick replied.

"I would very much like you to leave your current employment and come to work for me," Marcel said.

Rick laughed. "My current employer frowns on resignations," he said, "but I thank you for your kind invitation."

"Perhaps I can loan you Rick from time to time," Lance said. "As an interpreter or in whatever role you prefer."

"That might be interesting," Marcel said.

"But you must promise not to abscond with him," Lance said. "I would miss Rick terribly."

"We shall see," Marcel replied. "All right, Lance, I will be a friend to your Agency, at least for a while. We'll see how it goes."

"I'm delighted to hear it."

"Please remember," Marcel said, "that our channel must flow in both directions. I expect I'll hear from you, at times, with information that might interest me."

"Of course," Lance said. "I think you will find our friendship beneficial." Lance looked at his watch, then held out a hand. Rick placed the handle of his briefcase in it. "In the hope that we might reach an accommodation, I have brought you two gifts," Lance said, opening the case. He removed an iPhone and handed it to Marcel. "This operates as any other, but when you call one of our phones at the numbers listed on the favorites page, our conversation will be encoded in both directions. With anyone else, it will be an ordinary cell phone call. I am listed among your favorites as Jacques, and Rick is listed as Pierre."

"I see," Marcel replied, checking the page.

Lance removed a Mac Air laptop from the case. "Again, this computer operates as any other, except that when you e-mail either Jacques or Pierre, your message will be encrypted, as will our replies."

"It's all very simple," Marcel said.

"We look forward to hearing from you," Lance said, rising and offering his hand. "And now Rick and I must go. Stone, may we give you a lift?"

Stone felt this was more than an invitation. "Thank you, Lance, yes." He thanked Marcel for the lunch.

"Stone," Marcel said, "the Paris Auto Show begins tomorrow, and I will be introducing the Blaise to the world. I hope you will attend as my guest and stay for lunch, too. Lance, Rick, perhaps you can come as well?"

"I fear I must fly home this afternoon," Lance said, "but I'm sure Rick would be delighted. He loves cars."

"I certainly do," Rick said.

"I will send a car to the Plaza Athénée for you tomorrow at ten," Marcel said to Stone. "And Rick, perhaps you can hitch a ride with him."

"Perfect," Rick said.

The three of them made their good-byes and rode down in the elevator together.

"Stone," Lance said when they were secure in his car, with the glass partition rolled up to seal off the driver, "you have done very well."

Stone shrugged. "The opportunity was there," he said.

"And you will be rewarded," Lance said.

They came to a broad intersection a couple of blocks from the hotel and stopped for a traffic light.

"Stone, will you continue to have business with M'sieur duBois?"

"I expect I will," Stone said. "From what I've heard, he's the reason I came to Paris. Eggers and I met with him in New York." He didn't feel it necessary to tell Lance more than that.

"Well, I hope you will keep me abreast . . ."

Lance, who was sitting behind the driver, stopped talking and looked out his window. Suddenly he threw himself across the car on top of Rick, who was in the middle, and Stone.

Stone looked to his left in time to see an enormous truck grille hurtling toward the car. It struck with enormous force, shattering glass and rolling the large car onto its side. Even upended, the truck's engine was still roaring.

"Get out! Out!" Lance shouted.

"How?" Stone asked.

21

Incredibly, the truck's engine continued to roar. The car began to move again and rolled onto its back.

"Out!" Lance shouted again.

With the car on its top, Stone's door was now free. He got it open, but now his door faced the truck and was pressed against it. Then the truck's engine abruptly stopped, and there was shouting from outside the car.

"We're trapped in here," Stone said. "Lance, can you get your door open?"

"I'm working on it," Lance said. He grabbed Rick's briefcase and used it to batter the remaining glass from his window, then he crawled out into the street. Rick followed, then Stone. Stone noticed that they both held themselves low, looking around. Rick had a gun in his hand.

"I smell gasoline," Stone said. "We've got to get the driver out." He managed to get the front door open, and they dragged the man into the street. He had not been wearing a seat belt. Stone had hold of his jacket, and he could see the butt of a gun in a shoulder holster, so he grabbed it and tucked it into his belt.

Lance was on his phone, shouting the name of the intersection. "Chopper now!" he yelled. "And an ambulance!" He put the phone away and resumed watching the perimeter of people who stood gawking.

"Who are you looking for?" Stone asked.

"I don't know," Lance said. "Anybody with a weapon will do."

The sound of police cars could be heard in the distance, and, incredibly, a helicopter appeared, flying down the Seine, then hovering over the intersection.

Lance turned to Rick. "Deal with this," he said. "I've got to get to Le Bourget." He slapped Rick on the back, shook Stone's hand, and ran toward the descending chopper.

"Central Paris is a no-fly zone," Rick said. "Only Lance could manage that."

"Rick, do you have any idea what's going on?"

"Assassination attempt, I should think," Rick said.

"On whom?"

Rick chuckled. "You and I aren't worth bothering with."

The helicopter rose, turned 180 degrees, and headed back up the Seine.

Police were running toward them. "I hope you've got your diplomatic passport," Rick said, reaching for his and holding it up. "*Diplomate américain!*" he shouted.

Stone held up his passport, too. Rick entered into conversation in rapid French with the police, while Stone turned to the driver. He had a massive head wound, but there wasn't much blood. Stone felt the man's neck for a pulse but couldn't find one.

"This man needs . . ." he started to say, but he was pushed out of the way by a uniformed medical attendant.

Stone looked at the truck; the cab was empty.

An hour later Stone and Rick were in Stone's suite at the Plaza Athénée, having been given a lift there by the police. Rick was on the phone and had made half a dozen calls. Finally, he hung up. "Mind if I stay here for a while? Doug Hobbs thinks this is the safest spot, for the moment."

"Sure." Stone handed Rick the driver's gun. "You'd better have this," he said. "I don't need it."

"You don't?" Rick asked. "Oh, that's right. Lance armed you, didn't he?"

"Do you have any idea what happened back there?"

"I told you what I thought. Do you doubt it?"

"They were after Lance, then?"

"Who?"

"How the hell should I know? I'm the civilian here."

"They could have been after all three of us. I mean, it wasn't exactly a surgical attack, was it? Our driver is dead, and we could have been, too, if the car hadn't been armored. I don't know if you noticed, but the truck that hit us was a mixer truck, carrying a full load of concrete. That's quite a lot of mass."

"It's hard to know how it could have been heavier," Stone said. "Did you see what happened to the truck's driver?"

"There was no driver to be found," Rick replied. "I expect there's one in a ditch somewhere with a bullet in his head. Something else interesting: the station checked, and the truck belongs to a construction company owned by—guess who? Marcel duBois."

"You don't really think . . ."

"Who else knew we were in that car and where we were headed? Not even the station knew—the driver didn't call in."

"I think that's a bit fanciful, Rick."

"Let me ask you something," Rick said. "Did you buy your own air ticket for Paris?"

"No, it was delivered to my office, along with an envelope of expense money."

"Who sent it?"

"DuBois, I guess," Stone admitted.

"Did you choose your seat on the airplane?"

"It was already on the boarding pass that came with the ticket."

"So duBois knew what flight you were on and what seat you were in?"

"I suppose he did," Stone said slowly.

"What business were you here to discuss with duBois?"

"He made me an offer for a hotel in Los Angeles that I'm a partner in."

"The Arrington?"

"Yes."

"Did you accept his offer?"

"No, but we agreed in principle that he could build a number of Arringtons in Europe with our investment and cooperation."

"Why didn't you want to sell it to him?"

Stone told him what he had told duBois.

"One more question: do you think duBois might have a better chance of buying The Arrington with you out of the way?"

"Possibly. It was a very good offer."

"One last point: the drug you were given was pulled off the market years ago by the FDA. Do you know where it's still available?" He didn't wait for a reply. "France. And guess who owns a big chunk of the French manufacturer?"

Stone held up a hand. "Stop, you've made your point."

Rick's cell phone buzzed. "Yes? I'll be right down." He hung up. "They've sent a car for me."

"An armored one, I hope."

"Oh, nobody's after me—that would be you or Lance, or both. See you tomorrow at ten."

"You still want to go to the auto show, after all you've just told me?"

"Sure, we're not going to find out anything locked in this suite. Would you rather just get a plane home?"

Stone shook his head. "No, I want to get to the bottom of this."

"Yeah? Well, that's the difference between us," Rick replied. "I want to get on top of it." He walked out of the suite.

22

Stone was napping, exhausted, when the phone rang. "Yes?"

"I have Mike Freeman for you," a woman's voice said.

"Yes, of course. Mike?"

"Hey, Stone. I just got back from the coast and called your office. Joan said you're in Paris."

"I am," Stone said. "Bill Eggers and I had a meeting with a French industrialist named Marcel duBois about a week ago. Do you know who he is?"

"I've heard him referred to as the French Warren Buffett," Mike replied. "I don't know much more than that."

"Well, I had lunch with him today, and he

offered us a billion dollars for The Arrington. Not including the land."

"Wow," Mike replied. "That's a very serious offer. How did you respond?"

"I told him I liked having the hotel and suggested that we enter into an arrangement whereby he would build some more Arringtons in Europe, and we would invest and offer him design and staff training services."

"And how did he respond?"

"He said that was his fallback position. He owns a chain of cheaper hotels, and he said he could raze a dozen of them around Europe and build Arringtons."

"And how did you respond?"

"I told him I'd discuss it with you and Eggers."

"Well, off the top of my head, I'd say it's a sensational idea."

"That's pretty much what I thought."

"Are you going to talk with him about it further?"

"Are you kidding? The guy would skin me alive. We need to put a team on this. Any ideas?"

"Well, I know some awfully good lawyers, firm called Woodman & Weld. Why don't you ask Eggers to put a team together?"

"Okay, but before I do that I want to know

more about duBois, specifically his history of business practices. He seems like a good guy, but I don't want to find out he's a shark after I'm missing a leg."

"Okay, I'll run a full-blown background check on him, and I'll get my Paris office involved. Is there something in particular you're concerned about?"

"Everything. I've never been in business with a multibillionaire before, and it makes me nervous. I'd like to know how close he works to the line of legality and if he's inclined to cross it."

"I understand. When are you coming home?"

"I don't know—as soon as I get a handle on this, I suppose. A few more days."

"I'll get right on it. Take care." Mike hung up.

Stone felt guilty about not bringing Mike fully up to date about his experience, but the backstory didn't seem that relevant to what he had to do now.

He had been meaning to call Amanda Hurley and he did so now, only to be told that she had checked out of the San Régis. He didn't have a cell number or a New York number, so he let it go. His phone rang again.

"Yes?"

"It's Joan."

"How are you?"

"I'm okay, but what the hell am I supposed to do with this exotic-looking car? It's outside on a flatbed hauler."

"Oh, I forgot about that. DuBois said he was shipping it by air."

"Is this the one you paid two hundred and twenty-five thousand for?"

"One and the same. Please just go into the garage and rearrange things so it will fit next to the Bentley. Get the truck driver to help you. When you get it in there, call my insurance agent and add it to my policy, and list the value as three hundred and fifty thousand."

"Stone, is this an insurance scam? You only paid two hundred and twenty-five thousand."

"The replacement cost is three hundred and fifty thousand, maybe more. I got a deal."

"Okay, I'll get on it. See ya." She hung up.

He stood up and stretched and found that he hurt all over. The collision with the truck had shaken him up more than he had known. He resumed his nap.

At eight he met Helga at Le Grand Véfour, which turned out to be a spectacular monument to the Belle Époque, with a menu to match. He was going to have to start eating more simply if he wanted to preserve his waistline and his digestive tract.

"How was your day?" Helga asked, after the champagne had been served.

"I was involved in a traffic incident," he said, "and I guess I was a little shaken up, because I ache a lot all over."

"Poor baby," she said, patting his cheek. "I was trained as a masseuse, you know."

"I didn't know."

"I'll make it all better later."

"You're on."

"Did you have your lunch with Marcel?"

"I did."

"And how did that go?"

"Well, he made me a very good offer for our hotel, but I don't want to sell it. We may be able to do some business in Europe, though."

"You can't do better than doing business with Marcel," she said.

"Tell me the worst thing you've ever heard about him."

She looked at him, surprised. "The *worst*? I haven't heard anything worst. Everyone says he's a perfect gentleman."

"Do you know anyone who's ever been involved in a business deal with Marcel?"

"Yes, my former husband, in Stockholm."

"How did he find the experience?"

"Profitable."

"Did he enjoy dealing with Marcel?"

"How could one not enjoy knowing Marcel?"

"I don't mean his personal charm, I mean his business practices, his dealings. Did your husband like dealing with him?"

"Well, he never complained," Helga said. "Why are you asking this?"

"If I'm going into business with Marcel, I want to know more about him."

"He does have a reputation for getting what he wants," she said. "He will go to great lengths if he really wants something."

"What kind of lengths?"

"I don't understand."

"Is he ruthless?"

"I suppose anyone who has made as much money as Marcel must have a ruthless streak. Is that a bad thing?"

"It depends on how ruthless. Have you ever known anyone who has done business with Marcel, then regretted it later?"

"He does have a reputation for being very charming with people in his business dealings, then dumping them after he gets what he wants."

"Socially dumping, you mean?"

"Yes, but a man like Marcel has no more hours in the day than you or I. No busy person has time for everybody. After all, he's not a politician who has to keep everybody sweet."

The waiter came with the menu, and the subject changed, but Stone thought about duBois all through dinner.

23

Stone woke early and stretched. His soreness was gone, and he had Helga to thank for that. She was not in bed, and he could hear her in the bathroom, singing in Swedish. The doorbell rang; he found a robe and let in the room service waiter.

Helga came out of the bathroom in a robe, still singing. "How are you feeling?" she asked.

"Terrific," he said, "thanks to you."

"Anytime. I don't get chances often to maintain my skills."

"I'm happy to be your patient anytime," Stone said, then they turned their attention to breakfast.

"What does the day hold for you?" Helga asked.

"I'm going to the opening of the Paris Auto Show with Marcel."

"That should be very interesting. He's introducing the Blaise to the world, you know."

"Would you like to come with us?"

"Thank you, but I've already seen the Blaise—with you—and I'm not very interested in cars. I rarely drive mine. Will we have dinner this evening?"

"I'd love that, if you can find a simpler restaurant. The way we're going, I'll get fat."

"There are more than eight thousand restaurants in Paris, and very few of them are bad. I'm sure I can come up with something."

"Then you're on."

Stone got downstairs a little before ten to find Rick waiting for him out front, leaning against Marcel's Maybach. "Good morning, Rick."

"Good morning, Stone." He opened the door and let Stone in, then went around the car and joined him in the rear seat. "This cabin is more like an airplane than a car, isn't it?" he asked, playing with his seat adjustment.

"A good comparison," Stone said as the car moved away. "I'm surprised to see you this morning after hearing your theory yesterday. Don't you feel at peril?"

Rick smiled. "Always. It's part of the training."

"It must wear on the nerves to always feel at peril."

"One gets used to it."

"I like the new suit," Stone said. Rick was wearing a tan gabardine from Charvet.

"Thank you. Lance was very helpful. They didn't finish the whole order overnight, but I'm getting them at the rate of a suit a day."

"Have you heard from Lance?"

"I spoke to him last night."

"How did his escape from our company go?"

"The prefect of police complained to the ambassador about that. The morning papers are full of the mysterious helicopter that plucked an American from the midst of a traffic accident."

"Is that what they're calling it?"

"Yes."

"How did the helicopter get there so fast?"

"They were practicing instrument approaches at Le Bourget when the call came, so they were already in the air."

"I didn't know Le Bourget was still in use. That's where Lindbergh landed after his solo transatlantic, isn't it?"

"Correct. It's now a general aviation airport. All the business jets use it. Our Gulfstream 450 was waiting for him there, so he was out of the country before the ambassador could yell at him for his little faux pas."

"How well do you know Lance, Rick?"

"I worked for him when he was station chief of Europe."

"How did you get along?"

"He sent me to Africa, then the Middle East."

"As badly as that, huh?"

"Best thing that could have happened to me. You get a lot of street cred in the Agency for working the tough stations, and you get to serve in places like Paris later on."

"I'll bet you'll be back at Langley before long, serving the new director."

"He brought that up, but I told him that travel is broadening, and that I want to further improve my wardrobe before I go home."

Stone laughed. They drove on to some suburb Stone had never seen and approached a gate at the huge building where the auto show was being held. Swarms of uniformed police, armed with submachine guns, roamed the rear of the building, and flashing lights were everywhere.

"This can't be ordinary security for an auto show," Rick said. "Something has happened."

To their surprise, the Maybach was waved through without so much as slowing. After they got out of the car, they were escorted by policemen

into the building, where they were met by two
large, fit-looking men in black suits with some sort
of ID button in their lapels and escorted across
the crowded floor to the duBois exhibit, where a
phalanx of shiny new Blaises was on display. Marcel duBois saw them coming and waved them to
the rear of the exhibit, where there was a small
office.

"Before we go out there," he said, "let me tell
you what has happened."

Stone and Rick exchanged a glance.

"At four o'clock this morning I was awakened
to answer a phone call from your Lance Cabot. He
told me that information had reached him from
intelligence sources that an attempt would be
made to attack the auto show shortly after it
opened this morning."

"What sort of sources?" Rick asked.

"Cell phone traffic picked up by your National
Security Agency."

"Ah, yes."

"I called the prefect of police immediately and
put my chief of security and his people at his disposal. When my ten Blaises arrived here on trucks
at six o'clock this morning, they were searched
and two bombs were found and disabled."

"That's a relief to hear," Stone said.

"Every other car in the show was searched, but mine were the only ones affected."

"So this was an attack against your company, not the whole show?" Rick asked.

"I or my company—it's pretty much the same thing. I can tell you that never has a new association so immediately been of such great benefit to me, and I am very grateful to Lance and your Agency."

"I'll pass that on to him," Rick said.

"I have already phoned him and expressed my thanks."

"He is being sworn in today as director of Central Intelligence," Rick said.

"Then he has scored a coup on his first day," Stone said.

"I must tell you that it was not until I saw the morning papers that I heard of your terrible accident after you left my home yesterday, if an accident was what it was. I was extremely embarrassed to learn that a truck belonging to my construction company was involved. The driver was found unconscious at one of our building sites, and I was told that the man who stole the truck and crashed it into you was fired yesterday morning for being drunk on the job. He is being sought by the Prefecture of Police. Please accept my apologies for this terrible tragedy. I spoke to Lance again, and I am making a contribution to a fund being set up for your driver's family."

"That's very kind of you," Rick said.

"All these events have made me proud to be associated with your Agency," Marcel said. "Now, I must go to the platform and make a speech and give some television interviews, then we will have lunch. I promise to get you both home unmolested afterwards."

They followed Marcel back to the exhibit and listened as, bursting with pride, he introduced the Blaise to the world.

24

The lunch was held not in a grand ballroom but in a private dining room, and Stone was told that those present were the top people at each of the auto companies represented at the show. Marcel was the toast of them all, and Stone heard many complimentary things said about the Blaise.

Then, when they were seated at the best table, Stone looked across the room and saw, at a rear table, a familiar face. "Don't look now," he said to Rick, whose back was to that table, "but your friend Majorov is here."

Rick looked at him sharply. "How do you know that name, Stone?"

"You pointed him out to me at Brasserie Lipp."

"Yes, but I didn't mention his name."

"Amanda Hurley did. We saw him at Lipp the following day, and he followed us as we were gallery-hopping. Lance told me that ten minutes after she and I parted, someone took a shot at her."

"That sounds like Majorov," Rick said.

"Who does he work for?"

"That's a very good question. He's Russian, and earlier in his career he was KGB. It's said that he and Putin served together there, and that they have remained close."

"So he's a sort of personal representative of Putin?"

"I wouldn't go that far. We've heard rumors of Russian gang connections. He has an interesting background: his father was a KGB general and was said to have planned an invasion of Sweden back in the eighties, one that never came off."

"I remember that a Russian submarine ran aground near a secret Swedish naval base," Stone said, "and there were stories in the press about sightings of miniature subs in Swedish waters."

"All those sightings were connected to the putative invasion. Strangely enough, President Will Lee is connected to the story."

"But that was a long time ago."

"He was chief of staff to Senator Ben Carr of Georgia at the time and was also counsel to the

Senate Select Committee on Intelligence. He met his future wife when she was testifying before the committee about CIA funding. She was an analyst at the time."

"But how was he connected to this thing with the Russians?"

"He was on vacation. He took delivery in Finland of a new yacht for a friend of his and was delivering it to England for him. While still in the Baltic he ran into some weather and lost his mast. He put in to the nearest port and got himself arrested, because it was a Soviet naval base, the one from which the invasion was to be launched. He talked his way out of it, but he called Kate and told her about his experience. She was instrumental in exposing a CIA mole who was giving the Soviets information. That catapulted her into the top ranks at the Agency, and she eventually rose to director."

"Funny, I've never heard about that."

"It was kept quiet at the time, except for the part about the mole."

"And how is this fellow Majorov connected to all that?"

"His father was the commander of the Soviet naval base. Will Lee actually met him, I think."

"And now his son is living in Paris, taking shots at your agent."

"Former agent," Rick said. "I told you, Amanda was drummed out."

"Just between you and me," Stone said, "she wasn't. Lance told me she is still active as a sleeper."

Rick regarded him with amazement. "He told you that?"

"He did."

"He never told me that."

"Perhaps you didn't have a need to know."

"Let me know if Majorov leaves the room," Rick said.

"All right."

They finished a superb lunch, then Marcel came around to their side of the table. "I must do a little business here," he said. "Keep the car for as long as you like, I have other transportation." He wandered off with a small group of people.

Stone looked up and saw Majorov making his way out of the dining room. "Heads up," he said to Rick. "There goes your man."

"Let's go," Rick said. They got up and followed Majorov, at some remove, out of the dining room and across the main exhibition floor. He went out the same back door by which they had entered. As they got to the door the Russian was getting into the driver's seat of a large silver BMW sedan. They got into the Maybach.

Rick leaned forward. "What's your name, driver?"

"Fritz," the man replied.

"Well, Fritz, you see the silver BMW going out the gate?"

"Yes, I see it."

"Don't lose it, but don't get too close, either."

The man put the Maybach in gear and drove out the gate, in time to see the BMW turn a corner.

"You've always wanted to do this, haven't you?" Rick asked Stone.

"Not really," Stone replied.

25

They followed the BMW back toward the center of Paris, to Montmartre, past the old church and down a side street.

"Fritz?" Rick said.

"Yes, sir?"

"Have you done this before?"

"Only in my dreams, sir."

Rick laughed aloud. "Everybody wants to do it. Hang on!"

The BMW suddenly pulled to the curb in front of a row of shops and stopped.

"Keep right on going, Fritz," Rick said. "Take your next right, and circle back. Drive slowly past the BMW."

Fritz followed his instructions.

They came back into the street, and the BMW was gone.

"See him anywhere?" Stone asked.

They drove slowly past the shops, and as they did, the BMW pulled out of an alley behind them.

"Uh-oh," Rick said. "Did you see the gallery?"

"What gallery?" Stone asked.

"The Ulyanov Gallery, just behind us. There was a sign in the window announcing an exhibition of new Russian paintings, starting today."

"Maybe Majorov is going to the opening party," Stone suggested.

"Then why is he following us?" Rick asked. "No, he's curious as to who we are."

"He can't see us through these darkened windows," Stone said.

"Good," Rick said, "because I don't want him to know who we are. Fritz, let's go back to M'sieur duBois's offices."

"You want him to think we're duBois?" Stone asked.

"He'll run our number plate anyway," Rick replied, "and find that the car is registered to one of duBois's businesses."

Fritz drove dutifully to duBois's building.

"Through the gates and into the courtyard, please," Rick said. "Then pull over to the left, out of sight of the street."

Fritz did so.

"Now, Fritz, please go inside to reception and look out the street window—see if you see the BMW."

Fritz got out of the car and went inside.

"What are we doing?" Stone asked.

"I don't want Majorov to associate us with this car," Rick said. "And I don't want him to see either of us popping up all the time."

Fritz returned. "The BMW stopped for a couple of minutes, then drove off," he said.

"Thank you for your help, Fritz," Rick said. "Okay, out of the car." He handed Fritz a fifty-euro note. "Would you ask the receptionist to call us a taxi, please? Have him drive in here. I don't want him to see us leaving the building."

Shortly a taxi pulled into the courtyard, and they got in. Rick asked the driver to take them to the Plaza Athénée. Back in Stone's suite, Stone asked, "Rick, do you have some theory of what's going on here?"

"You mean a unified theory that covers everything from your trip to Paris up to the present moment?"

"That's exactly what I mean."

"No," Rick said, "I don't. There are too many fragments to put together. What about you?"

"I'm baffled," Stone said. "I still don't know who

drugged me on the airplane, let alone why. I don't know why Majorov would be interested in me."

"He wasn't interested in you until he saw you, first with me, then with Amanda."

"I didn't think he saw me with you," Stone said.

"The KGB trained him to walk into a room and see everybody," Rick said. "That's how the Agency trains us, too. They would walk us into a McDonald's, then out, and say, okay, describe every adult in the restaurant."

"And you could do that?"

"It's amazing what you can do if somebody in authority is insisting. Believe me, Majorov made us together, and after the Amanda incident, he has you pegged as CIA, whether you like it or not."

"If I have a choice, I don't like it," Stone said.

The phone rang, and Stone picked it up. "Yes?"

"It's Eggers."

"So you kept the satphone?"

"The pilot didn't want to leave without it, but I insisted. I don't think anyone had ever taken one of his toys."

"Poor guy. I'll bet he's having trouble explaining that."

"He'll get over it when I send it back to him. The reason I called is, I remembered that thing I couldn't remember when I talked to you before."

"Tell me."

"He said Warren Buffett recommended our firm to him."

"Have you ever done any business with Warren Buffett?"

"No."

"Do you know Warren Buffett?"

"No."

"Then why the hell would the man recommend us to Marcel duBois?"

"I have no idea. I'm still trying to figure it out. Why don't you ask him?"

"All right."

"But don't tell him we don't know Warren Buffett."

"You think it's better if he thinks we do?"

"It couldn't hurt."

"Bill, while I've got you, I need some help."

"Okay, what kind?"

"DuBois has made us an offer for The Arrington."

"How much of an offer?"

"A billion dollars, not including the land."

"Take it. Anything else?"

"Wait a minute—what Mike Freeman and I want to do is to sell him, say, twenty percent of the hotel, then invest the proceeds with duBois for building some Arringtons in Europe."

"Great! Do that!"

"What I need from you is a couple of guys from the firm to make up a negotiating team to do the deal."

"All you need is one guy," Eggers said.

"Who?"

"You."

"I've never dealt with somebody that rich before. I'm afraid he'd skin me alive."

"Stone, if this were somebody else's hotel, you wouldn't bat an eye. You're just nervous about playing poker with your own money. Sit down with the guy, trade a few lies about what you each think it's worth, and get another offer from him. Then you can check with me, and I'll tell you if you're crazy or if duBois is."

"Well . . ."

"You're wasting my time. There are moose waiting."

"Okay. How's the moosing going?"

"Not bad. I'll send you some steaks."

"Don't, please don't. I'll never eat them."

"You're suffering from a Bambi complex," Eggers said.

"No, I have no trouble with venison, but moose is something else again. I think it's their soulful eyes."

"Sissy." Eggers hung up.

Rick stood up. "All right, I'm leaving now. If anybody tailed us in the taxi . . ."

"We didn't see the BMW while we were in the taxi," Stone pointed out.

"What makes you think there weren't other cars following us?"

"What makes you think there were?"

"Majorov didn't go into that gallery for no reason. He could have collected associates there."

"You have a suspicious nature," Stone said.

"It comes with the territory. You might profit from being suspicious. Suspicion might keep you alive longer."

"Nobody's taken a shot at me," Stone said.

"The first one could be the last," Rick said, then left.

Stone stretched out on the bed for a ten-minute nap.

26

Stone was jarred out of a deep sleep by his cell phone making noises. He looked at his watch: half past five. Some nap! He got out of bed and found the phone. "Hello?"

"It's Holly."

"Hi, there."

"I hear you have one of our phones now, so we can talk."

"Is Lance director yet?"

"He is. Kate is hanging around for a few days more to help with the transition. They've held lots of joint meetings with key personnel to pass the baton."

"How's everybody taking it?"

"Lance's rivals are sulking, everybody else seems cheerful enough. Of course, the people at

Langley have a lot of affection for Kate, and they hate to see her go. She's trying to rub some of her mojo off onto Lance, but it may not take. You making any progress with your memory?"

"None at all. Lance sent a satphone to Eggers up in the North Woods, and Bill called and filled in a lot of the blanks. I thought that might jar something loose, but it hasn't. What are you up to?"

"I'm back in New York and working my ass off. That's what I wanted to talk to you about."

"Okay, go."

"First of all, I lied to you. Nobody pressed me to move out of your house, it was my decision. I'm sorry, I should have been straight with you."

"Go on."

"I've just had the promotion of a lifetime. I'm hanging on by my fingernails, and it's not going to get any better in the foreseeable future. As a result of the change in our charter, we're expanding the New York station, and it will be a model for other stations around the country. I can't take the time to think about anything else but that. If I can bring this off, I might be in line for Lance's old job next time it opens up, and that's a dream for me. The guy who Lance appointed is a couple of years from retirement, and everybody knows he's just keeping the chair warm. Lance has told me he would like for me to have it someday, but not now.

I'm going to need more weight in my résumé before that might be possible."

"So, no time for me, then?"

"No time for anybody," Holly said with finality. "I love ya, Stone, but I love my work more, and I can't keep you both happy."

Stone sighed. "I can't say that I like it, but I understand it, so all I can do is wish you well and stay out of the way."

"Thanks for that, baby."

He sensed that their conversation was over. "Take care of yourself, and good luck in the job, for all our sakes."

"Thanks. Bye-bye." She hung up.

Stone lay back on the bed and realized that there was now a big hole in his life where there hadn't been one before. He closed his eyes and tried to let go.

Dinner was back in Montmartre, at an outdoor table next to the park. It was simple: roast chicken, potatoes, and haricots verts, with a bottle of Beaujolais.

"Feeling better?" Helga asked when he was done.

"Much," he said. "One more three-star dinner and I would have exploded."

"You seem a little preoccupied this evening. Anything wrong?"

"I said good-bye to a friend this afternoon," he said.

"How good a friend?"

"A very good one."

"So you were dumped?"

Stone laughed. "I was dumped. The competition was too tough."

"I can't imagine you losing that kind of competition," she said.

"I wasn't competing with another man, just with her job, which is overwhelming her at the moment and probably will for a long time to come."

"Good," Helga said. "More time for me."

"All you want," he replied. "Let's take a walk."

They walked to the top of the hill, then down the side street where Stone and Rick had followed Majorov that afternoon.

"Are we going anyplace special?" Helga asked.

"How about to a gallery opening?"

"That sounds like fun."

He found the Ulyanov Gallery. It was brightly lit, and there was a crowd inside, some of them spilling out onto the sidewalk, holding plastic cups of wine.

"Russian paintings?" Helga asked. "Are they good?"

"Sometimes. I have a couple in New York." They got some wine and began to look at the pictures. Stone stole glances around the room, looking for Majorov, and he was relieved to find him not there. Someone else was, though.

"Look at the tall man in the back," Stone said to Helga. "Wasn't he talking to you at Marcel's party? The one where we met? I think he's Italian."

Helga looked at the man. "Oh, yes. He's . . . let me see, Aldo something or other. He's not Italian, though, he just pretends to be."

"What is he?"

"Albanian. He's said to be a nephew of Hoxha, the longtime dictator, now deposed and dead."

"Then why is Aldo running around loose?"

"The rumor is he had some important post with the intelligence service or the police, if there was any difference. They say he got out of the country with a lot of cash before the regime came tumbling down—euros, not whatever used to be cash in Albania. Now he flits around Paris in expensive clothes with no visible means of support, so he must have stashed the cash."

Stone stopped in front of a painting of a castle by a river. "Nice," he said.

"Are you going to buy it?"

"No, I don't think I want this gallery to have my name and address."

"I'll buy it for you. I don't care if they have mine."

"I don't want them to have yours, either."

"Excuse me," a voice behind them said. They turned to find the mysterious Aldo standing behind them. "I believe we met at Marcel duBois's house recently. I'm Aldo Saachi."

"Of course," Stone said, offering his hand but not his name.

"Yes," Helga said, and shook it, too.

"What brings you two to this opening?" Aldo asked.

"We had dinner in the neighborhood and went for a walk," Stone replied. "We saw the poster and thought we'd have a look."

"Seen anything you like?" Aldo asked.

"No, we haven't," Stone said, "and if you'll excuse us, we were just about to leave."

"Can I offer you a drink somewhere nearby?" Aldo asked, gazing at Helga's cleavage.

"Perhaps another time," Stone said. "Good night." He took Helga's elbow and steered her toward the door.

Outside, Stone hailed a taxi.

"Why did you want to leave?" Helga asked.

"I think maybe it was a mistake to go there," Stone said. "I thought we'd gotten away with it, then Aldo showed up."

"He's inoffensive," she replied.

"He's dangerous," Stone said. "On the advice of a friend, I'm going to be suspicious of him."

27

The following morning Stone sat at the breakfast table in Helga's suite and glanced through the Paris papers. Marcel's Blaise had been chosen best in show, and there were multiple photos of him in and out of the car. He was quoted in the *International Herald Tribune* as saying, "On to New York!"

"It looks as though Marcel has a major success on his hands," Helga said, reading over Stone's shoulder while massaging his neck.

"I'm sure it's not his first," Stone said, "but it must be very satisfying for him."

Helga's phone rang, and she picked it up. "Yes? Good morning." She listened for a moment. "That's very kind of you. Please hold for a moment." She turned toward Stone. "It's the ambassador's secretary at the Russian Embassy. They are giving an impromptu party for Marcel this evening, and we are on a list that he gave them to invite. Do you want to go?"

Stone shrugged. "If you do."

She turned back to the phone. "Yes, I'd love to, and you may check Mr. Barrington off your list. He'd like to come, too." She hung up. "Well, that's very interesting."

"How so?"

"Why would the Russian ambassador give a party for Marcel?"

"Perhaps he does some business in Russia," Stone said.

Stone spent his day calling Joan and dictating letters, then working out a framework for a deal with Marcel. Late in the afternoon Rick LaRose called.

"What are you doing?" he asked.

"Pretending to work," Stone replied.

"Want to go to a party tonight?"

"I can't. Helga and I are going to the Russian Embassy."

Rick laughed. "So am I."

"You want to be seen by the opposition?"

"I'm accompanying the ambassador as the commercial attaché. Marcel has very large business interests in Russia, so many of the guests will be business types in town for the auto show."

"You make it sound dull."

"I hope it won't be," Rick said. "About an hour after you arrive, we'll bump into each other, and I'll point out the players to you."

"Will that keep me awake?"

"I didn't promise you excitement. See you there." Rick hung up.

They took a taxi, and when they arrived at the Russian Embassy, they found a Blaise parked in the forecourt, on display. Both gull-wing doors and the hood were open, and a photographer was shooting it from every angle.

Inside there was a formal reception line, and they had to work their way through that; then there was caviar, chilled vodka, and Russian champagne on offer. By the time they got to Marcel, Stone had a vodka buzz going.

"Did you see the photographer outside?" Marcel asked.

"Yes, I did."

"The Russians are photographing the Blaise because they want to copy it."

"That seems like a stupid idea," Stone said.

"They have a history of this," Marcel said. "Do you know that during World War Two an American

B-17 bomber made a forced landing in Siberia, and the Russians—or should I say, the Soviets—dismantled it, copied every part of it, and when they assembled their new airplane, it was so heavy they couldn't get it off the ground?"

"Then let's wish them the same success with copying the Blaise," Stone said, raising his glass.

"Stone, have you given any thought as to how you would like to proceed with our Arrington business?"

"I have, and I'd like to get together with you to discuss it."

"Lunch tomorrow at my home, then?"

"Yes, fine."

"I'll send the car for you at noon."

"Oh, don't bother. I'll get a taxi."

"I'll send you home in the car, then," Marcel said.

Stone looked across the room and saw Aldo Saachi, ne Hoxha, talking with someone. While he talked he stared at Stone and Marcel.

"Marcel, do you know Aldo Saachi well?"

"Not very well. Why do you ask?"

"Helga and I met him at a gallery opening last night—the Ulyanov Gallery, in Montmartre."

"Ah, yes, I had an invitation but declined. It is a very odd gallery, no?"

"How do you mean?"

"First of all, 'Ulyanov' is the real name of Vladimir Lenin. An odd reference for a Russian art gallery in their time of democracy, yes?"

"Yes, I suppose so."

"And it is operated by a former citizen of Albania, who is close to Aldo."

"Oh?"

"Wheels within wheels. I think the business of this gallery is not art but something else. Perhaps something our friend who works in Virginia would like to know about?"

"A good opportunity to enlighten him," Stone said. "Then make him tell you something."

"Good advice."

Stone saw Rick enter with the American ambassador, waited a few minutes, then sidled over to him.

"Good evening," Rick said. He was wearing another of his new suits. He introduced Stone to the ambassador.

"Ah, yes," the ambassador said. "Mr. Barrington, you're one of Lance's, aren't you?"

"I'm a consultant to the Agency," Stone replied.

"Yes, of course," the ambassador said with a knowing wink. He turned to speak to someone else.

Stone turned back to Rick. "When you get a moment, will you kindly explain to the ambassador that I'm not one of you?"

"I would, but it would only confuse him," Rick replied.

Stone sighed. "All right, but now please, make this evening exciting for me."

"I'll do my best," Rick said. "This event is a hotbed of spies of all sorts—political and industrial. You see the short, heavy man over there with the Russian ambassador's wife? That's the German intelligence service's man in Paris. And over there is the Italian ambassador with a man from Ferrari, who is probably here just to sneer at the Blaise. And then there's Aldo Saachi. Remember him?"

"Yes, I do." Stone told him of the events of last evening.

"I wish you hadn't gone there," Rick said, "but now I don't suppose it matters because everybody in town has seen us together here. You will now be known by everyone as Agency, and there's nothing you can do about it, short of slugging me and walking out."

"Is that what you suggest?"

"No, no. The ambassador would have a cow. Just learn to live with it. And with the consequences."

"Consequences?"

"There will be some probing, I expect."

"I think I should just conclude my business in Paris and get back to New York," Stone said.

"I was going to suggest that, but I didn't think you'd go for it."

"I'm having lunch with Marcel tomorrow. I think after that I will wend my way home."

"And happy contrails to you," Rick replied.

28

Stone and Helga arrived back at the Plaza Athé-née and got on the elevator.

"Excuse me," Helga said, pressing both her button and Stone's, "but I'm tired, and I'd rather sleep alone. Please don't take offense."

"Of course not," Stone said. "That party made me pretty tired, too." The elevator arrived at his floor; he kissed her, then the doors closed, and she continued up to her floor.

Stone let himself into his suite, got undressed, and fell into bed. He was asleep almost instantly. He began dreaming.

He was back on the Air France flight from New York, sitting in his seat, reading a magazine and sipping a mimosa—orange juice and champagne.

Amanda Hurley was across the aisle, and the sixty-ish woman in the Chanel suit was making her way down the aisle. He turned and looked over his shoulder: Aldo Saachi was seated directly behind him. Then he looked across the airplane, past Amanda, and saw Majorov across the other aisle. The Chanel woman came closer, then suddenly a chime was ringing. He looked ahead at the sign on the bulkhead, expecting the seat belt light to be turned on, but it was not. The chime seemed to get louder. The Chanel woman came closer and seemed to lose her balance, teetering toward Stone.

He jerked awake, but the chime was still ringing, and someone was knocking loudly on his door. He got out of bed, grabbed a robe, and looked through the peephole. Two men in suits stood outside. "Yes?" he yelled. One of the men held up an identity card, and Stone was able to read the words "Préfecture de Police." He opened the door. "Yes?"

"Mr. Barrington?"

"Yes."

"We must speak with you. May we come in?"

Stone turned on the master light switch, illuminating his sitting room. "Yes, come in." What the hell could the police want with him?

"Please be seated, Mr. Barrington," the older of the two, a man in his forties, said. His companion, who was perhaps ten years younger, stood silently and watched, a notebook in his hand.

"Have a seat yourself," Stone said, and everybody got comfortable. "Now, how may I help you?" He glanced at the digital clock on the desk: 3:40.

"I am Detective Inspector Claire," the older man said. "Would you kindly account for your actions of earlier this evening?"

"Why? What is this about?"

"Please, Mr. Barrington, indulge us."

Stone sighed, then recalled that he had spent many an evening of his youth in their position. "I spent the evening at a party at the Russian Embassy," Stone replied.

"And who at the party can confirm your presence there?" Claire asked.

"Oh, let's see," Stone said, staring at the ceiling as if to concentrate. "The American ambassador; the commercial attaché at our embassy, Mr. LaRose; the Russian ambassador; oh, and M'sieur Marcel duBois."

At the mention of that name the younger detective, who had been writing in his notebook, stopped and looked up at Stone.

"Anything else?" Stone asked.

"Were you in the company of a woman at this party?" Claire asked.

"Yes, I was."

"And her name?"

"Helga Becker. She lives on the top floor of this hotel."

"Did you return to the hotel in her company?"

"I did."

"At what time did you arrive here?"

"I think around ten thirty."

"Did you go to her suite with her?"

"No, we took the elevator up together, but I got off at this floor, and she continued upstairs."

"Mr. Barrington, do you possess a firearm?"

Stone nearly said no, but reconsidered. Lying to the police was not a good idea. "Yes, I do."

"May I see it, please?"

Stone got up, went to the desk, opened a drawer, and removed the small pistol Lance had given him. He also picked up his passport and slipped it into the pocket of his robe before returning to his seat.

Claire accepted the pistol in its holster. He popped out the magazine and worked the action to be sure it was unloaded, then he smelled the breach and the barrel. "How is it that you, a foreign visitor, would be armed?"

Stone decided to give him a short version: "An official of the American government was concerned for my safety and gave it to me. Earlier that day, an apparent attempt had been made on our lives. A large truck rammed our car about one hundred meters from here."

"Ah, yes," Claire said, "I know of this event. Who else was in the car with you?"

"I'm sure you already have their names," Stone said. "Now, would you please tell me why you are calling on me at this ungodly hour?"

The two detectives exchanged a glance.

"We are investigating a homicide," Claire replied.

"A homicide where and who?" Stone asked.

"In Ms. Becker's suite," Claire replied.

Stone was startled. "Is Ms. Becker all right?" he asked.

"She is quite safe, I assure you," Claire said. "She is at the headquarters of the Prefecture of Police, helping us with our inquiries."

"Did she witness the homicide?" Stone asked.

"As far as we know, she was the only person in her suite besides the deceased."

Stone didn't like the sound of that. "And who died?"

"Are you acquainted with a person who calls himself Aldo Saachi?"

"Yes, I've met him."

"When, and under what circumstances?"

"We were first introduced at a dinner party at the home of Marcel duBois, then I ran into him the evening before last at the Ulyanov Gallery, in

Montmartre, at the opening of an art show. I also saw him at the party last evening at the Russian Embassy, though we did not speak. He seemed quite healthy at the time."

"You are friends, then?"

"Certainly not. On the two occasions when we actually spoke, we exchanged only a few words."

"Are you aware of the true identity of this man Saachi?"

"I've heard rumors that he is an Albanian named Hoxha."

"Ah, yes, quite so. You seem to know a lot about this Saachi."

"Only what I've told you. I am an attorney, a lawyer. May I go to your headquarters and see Ms. Becker?"

"Are you licensed to practice law in France?"

"I am not."

"Then you may not see her. However, I think it would be a good idea if you got dressed and came with us."

"For what purpose?"

"We wish to investigate your story and question you further."

Stone handed the detective his passport, reflecting that Lance Cabot had been prescient in giving it to him. "I'm sorry, but I must decline to accompany you. If you have any further questions of me, please ask them here and now, because the next time we speak I will be accompanied by my legal representative, who will, no doubt, advise me not to answer any questions."

Claire examined the passport with care. "Why do you have a diplomatic passport?"

"Your question is not relevant to your reasons for visiting me," Stone said.

"Please, sir, I will determine what is relevant and what is not."

"No, I will make that determination for myself," Stone said. "Now, if you have further questions, please ask them or leave."

Claire glanced at his colleague, who shook his head, then they both got to their feet. "We may wish to question you again," Claire said, "so do not leave Paris."

Stone walked to the desk, got a business card from his briefcase, and handed it to Claire. "I will go where I wish, when I wish," Stone said. "If I decide to leave Paris, you may contact me at my office in New York." He walked to the door, opened it, and stood back. "Good night—or rather, good morning—gentlemen," he said.

The two men left, and Stone closed the door behind them.

He found his iPhone and pressed the speed-dial

number for Rick LaRose. It rang several times before it was answered.

"Yes?"

"Rick, it's Stone Barrington."

"What time is it?"

"Nearly four a.m."

"What's going on?"

"Aldo Saachi has been shot and killed in Helga Becker's suite at the Plaza Athénée, and she is being held at the headquarters of the Prefecture of Police."

"*What?*"

"You heard me the first time. It sounds as though Helga is their only suspect. They wouldn't let me see her."

"Good God! It wasn't supposed to happen that way!"

Stone was speechless. By the time he had recovered enough to speak, Rick had hung up.

29

Stone drifted awake. He looked at the clock on the desk: 10:20 a.m., and his bedroom seemed darker than usual at this hour. He was aware that he had had two dreams, and he remembered both of them with absolute clarity. He couldn't remember ever having recalled a dream after waking. Then he realized that one of them had not been a dream: the one with the French policemen.

He went to the windows and opened the drapes. The Paris he had been experiencing for the past few days—one of crisp, sunny autumn days—was gone; it had been replaced by a darkened city whipped by gusty winds and lashed by pouring rain. He closed the drapes.

He shaved and showered, then phoned down a

breakfast order, then he picked up the phone, called the American Embassy and asked for Dr. Keeler. He didn't remember a first name.

"Dr. Keeler," the man said.

"Good morning, Dr. Keeler," Stone said. "It's Stone Barrington. I've had a dream I can't interpret."

"Freud I'm not," Keeler replied, "but tell me about it."

Stone told him about the dream of his Air France flight. "It's extremely unusual that I would remember a dream," he said. "In fact, I've hardly ever done so."

"I think what you have there is not a dream but a memory," Keeler said. "Congratulations, you're on the mend."

"Thank you. What do I do now?"

"Remember something else," Keeler said.

Stone thanked the man and hung up. His doorbell was chiming, and he shouted for the waiter to enter. The man wheeled in the table, and Stone started to eat.

The doorbell chimed again, and Stone shouted for the waiter to enter.

"I don't have a key!" somebody yelled from the other side of the door.

Stone opened the door and let in Rick LaRose. "Good morning, Rick. Would you like some breakfast?"

"Thank you, yes," Rick replied. "Belgian waffles, three scrambled eggs, bacon and sausage, and a pot of espresso."

Stone pointed at the desk. "Speak into the phone," he said.

Rick ordered his breakfast, then pulled up a chair to Stone's table.

Stone poured him a cup of coffee. "Have you heard anything about Helga?" he asked.

"I put her into a car a couple of hours ago," Rick replied. "By now, she's on a private jet to Stockholm. She'll be met there and driven to her divorce-won house on an island in the Stockholm archipelago. You won't be hearing from her."

"How did you get the Prefecture of Police to release her?"

"I didn't. The ambassador spoke to the prefect of police personally and did some explaining. That's the second time in less than a week he's had to do that for us, and he was very unhappy about it—to put it mildly."

"Do they have another suspect?" Stone asked.

"No."

"Then what could the ambassador possibly have said to the prefect of police that would secure her release? Is she something more than one of your assets?"

Rick sighed. "Let me put it this way: Helga is

something more than an Agency asset and something less than a CIA officer."

"What lies between?"

"Consultants and contractors."

"Which is Helga?"

"A contractor."

"And what is she contracted to do?"

Rick finished the coffee, and his breakfast arrived. He dug in.

Stone waited until he had finished everything and was on his first cup of espresso. "Why don't you weigh three hundred pounds?" he asked.

"I don't eat this way every day," Rick replied. "Only when I'm under stress and somebody else is buying."

"Back to my question," Stone said. "What is Helga contracted to do?"

"Helga was recruited as an asset about three years ago, then Lance felt that she might have what it takes to make an actual agent. She didn't make it through all the training at the Farm, but two things about her stood out."

"Was that an attempt at humor?" Stone said.

Rick ignored the question. "First, she turned out to be an excellent shot with a handgun and a rifle, and, being athletic, she was very good with other . . . tools, as well. Very strong, physically. And her psychological profile revealed her to be very strong mentally as well—cool under pressure, ruthless when motivated, and not much burdened by conscience."

"You're not telling me she's an—"

"That's right, I'm not telling you that, but she wasn't supposed to do it in her hotel suite. She came home and found Aldo Saachi waiting for her, expecting a roll in the hay, and he, you might say, insisted. Still, with no witnesses to support her story, the police were not inclined to believe her—thus the intervention of the ambassador."

"Well, that's a breathtaking story," Stone said. "I don't think I've ever . . ." He seemed at a loss for words.

"Fucked an Agency contractor?" Rick offered helpfully.

Stone shrugged. "You said something on the phone that puzzled me," he said.

"What was that?"

"You said, and I quote, 'It wasn't supposed to happen this way.' I take it you had plans for Aldo?"

"Aldo was a pain in the ass," Rick said, "but he became much more than that. He became a danger to, among other people, you."

"Wait a minute," Stone said, "don't hang this on me."

"And Marcel duBois."

"Do you mean he was an actual physical threat?"

"Aldo was in the employ of . . . I don't know quite what to call them—they don't have a name. A cabal, I guess, is as good as any word to describe them. They are a criminally oriented group of ex–intelligence officers—KGB and Eastern European services, formerly Soviet Bloc countries."

"With Majorov at the top?"

"Not at the top, but close."

"And who's at the top?"

"I dare not speak his name," Rick said. "Because we're not entirely sure."

"My memory has started to return," Stone said. "At least a slice of it." He told Rick about the group on the Air France flight.

"That was Lance's doing," Rick said. "He bought the empty first-class seats on that flight. You had already booked, so he left you in place, since you are contractually bound not to talk about what might have gone on."

"You mean Aldo was supposed to meet his end on that flight?"

"No, but what happened on that flight was supposed to make him easier to deal with. We had envisioned an interrogation."

"But I, ah, took his room reservation at the embassy?"

"You might say that."

"Rick, why are you telling me all this? Wouldn't Lance object to my knowing it?"

"Lance feels badly about what happened to you, and he wanted to help you fill in the gaps. He wants you happy."

"I'm puzzled," Stone said. "Why would he want that?"

"Because Marcel duBois is showing some reluctance to behave as an asset should. Lance said to tell you that, for the time being, he is *your* asset, not mine or Lance's."

"Oh, swell," Stone said.

"All you have to do is listen to him, then report in."

"That's all there is to it?"

"Well, there is the fact that, in spite of the demise of Aldo Saachi, M'sieur duBois is not entirely out of the woods, no pun intended." Rick drained his espresso cup. "Nor are you."

30

Stone checked the weather again before leaving the hotel. No change. He wished now that he had accepted Marcel's offer of his car. He got into his trench coat, unpacked a folding fedora, and carried it down to the lobby and out the front door. "Taxi, please," he said to the doorman.

The man was dressed in a yellow slicker with a hood. "I'm sorry, Mr. Barrington," he said, throwing up his hands. "There are no taxis, except those that might drop a passenger at the hotel. It could be half an hour or more."

"Then I'll walk," Stone said, putting on his hat and buttoning and belting his trench coat.

The man held out an umbrella. "Compliments of the hotel," he said.

Stone trudged down the street in the general direction of Marcel's building, leaning into the wind and sheltering himself as best he could under the umbrella. Twenty minutes later he walked into the building, dripping water onto the lobby floor. He gave the doorman his coat, hat, and umbrella. The man received them gingerly and hung them in a closet.

Stone's trousers were soaked from the shins down, and so were his shoes. He rode up in the elevator, adjusting his tie and making himself as presentable as possible. He arrived at Marcel's floor and was greeted by the man himself.

"My dear fellow!" Marcel cried. "Your trousers are soaked. Were you unable to find a taxi?"

"I should have accepted your offer of your car," Stone said.

Marcel turned to his butler. "Victor, find Mr. Barrington a robe and press his suit. Is your coat downstairs, Stone?"

"Yes."

"Dry everything and press his garments," Marcel said. "Please, Stone, go with Victor."

Victor showed him to a guest bedroom. "There is a dressing gown and slippers in the closet," he said. "Please give me your suit and shoes."

Stone got out of the clothes and turned them over to Victor, then he got into the cashmere dressing gown and soft leather slippers and went back to the living room, where Marcel waited.

"Come into the study," Marcel said. "Lunch will be ready shortly. Would you like a drink?"

"Perhaps some Perrier," Stone said. He took a chair and the footman brought him the water.

Marcel joined him. "Now," he said, "I hope you are comfortable."

"Quite comfortable," Stone said.

"The storm is very bad. De Gaulle is closed—until midnight, they say."

"I hope I might be able to get a flight to New York tomorrow," Stone said. "I hope we can conclude our business, one way or another, before then."

"I, too, hope so," Marcel said. "Have you thought about my offer?"

"Yes, and I've discussed it with two of our directors, as well. Here is what I am willing to propose to the board: to sell you fifteen percent of our stock for three hundred and fifty million dollars and to invest our net proceeds in a new company, which would operate hotels in Europe and, perhaps, elsewhere in the world."

"Well," Marcel said, "now it is my turn to think." The waiter entered and announced lunch.

"I thought some hot soup would be appropriate for the weather," Marcel said as they took their seats.

The waiter served a leek and potato soup, which Stone welcomed.

"I don't know if you have spoken to Lance," Marcel said.

"No, but I've heard that you are, perhaps, a little uncomfortable with your arrangement with him."

"On reflection, yes. I am French, and I am troubled that I might somehow go against my country's interests in being associated with him."

"I can quite understand that," Stone said. "I would certainly not enter into an arrangement that would go against my own country's interests."

"Also, I am reluctant to communicate through the means he has given me. I am hardly a Luddite, but I am a little distrustful of electronic devices in conveying sensitive information."

"Of course," Stone said. "If it would be helpful to you, I would be happy to act as a conduit between you and Lance."

Marcel brightened. "That is an interesting offer," he said. "Would you also convey in the opposite direction?"

"Yes, indeed. I don't imagine you will be contacting each other on a daily basis."

"That is unlikely," Marcel said.

"There is something that I should convey to you now, if I may."

"Please."

"I was visited by the police in the middle of the night," Stone said, and proceeded to describe Helga's situation.

"I am sorry for her," Marcel said, "but she will surely be safe back in Sweden."

"I believe so," Stone said, "but it has been suggested to me by Rick LaRose that you and I may not be quite so safe."

Marcel sighed. "I have been feeling a certain amount of pressure to enter into business dealings which are not attractive to me. This Aldo fellow has been the messenger, and I've had an instinctive distrust of him. The people he represents are eager to buy into my Blaise operation and to distribute the car outside of Europe and the United States."

Stone told him of Rick's assessment of Aldo's business associates.

"That is shocking," Marcel said, "but it confirms my worst suspicions, and more."

"It seems possible," Stone said, "that these people may employ more than business tactics in achieving their ends. You should be wary."

"I certainly feel wary," Marcel replied. "After all, there is the business of the bombs planted in my Blaises at the auto show."

"Do you have any personal security?" Stone asked.

"No, I have never felt the need," Marcel said. "Until now, perhaps."

"I serve on the board of a company called Strategic Services," Stone said, "run by an excellent man named Michael Freeman."

"I have heard of them, of course," Marcel replied. "Their reputation is excellent."

"Mike has a Paris branch, and I would be happy to introduce you to him."

"I would like very much to meet him," Marcel replied. "This would seem an opportune moment for me to get out of Paris for a while, I think, and it might be a good time for me to visit New York and see if we can come to some arrangement regarding The Arrington."

"I and my colleagues would be very happy to see you in America."

"Then tomorrow why don't you forsake Air France and fly with me to New York?"

"Thank you, that would be a pleasure. If you are uncomfortable staying in a hotel at this time I would be happy to have you as a guest in my home. We can make you comfortable and secure there for as long as you like."

"That is very kind of you, Stone."

"And there is room for others, if you wish to take some staff along."

"I usually travel alone," Marcel said.

"And I'll arrange for you to meet with Mike Freeman. I'm sure Bill Eggers would like to see you as well. He should be back shortly from his hunting trip in Maine."

"Then I will collect you at your hotel at ten tomorrow morning," Marcel said, "and we will drive to Le Bourget together. The storm will pass through tonight, and although the airline schedules may still be affected, we need not let that concern us."

When Stone left an hour and a half later his suit had been pressed; his shoes were dry, and so were his trench coat and his hat. He entered Marcel's car under shelter and drove to his hotel. As he returned the doorman's umbrella, the man seemed surprised to see him perfectly warm and dry.

As he walked into the hotel something caused him to turn and look back into the street. A black Mercedes sat idling, and Stone had the odd feeling that it had followed him from Marcel's building. He went upstairs to phone New York and make arrangements to receive Marcel duBois, thinking he was glad to be leaving Paris.

31

Stone stood in front of the Plaza Athénée, having paid his bill with Marcel's expense money, and watched the Maybach glide to a stop a yard away. He made sure that all his bags and his briefcase were put into the trunk and had a look at the street before sliding into the rear seat next to Marcel. He saw two vehicles, a black Mercedes sedan and a gray van, double-parked across the street. The van had steel beams where the bumpers usually were.

"Good morning, Stone."

"Good morning, Marcel. I see from the weather report that we have a good day for flying."

"Yes, the storm has moved off to the south. I believe that Lyon is feeling it by now." The car pulled away.

"I spoke to Rick LaRose last night," Stone said, "and told him of our conversation regarding communication with our friend in Virginia."

"Ah, good. I suppose when I return I will have to communicate through Mr. LaRose."

"You may if you wish, but if you phone me on the cell phone that Lance gave you, our conversations will be scrambled, since I have the same phone." He wrote the number on his business card and gave Marcel his personal card as well. "This is my address and various phone numbers in New York. Please feel free to give them to anyone who wishes to contact you while you're with us."

"Thank you," Marcel said, and tucked the card into his wallet.

They drove north along the Seine for a time, chatting idly. Marcel was making a phone call when Stone looked across the car and out the window to see a black Mercedes drawing up beside them and a rear window coming down. The morning sun glinted on the barrel of an automatic weapon as it was pointed through the open window by a man wearing a dark balaclava helmet obscuring his face. Stone was about to pull Marcel onto the floor of the car when there was a loud crash, and the Mercedes rocketed forward.

The gray van was behind the black car, and it accelerated again, slamming its bolted-on steel beam against the rear bumper of the Mercedes. Marcel's driver had slowed to remain clear of the two vehicles, and they watched as the van continued to assault the car. Then the van moved alongside the Mercedes and slammed, broadside, into the vehicle. The car hit the low railing and tipped over the edge, falling off the elevated roadway.

Stone looked over his shoulder in time to see the Mercedes ricochet off the lower level, ten feet down, then topple into the Seine. "Let's get out of here," he said to the driver.

Marcel sat rigid in his seat, his face drained of color, staring straight ahead. He said something in French that sounded to Stone like an oath, then he switched to English. "What happened?" he asked.

"Someone was about to fire a weapon at us from the black Mercedes, but a van struck it from behind repeatedly and dumped it into the Seine." He patted Marcel's arm. "It's all right now. Rick LaRose is driving the van, and he is behind us."

"How did someone know where to find us?" Marcel asked.

"The Mercedes followed me from your building to the hotel yesterday afternoon. Rick and I had a conversation about it last evening, and he told me he would take precautions for our drive to Le Bourget."

"You know," Marcel said, "I believe I have chosen the correct moment to leave Paris for a while."

On their arrival at Le Bourget, they drove through a guarded gate and drew up next to a Gulfstream 650 business jet, which already had one engine running, on the opposite side of the aircraft.

Stone got out of the car and found Rick LaRose waiting for him. "Nice driving," he said. "Is the ambassador going to have to have another chat with the prefect of police?"

"I think I can handle this one on my own," Rick said. "Enjoy your flight, and let me hear from you sometime."

Stone gave him his card, they shook hands, then Rick got into the van and drove away. Men appeared to take their luggage, and as soon as they had climbed the stairs and stepped into the airplane, the steps were taken away and the second engine started. A moment later, they were taxiing.

A uniformed young Frenchwoman showed them to seats at the rear of the airplane, an area arranged to look more like a comfortable study than ordinary airplane seating. Shortly after that the airplane accelerated, then they were off the ground and climbing steeply. The stewardess appeared with champagne and orange juice, and Stone had some of each.

"You know," Marcel said, "that was really quite a performance with the van and the Mercedes. I suddenly feel more kindly disposed toward your friends at the CIA."

"There are times when it's good to have friends," Stone said, picking up a phone on the table in front of him. "I'll see that we're met at the other end." He called Mike Freeman.

A couple of hours later, after reading the New York and Paris papers, they were served a good lunch, then Stone went forward to a reclining seat and had a nap. The stewardess awakened him as they were descending over Long Island toward Teterboro Airport in New Jersey, and five minutes later they were on the ground.

A car from Strategic Services pulled up to the airplane and received Stone and Marcel and their luggage, and another car followed as they were driven into Manhattan. Thirty minutes later, they pulled up to Stone's house. Two watchful men stood by the car as they got out and went inside, where Stone's secretary, Joan Robertson, and his housekeeper and cook, Helene, and her elder brother, Philip, waited. Philip was a retired butler and driver engaged for the occasion, and he showed Marcel upstairs to his room.

"I thought Philip could be useful during Mr. duBois's stay," Joan said.

"A great idea," Stone replied.

"Mike Freeman and Bill Eggers have arranged a dinner at the Four Seasons at nine o'clock," she said, "and Dino wants you to call him." She handed him a card. "He has a new office number."

Stone looked at the card, which announced that Dino Bacchetti was the new chief of detectives of the NYPD. "He didn't waste any time getting started after the honeymoon, did he?" Stone said.

"And Mrs. Bacchetti has already started her new job at Strategic Services. They'll be at the dinner tonight."

"It's good to be home," Stone said. He went upstairs to unpack and call Dino.

32

At eight o'clock, Stone rapped on Marcel's door. His guest was occupying the guest suite overlooking the garden, immediately below Stone's bedroom. Stone led him down to the study and offered him a drink.

"What is that you are drinking?" Marcel asked.

"Knob Creek, a small-batch bourbon. Knob Creek is where Abraham Lincoln was born in a log cabin, in Kentucky."

"I'll try it, then," Marcel said.

Stone poured the drinks and handed one to him. "You may find it peculiar at first, but the second one goes down more smoothly."

Marcel took a sip and wrinkled his nose. "Interesting," he said. He looked around the study.

"You have a great deal of very fine woodwork in your house," he said.

"Thank you. All of it was made by my father."

"He was a designer?"

"A woodworker who later became a designer."

"Tell me about him," Marcel said.

"My parents were from old families in western Massachusetts, to the north, in New England. My father had been enrolled at Yale, following in his father's footsteps, but he had always enjoyed working with wood, and he wanted to make a career of it. He and my mother were in love, contemplating marriage by this time.

"My grandfather was outraged that, instead of his son's following him into the family business, a woolen mill, he wanted to enter a trade. He also disliked my father's and mother's left-wing politics. Both sets of parents forbade them to marry, and when they eloped, they were disowned. My mother was a painter, and they settled in the Village, where my father earned a meager living, wandering the Village with a toolbox, knocking on doors and offering to do odd jobs. In the meantime, he was drawing the sort of things he wanted to build.

"My great-aunt Matilda, for whom my mother was named, was the only family member who would still speak to them. She built this house and engaged my father to do all the woodwork—paneling, library, doors—everything. The commission kept them alive for three years, and when it was done, all of Aunt Matilda's friends wanted my father's work. He became well known in New York, and my mother became a very fine painter. The picture there is one of hers." He indicated the painting over the sofa.

"She was very good indeed," Marcel said. "A lovely style."

"She has work hanging in the Metropolitan Museum."

"I'm not surprised. Who are the other people we're dining with tonight?"

"You've met Bill Eggers," Stone said. "He has been very important in my life. When I was in law school I worked in a summer program with the New York Police Department, and when I graduated I joined the police, instead of practicing law. I did that for fourteen years, then the department and I had a disagreement, and I lost. I had inherited this house from Aunt Matilda, and I was renovating it in my spare time, with a little help from outside contractors. I found myself unemployed with only a police pension for income and a big loan on the house.

"Then I ran into Bill Eggers, who had been a good friend when we were in law school together. He suggested I study for the bar examination, then come to work for Woodman & Weld. I did so, and I've been happy there ever since."

"And Michael Freeman?"

"Mike has a mysterious background in the world of intelligence. The founder of Strategic Services, Jim Hackett, also found Mike, and he became the number two man in the business. When Jim died, Mike succeeded him, and he has quadrupled the size of the company since then, to the point where they are the second-largest security firm in the world."

"And the other couple?"

"Dino Bacchetti and I were partners for many years when we were both policemen. He is still with the department and was recently promoted to chief of detectives, a very important position. His wife, Vivian, or Viv, as she's called, was also a detective. She retired from the department when they married, a few weeks ago, and has just joined Strategic Services. And those are our dinner companions."

The phone buzzed, and Stone picked it up, listened for a moment, then hung up. "My car is waiting for us outside," he said.

"Then I will have my second Knob Creek at the restaurant," Marcel said, rising. "Where are we going?"

"To the Four Seasons," Stone replied. "It's only a few blocks away."

They entered the Four Seasons from East Fifty-second Street and climbed the broad staircase, emerging in the bar, where the others in their party awaited. Stone gave Dino and Viv a hug, then made the introductions; then they moved into the main dining room, often called the "Pool Room" because of the large pool at its center. They were seated at a round table, and Stone placed Marcel between himself and Mike Freeman. Drinks were ordered.

"Marcel," Bill Eggers said when their drinks had arrived, "I see Stone has recruited you to bourbon."

"This is my second one," Marcel said, "and I'm enjoying it more and more." He turned to Freeman. "Mike, I would like to thank you for arranging our security at the airport," he said. "You've made me feel very secure in New York, something I had not felt recently in Paris."

"Stone told me about that," Mike replied, "and I was happy to help."

They ordered dinner, and the conversation flowed.

After dinner Stone's car, driven by Philip, returned them to his house. "Would you like a nightcap?" he asked Marcel.

"If you will forgive me, I think the time change is catching up with me, so I will retire. It is very late in Paris."

Stone put him on the elevator, then went to his

study, poured himself a cognac, and called Mike Freeman.

"I liked your guest," Mike said.

"And he liked you, I could tell."

"I've done a little looking into him, as is my wont, and I think he makes an ideal investor for us in the States, and an ideal gateway to Europe for us, too."

"Surely that isn't all you've found out."

"All right, he's worth something in the neighborhood of thirty billion euros, which puts him well up in the Forbes 100. The comparison to Warren Buffett is a perfectly valid one. Their careers and investing methods are similar, but not their lifestyles."

"Yes, I've experienced Marcel's lifestyle, and let me tell you, it is spectacular."

Stone's other line rang. "Hang on a minute, Mike." He pressed the hold button, then the second line. "Hello?"

"Stone?" A woman's voice, familiar. "It's Helga."

"Hold on, Helga." He pressed line one. "Mike, I'm going to have to talk to you tomorrow."

"Good night, then."

33

Stone returned to his second line. "Helga, are you all right?"

"Yes, at last," she replied.

"The Paris police woke me in the middle of the night to question me, but they refused to let me see you, so I called Rick LaRose."

"Rick was wonderful," she said. "I hadn't had any sleep, and the police asked me the same questions over and over, and I was exhausted by the time Rick turned up. He got me released and sent me directly to Le Bourget, where there was an airplane waiting to take me home to Sweden. I'm now at my house out in the archipelago, and it's very beautiful here, but lonely."

"I think I can fix that," Stone said. "Why don't

you come to New York for a while? None of the Paris complications will bother you here. Marcel is already here, asleep in my guest suite."

"Marcel in New York? He almost never goes to America."

"It seemed a good time to get him out of Paris." Stone told her about the attack on them along the Seine.

"I'm glad you're out—those people are very dangerous."

"Who are they?" Stone asked.

"A bunch of crazy Russians and East Germans left over from the Cold War days. They're working for a Russian oligarch named Vishinski. It's said that he's close to the Russian leadership. Vishinski is making business inroads into Europe, with Paris as his main target, and he seems to want what Marcel has."

"What happened with Aldo Saachi?"

"He was waiting in my suite when I got there."

"How did he get in?"

"He must have bribed a hotel staffer. He made advances, and I punched him in the nose, but he tore my dress on his way down. When he stood up he had a knife in his hand, so I shot him."

"Did the police find the knife?"

"Yes."

"Good, that will help clear your name."

"That won't be a problem. According to Rick, all records of my questioning will disappear, and they will think of some explanation for Aldo's death, so for all practical purposes, I am not involved."

"I'm relieved that you're all right. When can you come to New York?"

"Give me a few days to work on that. I'll need to get Lance's permission to come to the U.S."

"I'll have a word with Lance and let you know what he says. What's your phone number?"

"I have the same cell, the one that Lance gave me. We can talk on that without anyone hearing us."

"Then I'll be in touch."

"Please give Marcel my best."

"I will." They both hung up, and Stone went upstairs and to bed.

The following morning he had breakfast with Marcel in the kitchen, then went to his office, where he found a large stack of paperwork on his desk. He called Lance at Langley and left a message for him, then went to work answering mail and returning phone calls.

Just before noon Joan buzzed him. "Lance Cabot on one."

Stone pressed the button. "Good morning, Lance."

"Good morning, Stone. Did you have a pleasant flight?"

"We did indeed, except for the unpleasantness on the way to Le Bourget. Rick saved our bacon."

"A good man, Rick. He's destined for greater things."

"I'm glad to hear it."

"How is Marcel liking New York?"

"He's very happy here. He's staying with me, and we had dinner with Mike Freeman last night. Mike is going to help him with his personal security situation."

"He certainly needs help," Lance agreed.

"After Rick's intervention, Marcel's feelings toward the Agency have warmed considerably. I think you'll find him more cooperative."

"I'm extremely glad to hear that," Lance said.

"Lance, I've invited Helga Becker to visit me in New York. I hope you don't have a problem with that."

"Do you think you can avoid having her photographed in your company while she's there? I don't want her to turn up on Page Six—at least, not until everything has quieted down in Paris. Our two presidents have had discussions about the Aldo incident, and word has reached me that Aldo's friends are extremely angry."

"I think I can shield her from the press."

"I'm glad Marcel is staying with you. A lot of our friends seem to do that from time to time."

Stone knew he was referring to Holly, but he said nothing.

"I think it's time we augmented the security arrangements for your house," Lance said. "After all, after the events of a few weeks ago, al Qaeda is aware of you."

This had crossed Stone's mind, but he hadn't done anything about it. "What sort of augmentation?"

"If you're going to go on hosting people important to us, like the president and first lady, even after they're out of office, then we'll need to install a new security system, and we'll need to replace the exterior doors with steel ones and the windows with steel-framed armored glass."

"The New-York Historical Society will be alarmed to hear that, and you'll have to have their approval."

"Leave that to me. The doors and windows will appear identical to the ones they're replacing. We did the same thing with your cousin Dick's house at Dark Harbor, which you now own."

"You're not going to send me a bill for all this, are you?"

"Fear not, Stone, it will be done with dispatch, and you will be none the poorer for it."

"All right."

"A man named Joe will call and survey the place. He'll phone Joan first."

"And you'll take whatever steps are necessary so that Helga won't have any problems entering the country?"

"I will, but I don't want her flying commercial until I say so, and that could be a few weeks."

"Then I'll arrange something. How's the new job?"

"More hectic than I had imagined. Kate has been a great help with the transition. I'm moving into her offices tomorrow. Now I must go." Lance hung up without further ado.

Stone buzzed Joan. "A man named Joe, a friend of Lance's, is going to come to the house and make a nuisance of himself, and then he's going to put in a new security system and replace all the windows in the house."

"Is that all? Oh, it'll be fun!" She hung up.

Marcel rapped on the rear door to Stone's office and walked in. "May I?"

"Of course," Stone said. "How's the jet lag?"

"I'm feeling quite well," he said, "after a good night's sleep."

"When would you like to meet with Mike Freeman about your security arrangements?"

"Anytime at all. And we should invite Bill Eggers and discuss the Arrington proposition, as well."

"I'll do that. By the way, Helga called last night after you went to bed and sends you her warm regards. She's safe in Sweden, but she's going to come and visit me in New York."

"When will she come?"

"As soon as I can arrange a private air charter. Lance doesn't want her flying commercial until things have quieted down."

"My French attorney will come to New York if we can reach an agreement on the Arrington business. I can have him pick her up in Stockholm on his way."

"That's very kind of you, Marcel." And a reason to conclude our business quickly, Stone thought.

34

Stone and Marcel were driven to the offices of Strategic Services by Philip in Stone's car and were immediately shown into Mike Freeman's large office.

"Good morning, Marcel," Mike said. "Bill Eggers will be joining us in half an hour or so, but I wanted to talk with you about your security concerns in Paris."

"Thank you, Mike," Marcel said, sitting down on the sofa and accepting a cup of coffee.

"There are two immediate concerns, as we see it," Mike said. "First, there's the Blaise factory, which we have not had an opportunity to survey."

"Fortunately," Marcel replied, "we have had a considerable security presence at the factory, because of our concerns about keeping the operation secret. With the introduction of the car at auto shows around the world, I had planned to reduce that to the bare minimum."

"Are you pleased with the quality of the security personnel?"

"I believe they are good at keeping visitors away."

"Are they armed?"

"No."

"Then it is our recommendation, if you wish to continue with the same security firm, that you request an upgrade in the quality and training of the guards and have them armed with semiautomatic pistols, with assault rifles or shotguns readily available to them."

"I do not have confidence that the firm I'm dealing with would be able to provide such personnel."

"Then may we send our Paris station head to the factory to conduct a survey and make a proposal?"

"Certainly, and the sooner the better."

"Tomorrow at the latest," Mike said. "Now to your personal needs. Stone has described your living arrangements at the top of your office building, and we like what we heard. We recommend that you have two armed men in the building twenty-four hours a day, one at the front desk downstairs and one in your living quarters. Ideally, that man would answer the door when guests arrive, and he would ride in the front seat of your car with your driver when you move about Paris, then accompany you in a discreet manner when you leave the car."

"That sounds like a good plan," Marcel replied.

"Staffing that requirement twenty-four hours a day would require a team of eight to ten men." Mike handed him a sheet of paper. "This is a quote for such a complement."

Marcel read it quickly. "Agreed," he said.

"They will be on duty when you arrive back in Paris," Mike said. "We also recommend very strongly that you travel in a well-armored vehicle."

Marcel shook his head. "I don't want to move about in a tank."

"You drove here in Stone's car, which is a product of our armored vehicle division."

"The Bentley? That didn't seem like a tank."

"It would have protected you from the sort of assault that was attempted on your car on your way to Le Bourget," Mike said.

"How long would I have to wait for it?"

"Are you happy with your Maybach?"

"Very much so."

"We have existing templates for all the panels necessary to fortify your car. Stone says you are shipping Blaises by air to this country. If you can ship the Maybach that way, then by working around the clock on the car we can complete the work in eight days." He handed Marcel a quote for the job.

"I can ship it by air," Marcel said, "and I accept your proposal."

"Thank you, Marcel. In two or three days we will have a proposal for protecting the Blaise factory. In the meantime, I would suggest that you ask your current contractor to beef up security and, if possible, to arm them."

"I will telephone them today," Marcel said.

"How are you currently shipping Blaises to the U.S.?"

"In a former French military aircraft, two at a time."

"We have a contractor at Stewart International Airport, in Newburgh, New York, an hour's drive north of here, that operates a C-17. Do you know this aircraft?"

"No."

"It is a four-engine jet airplane that could transport perhaps two dozen Blaises and your Maybach on a single flight. Cars destined for other American cities could easily be transported by truck—enclosed truck, if you like."

"You can arrange this?"

"We'd be very glad to."

"Then please do so at your earliest convenience. I have six Blaises awaiting transport to the New York Auto Show next week, and a further dozen completed cars for our dealers in Palm Beach, Los Angeles, and San Francisco."

"Could you have all of them at Le Bourget the day after tomorrow?"

"Indeed, yes."

"I'll give you the cost later in the day."

Mike's secretary walked in, followed by Bill Eggers. Hands were shaken all around.

"That completes our security business," Mike said. "Now we can move on to the business of The Arrington."

"I have come prepared to make you an offer," Marcel said. "Stone has proposed selling me fifteen percent of the Arrington shares for three hundred and fifty million, then investing that sum in a European company. I offer to pay you that amount for twenty percent of the shares, plus a seat on the board. I will form a Swiss company with an initial capitalization of two billion euros for the purpose of handling the European expansion, and I suggest we satisfy our financial obligations to each other with an exchange of stock, which should redound to our mutual benefit through tax savings."

Stone, Mike, and Eggers exchanged glances and nods.

"That is acceptable to us in principle," Eggers said, "contingent on a determination of the value of your shares and other details."

"Then I suggest you draw up a deal memo," Marcel said, "and I will have my legal team here the day after tomorrow to hash out the details and help write the final contract. Do we have anything else to discuss?"

Mike spoke up. "If you have more time today, I'd like you to view a short film about Strategic Services, which will give you a good idea of the range of what we offer. Also, I'd like you to see the original designs that were made for The Arrington in Los Angeles, and meet some of the team that put them together."

"I have the rest of the day," Marcel said. "I need only to make a few phone calls to Paris to get the wheels turning."

"I must get back to my office," Stone said. "I'll leave you the car."

Marcel took him aside.

"I'll have my attorneys pick up Helga at Stockholm City Airport at noon the day after tomorrow. She should go to Grafair Jet Center at that airport."

"Thank you, Marcel, I'll let her know."

———

Eggers walked Stone out. "That went very well and very quickly," Bill said. "If Marcel is always that easy to work with, then this should be a delightful business venture for us."

"All we have to do," Stone said, "is keep him alive and well."

35

When Stone arrived back at his desk he had a note to call Lance Cabot, on what Stone assumed was a private line. He made the call.

"Good afternoon, Stone." No secretary.

"Good afternoon, Lance."

"Have you made any arrangements for Helga to fly to the States?"

"Yes, Marcel duBois's attorneys are flying to New York the day after tomorrow, and they will pick her up at noon at Stockholm City Airport, at Grafair Aviation. They will be landing at Teterboro."

"That is quite satisfactory," Lance said. "I will see that Helga is transported from her island home to Stockholm City Airport by helicopter that morning. Tell her the chopper will land on her front lawn at ten a.m., local time."

"I'll do that."

"How are your business dealings with Marcel proceeding?"

"Extremely well."

"Can you share some details?"

"I don't see why not. Marcel is buying twenty percent of our shares for three hundred and fifty million. He is establishing a European corporation for building hotels over there, and we will invest in this with an exchange of shares."

"You've moved quickly, then."

"Marcel is very easy to do business with."

"I have some news, too, but more troubling. The Russian contingent in Paris is extremely upset about the death of Aldo Saachi and the loss of one other man by drowning in the Seine. One of the men in the Mercedes survived, and he is very angry, too. His name is Yuri Majorov."

"Ah, yes, I've seen him in Paris. Is he the one who took a shot at Amanda Hurley?"

"He is, to our knowledge. A contact on the inside of his organization, which we have code-named SQUID, has told us that Majorov's masters have declared him persona non grata in Paris and that he is being dispatched to New York. Having failed to do so in Paris, perhaps we can dispatch him there."

"Good idea," Stone said. "Strategic Services will be providing personal security both here and in Paris for Marcel, and they will do a survey of his needs at the Blaise factory as well."

"What security arrangements have you made in New York for Marcel's protection?"

"He is staying in my home and being driven in my car, which is armored, and being guarded by two operatives from Strategic Services whenever he leaves the house."

"Ah, yes, the Bentley Flying Spur—a very handsome car."

"Marcel's Maybach is to be transported to New York by C-17, by a company in which you have an interest, then Mike Freeman's armoring division will transform it in eight days."

"Our C-17. Good to have some new business for it."

Strategic had sold the company owning the C-17 to the Agency. "Give Marcel a decent price, will you? Don't try to make the whole year's profit on this transaction."

"Well, I'll see that he's not overcharged, but he will have to pay what anyone else would pay. After all, he can afford it."

"Now," Stone said, "I think it would behoove

you to give me some tasty morsel of intelligence to pass along to Marcel."

"Well, let me see: I did mention that we think Majorov is coming to New York to kill him, didn't I?"

"I'm not sure that passing that along is quite the right thing to do," Stone replied. "Give me something more hopeful, more entertaining, even."

"Ah, I have just the thing: one of Marcel's German competitors, a rather unpleasant man named Horst Schnell, has suffered a financial loss of sixty million euros from a computer scam operated by our friends from SQUID. When Marcel has stopped laughing, you might mention that Strategic Services also offers an excellent computer security system. Tell Mike Freeman that we are quite willing to share what we know of how the scam operated with his tech people."

"Now, *that* is the sort of information that will entrance both Marcel and Mike."

"I thought it might. Oh, and our man Joe surveyed your house while you were out this morning, and he will be installing a very nice security system in your home tomorrow morning, early, that will include all the latest goodies."

"Lance, if I find out that you are surveilling me with my own security system, I will be extremely annoyed."

"Stone, it hurts me to think that you would have such an opinion of me. I should tell you, though, that there may be times when you might want such a service from us."

"If that time comes, I'll let you know," Stone said.

"Oh, and Joe has put a big rush on your new windows and doors. They'll be installed over the weekend, and Joe does very neat work, so he won't make a mess."

"Then I will be grateful to him," Stone said.

"Must run," Lance replied. "See you." He hung up.

Stone wasn't sure what time it was in the Stockholm archipelago, so he sent Helga a text message: *Good news, Marcel's attorneys are traveling to New York from Europe and will collect you at Grafair Aviation at Stockholm City Airport at noon, the day after tomorrow. Prior to that, Lance is providing a helicopter that will land on your front lawn at 10 AM, local time, to transport you to the airport. Try and get some rest on the airplane, because I will make you busy when you arrive. Please confirm receipt of this message. Stone.*

Joan came into his office. "Joe came and went," she said. "He'll be back early tomorrow to install your new security system. I gave him a key, so he won't have to wake you."

"Good work. I'm told Joe will be installing new windows and exterior doors over the weekend, so when you come back to work on Monday morning, you will be newly safe. Perhaps I'll take Marcel to Connecticut for the weekend, so he won't be disturbed."

The phone rang, and Joan went to answer it. "Mike Freeman, on one."

"Hello, Mike."

"Stone. Marcel is watching our video, goggle-eyed. I don't think he knew that such a company existed."

"Careful, or he'll buy you," Stone said.

"We'll give him lunch here, then he'll have his meeting with our design team. I'll return him to you around five, I should think."

"Good. I'll give him some news then that will make him want you to protect his computer systems, so be ready to make your pitch."

"Anything I should know first?"

"Marcel should know it first. He'll be in touch, don't worry." Stone hung up and buzzed Joan. "Make us a dinner reservation at Patroon at eight, and let the security people know. I don't want to surprise them. And ask Dino and Viv to join us."

"Consider it done," she said.

36

Stone and Marcel arrived at Patroon shortly after eight. They pulled up behind a black Lincoln Town Car with city plates, and Stone knew that Dino's promotion had won him a better car than his usual Crown Vic.

The owner of the restaurant, Ken Aretsky, greeted them in the dining room and showed them to a corner table, where Dino was waiting. He and Marcel shook hands warmly.

"Where's Viv?" Stone asked. "Don't tell me we have to put up with you alone."

"You do," Dino replied. "Viv is boning up on some Strategic Services operation manuals for her new job."

"What will she be doing there, Dino?" Marcel asked.

"She won't tell me," Dino said. "You'd think she had joined the CIA."

"Well, Mike comes out of the world of intelligence, and he insists on client confidentiality."

"I'm glad to hear that," Marcel said, "since he will invariably learn much about my business."

They ordered drinks, and to Stone's surprise, Marcel asked for a Knob Creek.

"Do you have a principal business, Marcel?" Dino asked.

"My father was a hotelier, and I worked in that business in my extreme youth. When he died I took over the hotels he owned and grew from there. I was helped by the fact that my father had established a chain of hairdressers in the hotels, and the cash flow from them was very useful to me. After that, I learned to invest well, in all sorts of businesses. My latest venture is my new car, the Blaise, named for my son, who was killed some years ago in a motor racing accident."

"What sort of car is it?" Dino asked.

"There's one in Stone's garage," Marcel replied. "I won't blunt the impact by telling you about it ahead of time." He turned toward Stone. "By the way, would you allow me to display your car at the

New York Auto Show next week? I would need it from Monday afternoon."

"Of course. Have someone pick it up, and Joan will give them the keys."

"Don't worry, it won't be driven, it will be flat-bedded."

"That's fine. By the way, some rather noisy work is going to be done on my house over the weekend, and I thought you might enjoy seeing a little of New England. I have a house in a small village called Washington, and Helga will be here as well. Would you like to drive up in the Blaise? I haven't driven it yet."

"That sounds delightful," Marcel said.

"Dino, would you and Viv like to come?"

"Sorry, pal, we've got plans."

"I saw your new car outside. How's the job going?"

"Yes, please tell me about your job," Marcel said.

"Oh, it's nothing to write home about," Dino replied.

"That's an outright lie," Stone said. "Perhaps I should tell you that Dino is the new chief of all detectives, in all five boroughs of New York City."

"Does that mean you have to be a politician as well as a detective?" Marcel asked.

"It better not mean that, because I'd be lousy at it."

"That's a somewhat smaller lie," Stone said, "but a lie, nevertheless. Dino has always worked the system very well, something I was never good at."

Their drinks arrived, and they looked at the menu.

"What do you recommend?" Marcel asked.

"Start with the Caesar salad, then choose whatever entrée sounds good," Stone replied. "The cooking is very good.

"Have any interesting cases crossed your desk, Dino?" Stone asked.

"Well, we have a Russian gangster somewhere in the city," Dino replied. "The feds had a stop order on him, but he got in before it hit the computers. Name of Majorov."

Stone gulped, but Marcel didn't know the name. "I'm sure you'll bag him," he said.

"I'll let the feds worry about him," Dino said.

"I have had my problems with Russian gangsters," Marcel said. "Stone, do you think this man Majorov has anything to do with that?"

"I'm afraid he does," Stone admitted. "I didn't want to worry you with it, but I spoke to Lance Cabot today, and he told me about it. Mike Freeman is taking all necessary precautions."

"Ah, good," Marcel said. "But I would be grateful if you would not keep information from me. I would rather be worried, but aware."

"I apologize," Stone said. "In fact, Lance believes that Majorov was in the car that attacked us on the way to Le Bourget."

Dino's face showed interest. "You were attacked?"

Stone told him about the incident with the Mercedes. "One man died in the Seine; the other, Majorov, survived."

"I'm extremely sorry to hear that," Marcel said.

"By the way," Stone said, "Lance asked me to pass along some information to you. He says that a German businessman of your acquaintance, one Horst Schnell, has had sixty million euros stolen from him in a computer scam perpetrated by the same people who have tried to do you harm."

"Well, it couldn't have happened to a nicer fellow," Marcel replied, laughing. "The man is a snake in the weeds—is that how you say it?"

"In the grass," Stone said. "Lance has recommended that you ask Mike Freeman to audit your computers and make security recommendations."

"I will ask Mike to do that tomorrow," Marcel replied. "And thank Lance for me when you speak to him again."

They ordered steaks, then the headwaiter appeared with a cart and a large wooden salad bowl and began to create a Caesar salad from fresh ingredients.

During dinner Stone got a text from Helga, saying that she would take the airplane from Stockholm as he had scheduled. He went to bed that night with fond memories of her lush body in his arms.

37

Two days later, Marcel had an early meeting with auto show officials about his display, and Stone was at his desk when three men arrived, carrying valises, boxes, and tools.

"I'm Joe," their leader said, offering his hand.

"Good morning, Joe. You want to tell me exactly what you're putting in?"

"The best security system in a private house in New York City," Joe replied. "If you can dream up a function, it can do it."

"All right, but stop by and explain it to me when you're done."

"Give me an eight-digit code," Joe said.

Stone gave him a familiar mix of letters and

numbers, and Joe and his colleagues went to work, starting at the top of the house.

Stone asked Joan to phone his Connecticut housekeeper and have her lay in groceries for the weekend, then Mike Freeman called.

"Lance Cabot called yesterday. A guy named Majorov from Paris has made it past immigration. I think Lance was ashamed to tell you."

"And well he should be," Stone said. "By the way, Marcel is going to call you about auditing his computer systems and making security recommendations. An acquaintance of his in Germany just got stung for sixty million euros."

"He has already done so. We're on it."

"I'm getting Marcel out of town for the weekend. Lance is having my windows replaced with more substantial ones, and I'm nervous about the presence of Majorov in New York."

"Good idea. I'll let my people know."

"We're going to drive the Blaise, leaving after lunch tomorrow, and I'd like your people to follow in the Bentley, in case something alarms us and we need shelter for Marcel."

"Good idea." They hung up.

It occurred to Stone that he was nervous for Helga's safety as well as Marcel's, since it was she who had taken out the Russians' man Aldo.

Joe suddenly appeared at his office door. "Mr. Barrington," he said, holding up something electronic-looking. "We've already found two bugs in your house. I take it you have enemies?"

Stone followed Joe upstairs and looked at the telephone panel he had opened.

"Right there," Joe said, pointing. "Your office line and your line one."

"Any idea how long?" Stone asked.

"It's not the latest stuff," Joe replied. "It could have been there for a couple of years."

Stone sighed. It seemed to him that anyone could bug his phones or his house whenever they felt like it. "Joe, I hope when you're done here it won't be as easy to bust into my system."

"Fear not," Joe said. "Only I could do it."

"I'm going to hold you to that," Stone said.

"Another thing, though," Joe said, holding up the bugs. "This equipment broadcasts a signal from your house that's not good for more than a block or two. Whoever was listening in was probably doing so within sight of your house."

"Where was the equipment made?" Stone asked.

"Well, it doesn't have 'Made in USA' stamped on it, or anywhere else, but it could as easily be European, Japanese, Chinese, or homegrown."

"I'll feel better when you're done and the windows are in," Stone said. "My guest and I are getting out of here Friday, and we'll be gone until Monday morning, so we'll be out of your way."

"I'll be all done when you get back," Joe said. "I'll brief you and your secretary on the system on Monday."

"Good," Stone said, then went back to his office. His cell phone buzzed, and he checked it. A text from Helga: *We are departing on time, ETA Teterboro 6 PM local. Marcel's lawyers will give me a lift into NYC. I have your address. Expect me in time for dinner and hungry.*

He texted back: *Received, understood and looking forward.*

In the late afternoon Marcel returned from his meeting.

"I think we'll dine at home this evening," Stone said to him. "Helga will be in around seven."

"I'll have a nap, then," Marcel said. "Wake me in time for drinks."

Stone went back to work.

It was nearly seven thirty when Philip answered the door. Stone was right there and Helga rushed into his arms. A heavily laden driver was right behind her, and Stone asked Philip to put everything on the elevator and take it to the master suite.

"I expect you'd like a bath," Stone said, "but you don't look as though you need one."

"I had a shower on the airplane," Helga said, "and it was very comfortable, so I'm well rested. I'm also starved and dying for a drink."

Stone took her to his study and rang Marcel to join them.

"You have a very handsome house," Helga said. "I'm impressed."

"I hope you'll be very comfortable here," Stone replied.

Marcel walked into the study and embraced Helga. "I was worried about you," he said.

"Well, now we are both out of Europe and entirely safe."

Stone sat them down, poured a martini for Helga and a Knob Creek for himself and Marcel. "Welcome to New York," he said, and they raised their glasses.

"This is my first trip to New York," Helga said, "and I'm so excited."

"I will be sure to show you the city," Stone said, "but I have to tell you that none of us may be as safe here as you had hoped. Majorov is already in the city."

Helga seemed unfazed. "Then I will be armed and glad to see him," she said.

Marcel burst out laughing. "Then I will be very well protected!"

"Helga," Stone said, "I'm afraid that you can't go packing in New York City. There are very strict laws against that. You must have a permit, and they are nearly impossible to obtain."

Helga dug into her handbag. "Oh, do you mean this?" she said, handing him a New York City carry permit.

"How the hell did you get this?" Stone demanded. "Is it a forgery? Because if it is . . ."

"Calm yourself, Stone," Helga said. "It's from Lance. The helicopter pilot handed it to me when he arrived at my house this morning. And my passport has a diplomatic visa stamped inside."

"Then Marcel is very well protected indeed," Stone said.

Philip came into the room. "Dinner is served in the kitchen," he announced, and they followed him downstairs.

38

Stone was at his desk just before noon when Joan buzzed. "Dino on one."

"Good morning, Dino."

"If you say so."

"You sound a little pissed off," Stone observed.

"Our plans for the weekend have been canceled. Viv has to work."

"The pains of employment in the private sector," Stone said.

"It's not all bad. She's been assigned to Marcel's security detail, so count on having both of us in Connecticut."

"Good news!" Stone said.

"If you say so."

"Don't worry, Dino, it's a strongly built house

with thick walls. Nobody will be able to hear your pitiful cries."

"What time?"

"We're leaving at one. Don't be late. And, Dino?"

"Yeah?"

"Pack—we can use the extra security."

"Will do." Dino hung up.

Stone buzzed Joan and asked her to warn the housekeeper that she would have a full house for the weekend and ask her to lay in Dino's scotch.

At a quarter to one, Stone, Dino, and Viv stood in front of Stone's garage door. While Viv turned her back to them and surveyed the street, Stone pressed his remote control, and sunlight flooded the garage.

"Good God!" Dino said. "What is that thing?"

Stone pressed a button on his key, and both gull-wing doors opened silently, exposing the interior of the car. He and Dino walked into the garage.

"How many cows died to make this happen?" Dino asked, fingering the leather.

"A herd," Stone replied. Stone started the car and backed up, double-parking in the best New York fashion. He got out and handed the Bentley keys to Viv. "Dino tells me you finished at the top of your tactical driving course," he said.

Viv accepted the keys with a grin. "Did he also

tell you that I finished at the top of my extreme driving class at Lime Rock?"

"He didn't mention that, and I'm sorry you did," Stone replied. "Just remember that the slightest ding on that car costs a fortune to repair—twenty-three coats of paint."

"I'll keep that in mind until I forget it," she said, and went to back the car out of the garage.

Philip loaded their luggage into both vehicles; Viv and her two colleagues got into the Bentley, and after introducing Helga to the Bacchettis, Stone, Dino, Marcel, and Helga got into the Blaise.

"Astonishingly comfortable for four people," Helga said.

"I insisted on that," Marcel said. "I prefer riding in the backseat."

Stone pressed the button lowering the gull wings, started the car, and drove to the West Side Highway. Traffic was light, and soon they were on the beautiful Sawmill River Parkway, built in the 1930s, winding north under a series of handsome stone bridges. They blew past the other traffic.

"You know," Dino said, "Rolls-Royce used to say that at sixty miles an hour, the loudest noise was the ticking of the clock. Why do I hear wind noise?"

"We're doing a hundred and ten," Stone replied.

"Holy shit," Dino muttered. "I guess you're

counting on me to use my badge when we get arrested."

"Absolutely," Stone said. After an hour and thirty minutes, Stone turned into his driveway in Washington, Connecticut. As they got out of the car, he reflected that he had never before made the trip in less than an hour and three-quarters.

Viv drove the Bentley in behind them and she and her crew got out. "That was one wild ride," she said. "Why do I feel like we just robbed a bank?"

"Sorry, it was the first time I've driven the Blaise, and I just had to throw it around a little."

"Has my hair turned white?" Dino asked.

"Not yet," Viv replied, "but you're working on it. Stone, we had a van behind us for a while, but by the time we left the Sawmill, he was so far back that he couldn't possibly know where we went."

"Describe the van," Stone said.

"Black on black with very dark windows. I don't think it was delivering anything."

"Let's put both cars in the garage, in case anybody drives by," he said, and they did.

Stone's housekeeper, Nellie, opened the front door and beamed at them. "We're all ready for you, Mr. Barrington," she said. "My daughter, Martha, is helping out."

Stone handed out room assignments, and everyone went inside to get settled in.

———

That evening they dined at the Mayflower Inn, widely heralded as the best country hotel in the United States, and as they left the inn after dinner to get into their cars, Viv tugged at Stone's sleeve and nodded toward the other end of the parking lot. A black-on-black van sat there. Stone couldn't tell if anyone was inside.

"You leave first," Viv said. "We'll block anyone from following you."

Stone did as he was instructed, and five minutes after the Blaise was in his garage, Viv and her colleagues pulled into the driveway and got out.

"Any problems?" Stone asked.

Viv shook her head. "We checked out the van. It was empty, but locked, so I expect the passengers are either staying at the inn, dining there, or both. I didn't see anyone suspicious in the dining room or bar, and believe me, I checked. They must be ordering room service."

"Did you run the plates?" Stone asked.

"No cell service around here. I'll call on your landline."

"Please do."

The men went into the little library, where Nellie had a nice fire going, and each settled in with a brandy.

Viv walked in a couple of minutes later. "The

plates on the van belong to a 1989 Buick," she said. "I've called it in to the Connecticut State Police, so their sleep will be disturbed soon."

"Have a brandy," Stone said. "You're officially off duty now."

"You talked me into it," she said, taking a seat.

"Stone," Marcel said, "this is a lovely house. You choose your residences well."

"Thank you, Marcel."

Five minutes later, Nellie came into the room. "Mrs. Bacchetti, telephone for you."

Viv left the room and came back a couple of minutes later.

"That was the state police. The van was gone when they arrived, but they've issued a bulletin on it."

"There's no reason to believe they know where I live, so we can relax."

They returned to their glowing fire and their brandies, which made them glow, too.

As Stone was going up to bed, Viv's two colleagues came into the house.

"We've had a look around the neighborhood," one of them said. "No sign of the black van."

"Good," Stone replied.

"One of us will be downstairs all night," the man said. "We'll do shifts."

Everybody else went to bed.

39

In the wee hours of the morning Stone felt fingernails running across his bare buttocks. He turned over to give Helga a better field of play. After a brief moment of fondling, she rolled onto her back and pulled him on top of her. Stone was groping for a point of entry when Helga said, "Oh, look, isn't that pretty?"

"What?" Stone asked, baffled.

"Out the window."

Stone momentarily abandoned his quest and turned his body so that he could see the window without straining his neck. "Good God!" he shouted. "Wake everybody and tell them to get their things out of the house."

"What's wrong?"

"The house is on fire!" Stone said, leaping out of bed and into his trousers. He found his shirt and a jacket, got into his loafers, and ran down the stairs, shouting, "Everybody up! Get out of the house!"

He ran into the kitchen and began looking in cupboards. Dino came padding in, his shoes in his hand. "What's going on? What are you looking for?"

"The fire extinguisher," Stone said, slamming a cabinet shut.

Dino opened the pantry door and held up a good-sized red bottle. "This fire extinguisher?"

Stone grabbed it from him and ran to the front door. He could see flickers from the side lights. He flung the door open and was driven back by flames.

"Use the goddamned thing!" Dino shouted.

Stone tore off the seal, pointed the extinguisher at the flames, and pulled the trigger. It worked faster than he had thought. He ran out the door, dousing flames as he went, then ran around to the back of the house. A column of flames was making its way up the rear wall, licking at his bedroom window. Stone pointed the extinguisher at the base of the flames and put them out, then worked his way up the wall of the house. He stopped spraying. "I think that's it," he said to Dino. "I wonder why my fire alarm hasn't gone off."

But Dino wasn't there. Stone ran back to the front and found everybody standing on the front walk, looking confused.

"It's all right," he said to them. "Let's go back inside."

Dino trotted up. As the garage door opened, Viv backed out the Bentley. "Where are you going, baby?" Dino asked.

"For a ride," she said.

Dino piled into the backseat, and Stone called out to Helga to get everyone inside, then hopped into the front passenger seat.

Viv backed up. "Which way would you go if you had just set a house on fire?" she asked.

"That way," Stone said, pointing. "The other way is a dead end."

She drove the block to the main road. "And now?"

"Turn right. Left is into the center of the village."

She did so and started south out of the village green.

"Now it's either straight ahead or turn right," Stone said. "They would have done one or the other. Right is toward New York."

Viv made the right and floored the Bentley, and it rocketed up a hill and around the curve.

"Our best bet," she said, "if we've taken the

correct turn, is to drive like hell." And she did. "They'll think they got away clean, and they won't be going all that fast." She kept accelerating, hitting the apexes of the sharp turns and sometimes using the opposing lane, if she could see ahead. A big moon came from behind a cloud, and Viv switched off the headlights.

"What are you doing?" Dino hollered from the backseat.

"I can see, and I don't want them to see me coming." They rounded another curve and caught a brief glimpse of taillights ahead, before they disappeared around yet another bend.

"You've got them," Stone said. "They won't see you coming."

Viv sped up even more. "I'll catch up to them and ram them," she said.

"Don't even think that!" Stone cried. "This is not an NYPD Crown Vic! It's mine, and I don't want to lose my insurance company!"

"All right, all right," she muttered. "There they are!" The taillights were a couple hundred yards ahead. She accelerated.

"What's your plan?" Stone asked nervously.

"I'm going to scare the shit out of them," Viv said grimly.

"Oh, swell."

Viv was gaining fast now. She waited until she

was nearly on top of the van, then she turned on the lights and hit the BRIGHT switch. "Take that, you sonofabitch!" she yelled. "How do you like them xenon gas lamps?"

The van wobbled, then accelerated, but Viv stayed right on its bumper.

"Don't hit them," Stone said, almost to himself. "If you can get alongside them, maybe I can get a shot into the cab."

"Do you have a weapon?" Dino asked.

"Well, no, there is that."

"Then shut up and let me do this!" Dino slid across the rear seat and put down his window. "Stand on it, Viv!"

Viv pulled into the passing lane, then whipped the car back behind the van. A car zoomed by, headed in the other direction.

"What's that guy doing up at this time of night?" Stone asked nobody in particular.

Viv made another attempt to pull alongside, then suddenly steered into another sharp turn. "I didn't see that coming!" she yelled. "Where's the van?"

Dino stuck his head out the window and looked back. "They slammed on brakes and took a right into the woods!" he shouted.

Viv came to a short, straight stretch of road, stomped on the brakes, and whipped the car around 180 degrees. Amazingly, it did not roll over. Then they were going back the way they came, and they could see the van in the woods, upside down. Viv pulled into the side road the van had tried and failed to make and slid to a halt.

"You stay behind us, Stone!" Dino commanded as he and Viv led the way toward the upturned van. Viv had produced a small but powerful flashlight from somewhere, illuminating the van. One of its wheels was still turning.

Each of the Bacchettis took a side of the van, with Viv shining her light through the driver's open door.

"Empty," Viv said. "They're gone. Everybody shut up and listen."

Everybody did. They heard nothing.

"They're either running or hiding," Viv said, switching off her light, "and we're too good a target. Let's go back to the house and call the state police. They have a trooper stationed in the village."

They tramped back to the Bentley and were shortly headed back.

"Thanks for not bending the car," Stone said to Viv.

"Don't mention it," Viv replied.

They got back to the house and found the phones dead. "They cut the wires. That's why the fire alarm system didn't go off."

"How far do I have to drive to get a cell phone signal?" Viv asked.

"Go back to the main road and take a left, toward Washington Depot. Halfway down the hill there's a church on your right. Pull over there, and your phone will work."

Viv ran back to the Bentley and drove away.

Stone found everybody sitting in the library around a cold fire. "You might as well get some sleep," he said to them.

40

Stone awoke a little before eight to the smell of bacon wafting up the stairs from the kitchen. He showered, shaved, and dressed while Helga slept on like a gorgeous Swedish statue, then he went downstairs. Dino and Viv were at the table.

"Morning," they said.

"Good morning. Helga is still out like a light. Is Marcel still asleep, too?"

"No, Marcel is awake," a voice said from the door behind him. Marcel came into the kitchen, sat down, and helped himself to muffins, eggs, and bacon. "I don't know why," he said, "but I slept like a child."

"It's the country air," Stone said.

"I suppose so. Anything new?"

Viv spoke up. "I got ahold of the state police last night and went with them to check out the van. It was gone."

"Gone?" Stone asked. "Where would they have got a wrecker in the middle of the night?"

"We reckoned they must have just rolled the van upright and driven it away."

"Then there was more than one of them."

"Probably more than two," Viv said. "It was a big van."

"Did you see anything inside it that might help us find it?" Stone asked.

"No, we were concentrating on the people who had been inside. I expected that the state police would haul in the van and go over it properly. They put out an alert for it, but the van was probably back in New York by the time we got to the scene. Oh, I reported your phone out, so somebody should be here soon to reconnect it."

"Thanks."

"So what do we do now?" Dino asked.

"How about just enjoy our weekend?" Stone suggested. "My house won't have any windows in it until Monday morning, so there's no point in going back to the city."

"How should we enjoy our weekend?" Dino asked.

"I don't know—lunch at a country inn and some antiquing?"

"Antiquing?" Dino said. "My favorite thing!"

"Dino," Viv said, "we're apartment hunting, remember? We're going to need new things to fill up a bigger place. Antiquing sounds good to me."

"Then there's golf," Stone said.

"Ha!" Dino said. "Viv, you antique, we'll golf."

"I'll go with Viv," Marcel said. "I've never seen any of New England."

"Okay," Stone said, "drinks at six, followed by dinner in Litchfield. I booked a table at the West Street Grill before we left. Viv, you and Marcel take the security guys with you."

"Done," Viv said.

"I wonder if Helga plays golf," Stone said.

Helga, as it happened, played to a six handicap and won all of Stone's and Dino's money. They got back to the house just in time to clean up and have drinks.

"I won!" Helga said as she walked into the library.

"Gloating is unattractive," Stone said.

"Gloating is fun!" she cried.

"How was the antiquing?" Stone asked Viv. "To change the subject."

"It was spectacular!" she replied. "I found a

couple of good pictures, a beautiful set of china, and a dining room table and twelve chairs! I couldn't believe it!"

"I don't believe it now," Dino said. "We don't have a dining room."

"We will have, and they've agreed to deliver when we move in."

"Where are you looking?" Stone asked.

"Upper East Side," Viv replied. "I've already seen a dozen places. Dino has seen two."

"I work for a living," Dino said.

"I work for a living, too," Viv said. "He just doesn't like the idea of moving."

"I like my place."

"It was a great bachelor apartment, Dino, but you're not a bachelor anymore, and there isn't enough closet space or a dining room or a study for you and one for me."

"I would like a study," Dino admitted.

"Also, now that you're in the NYPD hierarchy, we're going to have to entertain a lot."

"Now and then," Dino said, "not a lot."

"She's right, Dino," Stone said. "You're going to have to have the commissioner over a lot, maybe even the mayor, and a lot of people whose friendship the department needs. It will be expected of you."

"I hate it when they expect stuff from me," Dino said grumpily.

"You don't hate going to other people's houses and eating their food and drinking their scotch," Viv said.

"Yeah, I like that okay."

"It'll be more fun in your own home. I'm looking at a place Monday on Park in the Sixties, and I just have a feeling . . ."

"Uh-oh," Dino said. "*The feeling*. I've learned that *the feeling* is irresistible."

"My lawyers are meeting with Bill Eggers over the weekend," Marcel said. "By Monday, we should have a contract."

"You're very easy to deal with, Marcel."

"When both sides know they want the same things, it's easy to agree. I've cultivated a reputation for being easy to deal with. It makes others easy to deal with, as well. You don't learn that in your business schools over here. Your businessmen look upon a negotiation as a fight. I look upon it as making everybody happy. And achieving agreement is cheaper than fighting."

"You should write a business book, Marcel," Stone said.

"I've already written thirty chapters," Marcel replied. "And I don't have to worry about getting it accepted by a publisher, because I own a publishing house."

Everybody laughed.

"There, laughter," Marcel said, "that's a nice sound. I haven't heard that sound since dinner last night."

They had a good dinner, followed on Sunday by sitting around and reading the *New York Times* and the *Wall Street Journal*, then more golf and more antiquing, followed by dinner at home, prepared by Viv and Helga. They got up early Monday morning, had a good breakfast, and drove back to the city, unthreatened by black vans.

As they drove up to his house, Stone stopped before opening the garage door and looked at the building. "Nothing has changed," he said. "They didn't install the windows."

"Or," Dino said, "maybe they did such a good job that you can't tell the new windows from the old ones."

Dino turned out to be right.

41

Stone was struck by how quiet the house was. Traffic was roaring away on Second and Third avenues, and he could hear none of it. He figured out how to unlock a window, opened it, and the noise came rushing in. He felt a pane on both sides and reckoned that the glass was at least half an inch thick. He closed the window, locked it, and the noise vanished.

Helga unpacked her clothes and put her laundry in the chute for Helene to deal with. "Time for shopping," she said. "Where do I shop?"

"The best shopping mall in the world is Madison Avenue between Fifty-seventh and Seventy-second streets," Stone said, "from Bergdorf Goodman to Ralph Lauren, but you'll have to wait for Marcel to finish with the car. He has another meeting about the auto show, and late this afternoon we're scheduled to go over the contracts on our deal and, possibly, sign them. You can have the car and the guards from the time Marcel gets back until we leave for the meeting—say, four hours."

"I can do much damage in four hours," Helga said, "but why can't I take a taxi?"

"Because people are trying to kill you."

"Oh, that."

"The Bentley will repel small-arms fire—you will be safe inside it."

Helga sighed. "I was better off on a remote Swedish island."

"How was the shopping there?"

"Oh, all right!"

Joan buzzed Stone. "Yes?"

"Joe is here to tell us how to operate the new security system."

"I'll be right down." He found Joan and Joe in her office, staring at the computer screen.

"Okay, everything is right here," Joe said. "You can operate the system from any computer in the house, including an iPhone or iPad. Each part of the system is shown on-screen. You can choose which parts to turn on, like the doors or windows as a group, or one at a time if you like, or you can click on the 'arm' button, which turns on everything, and you have sixty seconds to get out of the house. The code is the one you gave me, and the false alarm code is the reverse of that number. Simple enough for you?"

"I got it," Stone said.

"Me, too," Joan echoed.

"I'd like to point out something," Joe said. "The windows are terrific, but they're useless unless they're locked. Please remember that."

"I'll remember," Stone said.

"So will I," Joan replied.

"Okay, folks, my work here is done. Your old doors are in the cellar. They're beautiful, so if you ever want to sell them, here's my number." He handed Joan his card. "Enjoy the peace and safety of your new system." He shook their hands and left.

"Why isn't everything in this house that easy?" Joan asked.

"Because nothing else was installed by the CIA," Stone explained. "The price was right, too."

Joan's outside bell rang, and she used the intercom. "The people are here to transport the Blaise to the auto show," she said.

"Be sure to get a receipt," Stone reminded her.

The phone rang, and Joan got it. "It's Lance Cabot, for you," she said.

While Joan dealt with the car transporter, Stone went into his office and picked up the phone. "Good morning, Lance."

"Good morning, Stone. How do you like your new security arrangements?"

"They are superb," Stone said, "thank you very much."

"I understand you had a bit of bother in Connecticut," Lance said.

"How did you know about that?"

"We have people who are in touch with the state police up there, along with a lot of other police departments. I'm beginning to think we should do something about the security arrangements in your house in Washington."

"Please don't bother. My builder is dealing with the fire damage, but it's mostly just shingle replacements."

"Perhaps when you have guests who are the subjects of attempts on their lives you should take them to your home in Maine, where the security is built into the house, and Penobscot Bay surrounds you."

"Perhaps you're right," Stone said.

"I've asked Holly to have her people take over the current protection of your New York house," Lance said.

"The last time you did that, you lost two men," Stone reminded him.

"That was a measure of the threat," Lance said. "I do not anticipate anything like that in these circumstances. After all, we're dealing with criminals, not political zealots."

"I very much hope you're right," Stone said. "Thank you for the extra security, Lance."

"You are very welcome. They are outside your house now, watching your beautiful new car being hauled away. I've heard so much about the Blaise—you must let me drive it the next time I'm in New York."

"Maybe," Stone said.

"Good-bye, Stone." Lance hung up.

Stone hung up and sent an e-mail to Holly. *Thank you for your help. I hope you are well and happy.*

A few minutes later, he got a reply. *I'm well, thank you. Watch your ass.*

She's well, he reflected, but she didn't mention happy.

42

Joan came into his office. "Okay, the car is on its way, there's nothing I can do to protect it now."

"We'll have to leave it to the gods," Stone said.

"What did you think of the special section on the auto show in the Sunday *Times*?" she asked.

"I didn't see it," Stone said. "It must not have been included in the Connecticut edition."

"I thought not," she said, handing it to him.

Stone put it aside. "I'll read it later."

Joan picked it up and handed it to him again. "I think you'd better read it now."

Stone picked up the section and there, taking up the front page above the fold, was a photograph of Marcel with one of his Blaises.

"Be sure and read all of it," she said, then went back to her office.

Stone began to read, and two paragraphs down, his jaw dropped. *Marcel duBois, on a rare visit to New York, is staying at the home of his friend, attorney Stone Barrington, in Turtle Bay.* There followed a long interview with Marcel recounting their meeting in Paris. Stone had an odd feeling in the pit of his stomach.

Joan buzzed. "I've got Mike Freeman on one and Lance Cabot on two," she said.

"Tell Mike I'll call him right back." He pushed two. "Yes, Lance?"

"I've just seen the city edition of yesterday's *New York Times*," Lance said drily. "Is this your idea of securing Marcel duBois's safety?"

"I knew nothing about it, Lance. I was in Connecticut, remember? It didn't appear in the national edition. However, I don't see that it much matters, as Majorov and his friends already know where to find us."

"Granted," Lance said, "but suppose the threat lies elsewhere? Marcel has just imparted to that part of the population of New York City who can read, which I assume is most of them, exactly where to find him—at the auto show tomorrow and at your home the rest of the time. All that's missing is a photo of Helga draped nude over the hood of his car."

"I'm not happy about it either, but what can I do?"

"Move?"

"Thanks to you, we're so well protected here."

"Good luck, Stone." Lance hung up.

Joan buzzed back. "Mike's on line one. He insisted on waiting."

Stone pressed the button. "Sorry to keep you waiting, Mike."

"Are you out of your fucking mind?" Mike asked pleasantly.

"I know, I know, but I didn't know until a moment ago. Do I have to explain?"

"It's too late for explanations," Mike said. "We're meeting at four in Bill Eggers's office to sign the contracts. Try and keep Marcel alive until then."

"I'll do my best," Stone said. Mike hung up.

Marcel and Helga walked into Stone's office, arm in arm. "I'm back from my meeting," Marcel said.

"And I'm off shopping," Helga chimed.

"Please have the car back by three thirty," Stone said. "Marcel and I have an important meeting."

"Of course, my dear," she replied, waving over her shoulder as she headed for the door.

"Please have a seat, Marcel," Stone said, and Marcel took a chair across the desk.

"My cars arrived at Stewart International this morning and are on their way to the Javits Center,"

Marcel said, then he squinted at Stone. "You look upset. Is something wrong?"

Stone handed him the auto show section. "Have you seen this?"

"Oh, yes, they showed it to me at the meeting this morning. Everyone was thrilled."

"So is anyone who might like to do you harm," Stone said, trying to keep the scold out of his voice.

Marcel's eyebrows shot up. "Ahhhh," he breathed. "I see your point, if a bit too late."

"We are now imprisoned in the house," Stone said, "until Helga comes back with the car."

"Well, there are worse places to be imprisoned," Marcel said. "May I borrow something from your library?"

"It is at your disposal," Stone said. "Anything you like."

Marcel got up. "See you for lunch?"

"Of course."

"What time?"

"Twelve thirty?"

"In the kitchen?"

"Yes."

Marcel departed.

Joan came and stood in his doorway, arms crossed. "I take it I'd better have my .45 at the ready."

"Please do."

"Have you noticed how quiet it is in this house with the new windows?"

"Yes, I have."

"I'm having trouble with it. I can't even hear traffic going by in the street."

"I know how you feel. It's quieter than the Connecticut house, but we'll get used to it."

"Why do people want to harm Marcel?"

"They want his business—ah, businesses. They figure that Marcel will be easier to deal with if he's dead."

"And Helga? Is she in business with Marcel? Is that why these people want her dead?"

"No, Helga had a little social problem in Paris that offended certain people."

"Dare I ask?"

"You dare not. Be careful who you let in the office door."

Joan looked over her shoulder. "Funny you should mention that."

"Something wrong?"

"Federal Express just pulled up."

"I have it on good authority that they are harmless," Stone said.

"Trouble is, they delivered an hour ago. They've never shown up twice on the same morning."

Stone opened his desk drawer and rummaged around until he came up with his little Walther .380.

"I guess it's time to unearth my .45," Joan said.

"Don't try firing through the window," Stone said. "The glass is very thick and heavily armored."

"Well, I'm not opening the door," Joan said, starting for her desk.

Stone followed close behind.

43

Stone stood in the doorway to Joan's office, the Walther in his hand but out of sight. All that the man approaching the door would be able to see was the left side of Stone's body. Joan took the .45 from her desk drawer, racked the slide, and flipped off the safety. The doorbell rang. "Yes?" Joan said over the intercom.

"Federal Express," the man replied.

Stone could see that he was wearing dark trousers, a dark shirt, and a FedEx baseball cap—not a standard uniform.

"Just leave it outside," Joan said.

"Can't. I'll need a signature."

Stone could see that he had a clipboard under his arm and a small FedEx box in the other hand.

"I can't come to the door right now," Joan said. "Deliver it later."

"Can't. I'm on my way back to my office."

"Then we'll just have to live without it," Joan said.

"I can see a guy standing in there. He can sign for it."

"I'm sorry, he doesn't know how to write his name."

Then Stone saw that the man was not holding the box in his hand; his hand was *inside* the box. He held it in front of him and the box exploded, but the paned door he was aiming at did not. Now a 9mm semiautomatic pistol could be seen in his hand. He fired twice more at the door, then stepped sideways and fired into Joan's window with the same effect. Stone had time to think that he could hardly hear the gunfire.

"Where the hell are the outside guards?" Stone asked.

"Good question," Joan said from under her desk.

Then Stone heard other shots softly firing, and the fake FedEx man spun around and collapsed in a heap. The FedEx truck suddenly rocketed forward and out of Stone's line of vision.

Stone walked to the door and opened it. Two men in civilian clothes were making sure the deliveryman was dead. "His accomplice just drove away in the FedEx van," Stone said to them. "Call it in."

"Yessir," one of the men said, then raised a fist to his lips and spoke into it. When he had finished, he looked at Stone. "We've got this," he said. "The body will be out of here in a minute and a half."

"I'll time you," Stone said, "and thanks for your help." He closed the door and went back into Joan's office. "You can come out now," he said to her.

Joan crawled out from under the desk and stood up, brushing her skirt with the hand that wasn't holding her .45. "I see they're on top of it," she said, looking out the window. The two men were zipping the corpse into a body bag. A van outside opened its door, and they shoved the bag inside and watched the door close. Then they returned to wherever their posts had been before the incident, and the van drove away. All was as before.

"That was smart of you to notice that FedEx came twice," he said to Joan.

"Hard to miss," she said, popping the magazine on her .45, then racking the slide and returning the ejected cartridge to the magazine before putting the weapon back into her desk drawer.

Stone returned to his desk and put the Walther into a drawer containing less stuff to hide it from him. He sat down and reviewed the incident in his head. The windows had worked; the bullets had left nothing more than little scratches where they had struck, and everything was still intact. Not a bad morning, if you didn't count the corpse.

A couple of hours later, as he was about to go to the kitchen for lunch, Joan buzzed him. "Holly on line one."

Stone picked up. "Hi," he said. "Your men did an excellent job."

"Thank you. I thought you'd like to know that the dead guy was carrying no identification, and his body contained no distinguishing marks. His dental work, however, was Russian and Eastern European. He'll be in potter's field by sundown."

"Very efficient," Stone said.

"How did the armored glass work?"

"Like a charm. I hope they don't come back with a bazooka."

"Lance will be thrilled to know," she said. "Is Joan all right?"

"She's just fine. Her .45 is back in her desk, and I hear computer keys clicking."

"Give her my best," Holly said. "You, too."

"I'll do that."

She hung up.

Stone found Marcel in the kitchen, sipping a

glass of white wine. "I like your California wines," he said. "Of course, if I served them to my guests in Paris, they would be outraged."

"No doubt," Stone said.

"The cars have reached the Javits Center," Marcel said, "and they do not have any bombs installed. I have had them place your car on a revolving stand high enough so that the unwashed will not get so much as a fingerprint on it."

"Thank you."

"And Mike's people took charge of my Maybach at the airport and drove it to God-knows-where to start work on it. I am very impressed with Mike and Strategic Services. Do you think I should buy it?"

Stone laughed. "I warned Mike that you might try, but I don't think he'll want to sell. It's privately held, but one of these days I suspect he'll take it public and make a killing on his stock."

"Ah, well, I suppose there are some things I can't own."

"You seem to do quite well at owning things," Stone remarked. "How many companies do you have?"

"About a dozen outright, major positions in about sixty others."

Helene served lunch.

"Marcel, you've spoken of your son, but never of your wife."

"She never recovered from Blaise's death," Marcel said sadly. "She went into an immediate decline and died less than a year later. She was forty-six."

"I'm so sorry for your loss."

"You have had a loss, too," Marcel said.

"Yes, but my son is well."

"What does he do with himself?"

"He will graduate from the Yale School of Drama soon, then go to California to work in the film business."

"Ah! I hear that is like swimming in a shark tank," Marcel said.

"He's going to have to figure that out for himself, but his partner—Dino's son, Ben—is going to be a very smart businessman, I think. The two of them together should make their way in Hollywood just fine, and Peter's girlfriend, Hattie, will be there to keep their feet on the ground."

"I shall look forward to seeing their films," Marcel said.

"So shall I," Stone said, glancing at his watch. Three more hours before Helga was due back.

44

It was three thirty, and Helga had not returned from shopping. Stone was loath to take a taxi, given the events of the morning. He went upstairs to his dressing room, opened his safe, and removed a compact .45 automatic and its holster. It had been custom-made by Terry Tussey and weighed only twenty-one ounces, compared to the thirty-nine of the standard Colt.

With the gun on his belt, he went down to the living room in time to see the Bentley pull up outside. Stone called the car and told Philip not to allow Helga out until they were in the garage with the door closed.

He collected Marcel and went to the garage.

Helga was emptying the trunk of many shopping bags, and Philip was taking them into the house.

"I did much damage," she said to Stone.

Stone kissed her and motioned for Philip to get behind the wheel. "We're running late," he said.

They arrived in the underground garage of the Strategic Services building and took the elevator to the top floor, where Mike Freeman greeted them. "I think we're all ready," he said.

He led them into the conference room where Bill Eggers and two French lawyers awaited. Eggers was reading the last page of the contract.

"Looks good to me," he said.

"I read it online this morning," Marcel said. "I'm ready to sign if you are."

"We are," Stone said.

"I have the signatures of the board on a draft," Mike said, "so you and I can sign for the company."

They sat down, and Stone took out his pen. "I think we'll remember this moment for a long time," he said, and signed three copies of the document. He passed it to Mike, who signed, then Marcel inked them as well. The copies were distributed, then Marcel looked around. "Have we any further business to conduct?" he asked.

"Nothing else," Mike said.

Marcel stood. "Then, if you will excuse me, I

would like to return to have a last look at our area of the auto show. Stone, would you like to come?"

"Thank you, no, Marcel. I'll see it tomorrow at the opening. Please take the car."

The meeting broke up, and Mike got onto the elevator and rode down with Stone. "We have special transportation for you," he said. "The first of our newest armored vehicle." The elevator arrived at the garage level, and they got out.

A large Mercedes van awaited them, its windows mirrored, and the side door slid open. Inside the richly furnished cabin four seats, two forward and two aft, awaited. Lance Cabot was sitting in one of them, and Rick LaRose was in another.

"Welcome aboard, Stone," Rick said. "Have a seat."

"I'll leave you two gentlemen to your trip," Mike said.

The door slid silently shut, and the van began to move.

Stone shook the men's hands. "Welcome, Rick," Stone said. "What brings you to New York?"

Rick looked at Lance, who ignored him.

"What do you think of our new conveyance?" Lance asked.

"Very handsome," Stone replied. "I hear people

are driving these things to the Hamptons for weekends."

"Not exactly like this one," Lance said. "It's quite heavily armored."

"Mike says it's his newest effort."

"Indeed. We'll make another stop," Lance said. "Then I will chopper to Langley, and the van will drop you at home."

"All right."

"It's a good opportunity for us to talk, Stone," Lance said.

"We've been doing quite a lot of that the past week," Stone reminded him.

"There's more to say, I'm afraid."

"What are you afraid of?" Stone asked.

"I have some things to tell you," Lance said, "and you're not going to like them."

Stone felt a pang of anxiety in his gut; he didn't like the sound of this. "Go on, Lance."

"I'm afraid that I and Rick and some of our colleagues have found it necessary to mislead you."

"Oh?"

"I'll get to the root of the matter," Lance said. "Marcel duBois is not the target of the attacks you have seen, beginning in Paris and continuing here."

"I don't understand."

"I know you don't. Tell me, have any further

parts of your memory returned since you've been back in the city?"

"No," Stone said. "Just the memory of who was on the airplane, the one I told your doctor about."

"I had hoped it would all come back to you," Lance said. "It would have been simpler than what I have to tell you."

"Lance," Stone said, "if Marcel is not the subject of the attacks, then who is?"

"You are," Lance said.

That stopped Stone in his tracks.

"I expect you thought that it was I who may have been the target in the attack on our car in Paris," Lance said.

"It crossed my mind."

"No, it was you."

Stone started to speak again, but Lance held up a hand. "No, please, let me continue. The shot that nearly struck Amanda was aimed at you. It was silenced, and you didn't see the bullet strike. The attempted attack on Marcel's car was aimed at you as well. And Aldo Saachi did not try to rape Helga— he was waiting in her suite, expecting you to return with her from the party at the Russian Embassy. He planned to kill you both, but mostly you. Helga would have been just collateral damage."

"I'm waiting to hear why all this is true," Stone said.

"Rick?" Lance said. "You tell him."

"Majorov and his friends were not after Marcel's businesses," Rick said. "They want The Arrington. Aldo Saachi approached Eggers right after the two of you met with Marcel, and Eggers rebuffed him."

"Why didn't Eggers tell me that?" Stone asked.

"Because he thought you knew. He's not aware of your amnesia attack, or at least, of the full extent of it. To continue, Marcel flew home that night, then the following day he called you and asked you to come to Paris for further talks. He arranged your travel and hotel and sent your ticket and expense money, and you departed that evening. We had a watch on Aldo, and we saw him onto the airplane. Lance had arranged for the first-class compartment to be confined to our people, Aldo, and you. Aldo was to have received the drug that rendered you unconscious, as Lance explained to you earlier. As it was, the ambulance we had arranged for him was used to transport you to the embassy."

"So that business about the cabdriver delivering me was a fiction?"

"It was."

"And it was Aldo who was to occupy the room given to me?"

"Yes, but he managed to elude us at the airport. Dr. Keeler, whom you met, is a forensic psychiatrist, who would have been in charge of the interrogation of Aldo. But he was quite interested in the effects of the drug on you, so it wasn't a total loss for him."

"I'm so happy to have been of help," Stone said drily. "What now?"

"Ah, now," Lance said, "there is more to do."

45

The van pulled into another garage, and the door closed behind it. Stone could see armed guards inspecting them.

"You've been here before," Lance said, getting out and leading the way to the elevator.

"Yes," Stone replied.

The elevator stopped on the top floor, and they stepped into a broad hallway. Unlike Stone's previous visit, when the building had seemed practically empty, it now teemed with life. He followed Lance down the hallway to Holly's large office at the end.

Holly got up from a group at her conference table, kissed Stone on the cheek, and shook Lance's and Rick's hands. "Please have a seat," she said.

Everybody sat, and a coffeepot was passed around.

"Everybody, please excuse me," Lance said, "while I bring Stone up to date." He turned toward Stone. "Now that we have in place the necessary changes to our charter, we are conducting our first operation against a criminal enterprise, in New York, London, Paris, and Los Angeles. Rick is here to coordinate with the three teams.

"Yuri Majorov, whom you have sort of met, has been identified as the leader of this group, at least outside of Moscow, and he is charged with both finding legitimate businesses and taking them over on terms very favorable to his group, which, as you know, we are calling SQUID. It's not an acronym, so don't waste time trying to figure out what it means. The squid overpowers large prey in its tentacles, then uses its very sharp beak to kill it, so the name is not inappropriate, given their tactics.

"Having been rebuffed in Aldo's meeting with Bill Eggers, they identified you as the key player in the Arrington business, since you, together with your son's trust, are the largest shareholder. They reason that, with you taken out of the picture, the board members would become rattled, fearful of their personal safety, and thus more inclined to accept an offer, albeit a very lowball one. We have learned that they are now preparing to take further steps, after they have dispatched you.

"In short, there will be, if their plan is successful, a significant 'accident' at the hotel, one big enough to frighten the paying guests and shake the board's confidence. Our Los Angeles station is alert to that possibility and working hard to see that it does not take place."

"So, Lance," Stone said, "what do you want me to do?"

"We want you to stay alive," Lance replied.

"I assure you, that is uppermost in my mind."

"Yes, but thus far, your attention has been redirected to protecting Marcel, who, as it turns out, is in danger only to the extent of his proximity to you."

"Do you want me to move him out of my house, then?"

"No, we have sufficiently fortified your residence, as recent events have shown, that we are happy for him to remain there."

"That's fine with me."

"We'd like you to move about separately, for you to give him and/or Helga the free use of the Bentley and for you to rely on our van for personal transportation."

Stone shrugged. "All right, I don't object to that."

"We would like for you to be armed at all times as well."

"I am armed," Stone replied.

"Please remain so. The driver of the van and one other man aboard will be heavily armed and prepared to deal with any attack."

"Oh, good."

"Stone, I would appreciate it if you would take this seriously."

"I assure you, I do," Stone said. "Anything to do with the preservation of my life will have my full attention."

"We think it best that you do not attend the opening of the auto show," Lance said.

"I was looking for a way out of that, anyway. I've already been to the Paris show, and they'll have mostly the same cars."

"Now, let me try to be delicate," Lance said.

"Please do."

"While we wish you to be at all times concerned for your safety, we also wish . . ." He seemed to struggle for the word.

"You want me to be the bait to draw out the Russians?"

"Well, yes. I would not have employed that word, but it will suffice. We would like you to maintain your movements around town, dinners out and such, and not just hole up in your house."

"All right," Stone said cautiously.

"And we are prepared to provide you with nearly unnoticeable body armor—the very latest thing, as it were. We have your size in stock."

"How much body armor?"

"Upper and lower body."

"So you're as much worried about my balls as my internal organs?"

"As it were," Lance said primly.

"All right, I'll give it a try."

"Good," Lance said. "I'm glad we're all on the same page."

"Please remember, Lance, that pages turn."

When the meeting broke up Holly pulled him aside. "How are you, Stone?"

"You mean without your company?"

"No, I meant how are you?"

"I'm sorry, that was churlish of me, but Lance always has a grating effect."

"I'm well acquainted with that characteristic, and I'm happy to be based in New York instead of at Langley."

"Straight answer: I'm annoyed, but otherwise fine. I look forward to the end of this episode and to being alive to see it."

"We've pulled out all the stops on this one," Holly said. "You probably won't see the other people involved, as they'll hang back a bit."

"Waiting for the Russians to go for the bait?"

"I'm afraid so. We want to bag every single one of them. What Lance didn't say is, if they take you out, Marcel duBois will be next. They'll use your death to cow him into letting them into his business empire."

Stone nodded.

"We're doing everything we can, but you have to take care of yourself, too."

"Don't worry about that." Stone kissed her and walked to the elevator. The big van was waiting with its door open and an athletic young man with no hair standing next to it, looking for enemies in his own garage.

Stone sighed and got in.

46

Stone arrived at home in the van and was told to wait inside it for a moment. He tried to relax as the two young men up front got out and surveyed the neighborhood. Finally, the bald one opened the door for him.

Stone got out. "What's your name?" he asked.

"Stanley," the young man said. "Now you'd better get inside."

Joan buzzed him in through the outside office door. There was a young woman sitting in a chair beside her desk.

"Who's your friend?" Stone asked.

"A friend of your friend outside," Joan said. "It seems I'm valuable enough to rate a guard."

Stone kissed her on the forehead. "You bet

your ass you are." He went into his office and looked for something to do. There wasn't much, but he did it. After he'd done it, he called Dino.

"Chief Bacchetti's office," a woman's voice said.

Stone was accustomed to getting Dino directly. "This is Stone Barrington. May I speak to the chief, please?"

"What is your business with the chief, Mr. Barrington?"

"Nefarious and disreputable. Just tell him I'm on the line."

She put him on hold for quite some time. Finally, she said, "The chief will speak to you now," and put him through.

"Hey, Stone."

"Hey, yourself. Who's the barricade?"

"That is my new secretary. I also have a detective assistant, a deputy chief, and some guy from public affairs in my offices."

"Why do you sound so pissed off about it?"

"I'm used to a glassed-in cubicle with a view of a dozen guys sitting at worn-out desks. Now I've got a view of the city, featuring two large office buildings that are no longer there, and a lot of mahogany paneling. All that's missing is a grand piano."

"Ah, I can see you're suffering from a bad case of cultural overindulgence."

"That pretty much sums it up."

"You and Viv want to get some dinner tonight?"

"Okay by me. I'll check with her. Where you want to do it?"

"Patroon all right?"

"Sure. See you there at what, eight?"

"Tell you what, I'll pick you up at home. I've got a new ride."

"An M1 tank?"

"Something like that. I'll be outside your door at eight." They both hung up.

It was nearly six before Marcel returned from his meetings at the auto show, and Stone took him into his study for a drink. He handed him a Knob Creek. "Would you like to join the Bacchettis and me for dinner this evening?"

"Thank you, Stone, but I'm tired, and I'd just like for Helene to give me some dinner and put me to bed."

"That is easily arranged," Stone said. "I heard some good news for you this afternoon."

"I can always use good news."

"Turns out you're not the target of all this attention from our Russian friends. I am."

"Oh, how nice for me!"

"Lance Cabot has given me my own transportation, and they'd like for you and me to travel separately. The Bentley is yours and Helga's for the duration."

"Fine. Where is she?"

"Right here," Helga said from the doorway. "There's a Black Maria parked in front of the house. Is someone being arrested?"

Stone laughed. "That's how I'll be traveling for a while. We're joining the Bacchettis for dinner, picking them up at eight, so after I get a drink into you, can you be ready to leave at seven forty-five?"

"That sounds awfully exact," she said, accepting the drink.

"It was meant to. Dino and I are accustomed to being punctual with each other, unless his work gets in the way."

"Then I will make the effort," she said, setting down a Chanel shopping bag and sitting next to Marcel on the sofa.

"I spent the afternoon with your masters from the Agency," Stone said. "I should warn you that traveling around town with me may put you in a certain amount of danger."

"Then I shall be well armed," she said.

They finished their drinks and Marcel went to find Helene.

Stone fixed them another drink. "One of the things I learned this afternoon is that I'm the target, instead of Marcel. The Russians want The Arrington, and they're willing to wait until I'm dead before going after Marcel."

"That's very interesting," Helga replied.

"I also learned that Aldo was waiting in your suite to kill me, not for amorous purposes. Of course, he would have to have killed you, too."

"Then I'm still glad I shot him," she said. "It's just more satisfying now. I would take grave exception, and I mean *grave*, to anyone who meant you harm."

"That makes me feel warm all over," Stone said.

"Are we quite alone?" Helga asked.

"Yes, why?"

"Because I feel a sudden urge to have sex in a leather armchair." She stood up and began peeling off her clothes, then she pulled Stone to his feet and undressed him.

The armchair accommodated them both quite nicely.

At eight o'clock sharp, Stanley opened the van's sliding door and admitted the Bacchettis.

Dino looked around him. "What is this beast?"

"An M1 tank disguised as a land yacht," Stone said.

Viv looked around her. "This is more like the interior of a corporate jet than a van," she said.

"A good comparison," Stone said. "It's how I'm traveling these days, until the Agency has corralled the Russians."

"Can we expect to be shot at?" Viv asked.

"At the very least," Stone replied.

"Oh, good." She removed a 9mm pistol from a shoulder holster, inspected the magazine, and found it full. She pumped a round into the chamber, then returned the weapon to its holster.

"I don't have to check mine," Dino said. "It's never been unloaded, except through the barrel."

They pulled to a stop in front of Patroon. "Sit tight for a moment," Stone said to his guests. "Stanley has to case the joint before we can expose ourselves."

A moment later, the door slid open, and Stanley assisted the ladies out. "How long?" he asked Stone.

"A couple of hours," Stone replied.

"Then we'll park the van, and I'll be inside with you."

"Whatever makes you comfortable, Stanley. By the way, three of us are armed."

"Please don't shoot me," Stanley said.

47

They dined well and sipped an after-dinner brandy while Dino complained about his new job.

"I have to go to three or four meetings every day," he said.

"You've been to meetings before," Stone said.

"Not three or four a day. I can't stay awake, so I have to drink coffee before every meeting, and that means I have trouble getting to sleep at night."

"Clearly, the job is ruining your health," Stone said.

"All right, Dino," Viv said, "we all know you hate your job, so you can shut up and listen—I have news."

"Tell us," Stone said. "Is Dino pregnant?"

"Better than that," Viv said. "I bought an apartment."

Dino sat bolt upright. "You did *what*?"

"I bought an apartment."

"Without consulting me?"

"I've been consulting you for weeks about this, and you won't listen, and you won't look at apartments, so I bought one. I said 'I,' not 'we.'"

"She likes to lord it over me that she's rich," Dino said. "Ever since she collected that reward."

"Well, I'm not rich anymore," Viv said. "Now most of it is tied up in real estate."

"Where?" Stone asked.

"Park Avenue in the Sixties."

"A snotty neighborhood," Dino said.

"Prewar building, four bedrooms, living room, dining room, library, kitchen, butler's pantry, and two maids' rooms."

"What are we going to do with four bedrooms?" Dino asked.

"We're going to sleep in the master suite, which has two bathrooms and two dressing rooms, then we'll have a room for Ben when he and his girl visit, one for guests, and I'll turn one into my study. You can have the library."

"How much did you . . . Oh, never mind, I don't want to know."

"You're going to love it."

"When do we have to move in?" Dino asked.

"When I say so, and not before. It has to be painted, and one or two other things done, then it has to be furnished, and when it's ready, I'll tell you, and we'll move in. And I put your apartment on the market today."

"Oh, God, what if it doesn't sell before we have to move?"

"So what? You don't have a mortgage payment. Anyway, the broker thinks it will go fast."

"I'm being uprooted," Dino said.

"You're being transplanted," Viv replied, "and to a better home."

Dino excused himself to go to the men's room.

"What Dino doesn't know," Viv said, "is I bought the apartment the day after we got back from Connecticut. The co-op board approved me the following day, we closed quickly, and it's already been painted. I've been furniture shopping all week, and things are already being delivered. I've kept the curtains from the previous owner, and I bought a few pieces of their furniture and their piano, too. They're elderly and they're downsizing. I'll let you know when the housewarming is."

"We'll look forward to it," Stone said. He looked up to see Dino returning and gave Stanley the nod to get the van brought out front. Stone paid the check, and they got up and started for the door.

Stanley came back through the front door, breathless. "The van has been shot up, and our driver is dead," he said. "Go back to your table. I've already called it in, and reinforcements and a new vehicle are on the way."

They went back to the table. Dino got out his cell phone and called the local precinct. He hung up. "NYPD is on the way," he said.

After ten minutes of grim silence, Stanley returned. "Let's go," he said. "I've got a car waiting at the back door."

They followed him outside and got into a stretch Lincoln.

"How did they shoot the driver?" Stone asked.

"He was smoking and had the window down, and that's definitely not procedure. The van took everything they threw at it and looks good. They'll need to touch up the paint here and there."

They pulled out of the alley and were bracketed by two black SUVs that followed them, first to Dino's building, then to Stone's house. There were half a dozen heavily armed men around them when they got out of the car and went inside.

"I am unaccustomed to being guarded by men with machine guns," Helga said as they walked into the master suite.

"So am I," Stone replied.

"I think it is time for me to return to Sweden, where things are quieter."

"I couldn't blame you," Stone said, "but I would miss you."

"Why don't you come with me?" Helga asked as she got into bed. "You will like my island."

"I have an island of my own, in Maine," Stone said, "called Islesboro. I think it's time I got out of town. When the auto show is over, I'm going up there. Why don't you wait another week and come with me? I'll invite Marcel also."

"I'll sleep on it," Helga said.

But they didn't get much sleep.

There was a message on Stone's desk from Mike Freeman, and he returned the call.

"I hear you had a bit of a rumble last night," Mike said.

"You could say that."

"You'll be happy to hear that our van performed brilliantly. It's at our factory in New Jersey. It needs a few holes in the bodywork filled and painted, but the Kevlar panels stopped everything. A pity about the driver."

"He had the window down," Stone said.

"That's what I heard. You'll have the vehicle back late this afternoon without a scratch on it."

"Lance will be so pleased," Stone said. "He's besotted with your van."

"I wish he could do a commercial for us," Mike said. "We'll do very well on sales to the government, even without that. I've had a lot of pictures taken of the van before we started repairing it."

"You may get an offer from Marcel for Strategic Services," Stone said. "Even though I've told him you won't sell."

"Good. That will give me some idea of what we're worth."

Stone hung up and called Dino. "I'm getting out of town for the weekend," he said. "You and Viv want to come up to Maine?"

"Viv's working," Dino said. "She's gotta travel somewhere with a client, but I'm in."

"My house at two on Friday?"

"I'll see if I can give myself the afternoon off."

48

Stone had a day in the house with no company except Joan. Marcel and Helga did the auto show and didn't get home until late. Helene made dinner.

"Everybody ready to leave for Maine tomorrow at two?" he asked his guests.

"I'm always ready to travel," Marcel said.

"What sort of clothes will I need for Maine?" Helga asked.

"*Very* casual," Stone replied. "You'll need a sweater in the evenings, and maybe in the daytime, too, and a light jacket, just in case."

"Will we be swimming?" Helga asked. "I didn't bring my bikini."

"Not unless you like your water temperature in the forties."

"How much is that in centigrade?"

"I have no idea, but it's cold enough to freeze body parts. You would not enjoy your swim, although we would enjoy seeing you in a bikini."

"I'll do some shopping tomorrow morning, just in case," Helga said.

"Whatever you wish."

At two the following afternoon the van awaited, and Stanley rang the bell and told them the luggage had been loaded. They made it into the van without being fired on, and Stone gave the driver his instructions.

"Are we not driving?" Helga asked.

"No, that would take about eight hours, including a ferry ride to the island. I have an airplane at Teterboro, where you landed when you arrived."

"Ah," she said.

Half an hour later they passed through the security gate and pulled up to Stone's Citation Mustang.

"How cute!" Helga said, getting out of the van and regarding the little jet. "Is there room for all of us?"

"There is," Stone said. Dino loaded the luggage while Stone did a preflight inspection, then settled Helga and Marcel in the cabin of the airplane.

"Where are the pilots?" Helga asked.

"You're looking at him," Stone replied.

"Just you?"

"Dino will help."

He showed them the earphones for music, then closed the cabin door and began working his way through the checklist, while Dino watched carefully, as he always did, to see that Stone missed nothing.

Stone got a clearance, then taxied to Runway 1. There was a short wait while another airplane landed. Stone did his final checklist, then was cleared for takeoff. He taxied onto the runway, stopped, set the heading and pitot head, and switched on the relevant light switches, then he pushed the throttles forward and watched the airspeed as they accelerated. He rotated, climbed to seven hundred feet, then switched on the autopilot. He said good-bye to Teterboro tower and switched to the departure frequency, then was given a climb by New York Departure, then cleared to his first waypoint. Twenty minutes later they were at flight level 310, where Stone leveled the airplane and switched on music for the passengers.

Helga got up and came forward. "This is very interesting," she said.

Stone asked Dino to switch places with her, and she sat down in the copilot's seat.

"I hope Dino won't be offended to give me his seat," she said.

"Once Dino has willed us into the air without crashing, he's happy to leave the cockpit," Stone said. He began explaining the three large color displays that told them everything about the condition of the airplane and their route.

"This is where we're headed," Stone said, showing her Islesboro on the large map display.

"And you can land this airplane there?" she asked.

"Oh, yes, there's a paved runway." He didn't explain that it was only 2,450 feet long.

"How long will it take us?"

"Less than an hour."

"And it would take eight hours to drive?"

"Right."

"An airplane is very convenient to own," she said.

Half an hour later ATC gave him his descent, and he began pointing out things to Helga. "The bay in front of us is Penobscot Bay," he said, "the largest in Maine." He changed the range on the map display, and the island got larger. Twenty miles out he canceled his instrument flight plan, then made his final descent to Islesboro. He checked the windsock to see which end of the runway was favored and he lined up on it, dropping the landing gear, adding full flaps, and slowing dramatically. On such a short runway, a pilot did not want to land hot.

Suddenly they were on the ground, and Stone was using the speed brakes to dump lift and braking hard.

"That was wonderful," Helga said. "Now what do we do?"

Stone turned the airplane around and pointed to a man leaning against a 1938 Ford station wagon. "That's Seth, my caretaker. He'll drive us to the house, and his wife, Mary, will give us our meals."

Stone parked and set the brakes, then went through the engine shutdown checklist. Then he, Dino, and Seth transferred the luggage to the station wagon, and he introduced Seth to everyone.

They drove to the village of Dark Harbor, then to the house, which was situated on the little harbor, within sight of the small yacht club.

Mary greeted them and showed the guests to their rooms.

Stone grabbed a pair of binoculars and walked out onto the porch overlooking the harbor. He looked at every boat moored there, remembering that his friend Jim Hackett, the founder of Strategic Services, had been shot on this very porch on a calm day by a sniper eight hundred yards out on a boat. He saw nothing unusual, but still, he went back into the house to his study and got the keys to the secret room that the Agency had built and equipped for his cousin, Dick Stone. Dick had recently been appointed deputy director for operations when he was murdered. Lance Cabot succeeded him.

Dino came down the stairs and found him there. "I thought you'd be in here," he said, looking at the half dozen weapons hanging on one wall. "What are you going to give me?"

"Can you still hit a man at a thousand yards with a good rifle?"

"I can."

Stone took down a military sniper's rifle with a large scope and silencer and handed it to him, along with a loaded magazine. "I've had a look at the harbor, and I didn't see anything, but I think we need to keep our people off the porch."

"You're remembering what happened to Jim," Dino said, sighting through the rifle and checking its condition.

"I certainly won't forget that. He was sitting right in front of me when he was hit."

Dino placed the rifle behind the living room curtain, while Stone found himself an assault rifle and did the same.

Everybody came down for drinks at five. Stone and Dino were one ahead of them.

49

Stone was awakened in the wee hours by a small noise. He disentangled himself from Helga without waking her, grabbed a robe and a pistol, and padded slowly down the stairs. When he reached the living room he could see in the moonlight that the door to the back porch stood open. That had been the noise.

Silently, he checked that there was a round in the chamber, then he made his way across the living room, checking around him for company, until he came to the open door. He looked around the porch and carefully stepped outside. The chilly night air crept up his bare legs.

"You couldn't sleep?" a voice asked.

Stone jerked in its direction, the pistol out in front of him.

"Relax, pal." Dino was sitting in a corner of the porch, hidden in a shadow made by the moon, the sniper's rifle across his lap.

"You scared the shit out of me," Stone said.

"I got up to pee and thought I saw something in the harbor." Dino got up, walked over, and handed Stone the binoculars. "See the buoy way out there? Check the third boat to the left of it."

Stone stuffed the pistol in the pocket of his robe, took the binoculars, and trained them on the buoy for focus, then swung slowly to his left, to a third boat. "Looks like something fast, around forty feet. There's a rubber dinghy aft, resting on a boarding platform."

"It arrived ten minutes ago without lights. I thought that was odd."

"You were right," Stone said, "it is odd, a boat running in the dark without lights. It's pretty bright out from the moon, maybe he just forgot to turn them on."

"Maybe," Dino said, "or maybe not. He used a very bright flashlight to pick up the mooring. I think there are two aboard."

"I don't see anybody on deck now."

"Who knows we're in Maine?" Dino asked.

"Only Joan. I didn't tell anyone else. Except Stanley, when he dropped us at Teterboro. He was disturbed that we were going somewhere without him and his boys."

"What's Stanley's last name?" Dino asked.

"I heard one of the other guards call him Manoff."

"That's Russian, isn't it?"

"You're a suspicious man, Dino."

"I'm professionally suspicious, like you used to be."

"You think I'm less suspicious than I used to be?"

"Yeah, since you left the department, you're Sunny Jim."

"That's ridiculous."

"No, it's not. Is Stanley Agency?"

"I think he's one of a group of civilian security people that the Agency employs to guard their buildings and people. I doubt if he's a Company officer."

"Then who knows where his loyalties might lie?" Dino said. "And what effect an important sum of money might have on those loyalties?"

"You have a point," Stone said, peering through the glasses. "I just caught a glimpse of a red light through one of the boat's ports," he said. "It came on for a second, then went out."

"Some of those little lithium-powered flashlights

have a red bulb. Red light doesn't screw up a person's night vision."

"I can see ripples," Stone said. "They're moving around inside the boat."

"So they didn't just get in, all tired, and go right to bed."

"I guess not." Stone braced himself against a porch post to steady the binoculars. "Uh-oh," he said.

"What?"

"They're in the cockpit, two of them."

Dino raised the rifle and peered through the scope at the boat. "And one of them has the moon glinting off his bald head," he said. "And they're launching the dinghy."

Stone ran lightly upstairs, got his cell phone, and came back. He pressed a speed-dial number.

"Are you calling Stanley?" Dino asked.

"Nope."

"Hello," a sleepy woman's voice said.

"Holly, it's Stone."

She was instantly awake. "What's up?"

"We're at the Maine house."

"How did you lose Stanley?"

"We may not have lost him," Stone said. "We said good-bye at Teterboro, and now there are two men on a fast boat in the harbor, one of whom is as bald as an egg."

"I'll call you back," Holly said, then broke the connection.

"Did Holly send Stanley up here?" Dino asked.

"I don't think so," Stone said. He looked through the binoculars again. "They're rowing in," he said. "I think there's an outboard on the dinghy, but they're not using it."

Dino braced his rifle against a porch post and looked through the scope again. "The bald guy is sitting in the stern, while his buddy does the rowing. And the bald guy seems to have a rifle slung across his body. I could take him out right now."

"If you do that, it will turn out to be the commodore of the yacht club coming back from a midnight cruise."

"Yeah, well."

"Interesting, though—they don't seem to be aiming for the yacht club dock. It's more like they're aiming for mine."

"Why don't we go down there and greet them?" Dino said.

50

Stone ran back into the living room and retrieved the assault rifle he'd left behind the curtains, then he joined Dino on the front porch.

"Are they still coming?" he asked Dino.

"Yep. Let's go."

They ran lightly across the backyard, using trees and shrubbery to keep from being seen. At the head of the ramp to the dock, there were two tall evergreen shrubs, and they took up positions behind them. Soon, Stone could hear the sound of the dinghy's oars and some unintelligible whispering. A couple of minutes later there was the sound of rubber squeaking against the dock, and Stone could see the dock move as the two men alit from the dinghy. They padded down the dock and started up the ramp. "There's the house," one of them said.

As they stepped onto the grass and walked past the evergreens, Dino said, in his best cop voice, "Freeze, NYPD."

Stone thought the NYPD was superfluous, so he racked the slide on his weapon for emphasis.

They froze.

"Now, we're going to do this very carefully so that nobody gets a bullet in the spine," Dino said. "First, on your knees."

The two men dropped to their knees.

"Hands on the back of your heads."

The two men complied.

"Now behind your back." Dino handed Stone a set of plastic tie cuffs and they secured both men. Dino lifted the assault rifle over the head of the bald one and looked at it. "Banana clip," he said. "These guys are loaded for bear."

Stone took a MAC-10 from the other man and tossed it away. "So, Stanley," Stone said, "you must have missed me terribly."

"Mr. Barrington?" Stanley said, sounding surprised. "What are you doing here?"

"That's my line, Stanley."

"I'm here to protect you," Stanley said.

Dino raised a foot and kicked Stanley onto his face in the grass. "So you arrive here in the middle of the night and sneak up on the house? That's how you protect him?"

"It's my job," Stanley said.

"Then why doesn't Holly Barker know you're here?" Stone asked.

"I didn't tell her I was coming. We have a different command structure from the people at the station."

"And who do you report to?" Stone asked.

"Carlton. He's in charge of our unit."

"And did Carlton tell you to come up here and sneak up on my house?"

"Not exactly," Stanley said.

"How did you find us?"

"I checked the flight plan you filed with flight services. The address of the house was on the information sheet Carlton gave me."

"Clever fellow," Stone said. "Tell me, Stanley, are you Russian?"

"I'm first-generation American," Stanley said.

"Where from?"

"Brighton Beach."

"A hotbed of the Russian Mob, is Brighton Beach," Stone said.

"I'm not Mob. I hate those guys."

Stone's cell phone vibrated in the pocket of his robe. "Yes?"

"It's Holly. Stanley is on his way to you."

"Oh, he's arrived."

"Well, that's a relief," she said.

"Funny, I'm not relieved."

"Well, you should be. Stanley is our guard team's best man. I just spoke to his commander, Carlton, and he dispatched Stanley when he learned you'd abandoned him at Teterboro."

"I see," Stone said.

"I hope to God you didn't shoot him."

"Not yet, but I'm thinking about it."

"Stone, the man is doing what he was assigned to do, and you ought to be grateful to him, instead of just leaving him on the tarmac at the airport."

"All right, I won't shoot him. Sorry to get you up." He ended the call. "Okay, Stanley, on your feet."

The two men got up. "This is Lewis," Stanley said, nodding at his companion. "He's a local asset, knows the territory."

"How did you get here?"

"Once I found out where you were and got permission, I chartered a light plane at Teterboro and flew to Rockland. The rest of the team is assembling there."

"How many men are we talking about?" Stone asked.

"Eight. They're ready to chopper in here as soon as I call them on the radio."

"Stanley," Stone said, "call them on the radio and tell them to find a place to sleep. We're not going to need them."

"I can't proceed on that basis," Stanley said.

"Stanley, Dark Harbor is a small community. Everybody here knows everybody else, and strangers tend to stand out. Heavily armed strangers in riot gear rappelling from a helicopter *really* stand out, and we don't want to frighten the summer folk. As you should have learned on the boat trip over, we're isolated here, and quite safe. There is no way anyone could find us."

"I found you pretty easily," Stanley said.

"All right, I'll give you that, but you had my file, didn't you?"

"We were followed to Teterboro," Stanley said. "We didn't lose them until we passed through the security gate."

That gave Stone pause.

"No reason why they couldn't check your flight plan, just as I did, and I'll bet you're listed in the phone book up here. That's how they found you in Connecticut."

Stone winced. "All right, Stanley, we'll talk about it in the morning. Right now, call your people and tell them to stand down and get some sleep. We'll see how the cold light of day looks on this problem."

Stanley called his people and told them to stand by and get some sleep.

"That's the guest house over there," Stone said. "You and Lewis go over there and get some sleep, too, which is what Dino and I plan to do."

"I'm not comfortable with that," Stanley said.

"Stanley, I'm losing my patience with you. You can take turns staying awake, if you like, but you need rest just like everybody else, and you'll be useless tomorrow if you're exhausted."

"As you wish, Mr. Barrington. Lewis, I'll take the first watch. I'll wake you in four hours."

"Right," Lewis said.

"The back porch has a fine view of the harbor," Stone said, pointing. "Take a rocking chair, and it's okay if you doze off."

"Good night, then," Stanley said.

"And no helicopters, unless I say so," Stone said.

Stone and Dino trudged back to the house and went to bed.

51

When Stone awoke it was nearly ten o'clock, and Helga was not in bed. He showered and shaved and went down for breakfast. Helga and Marcel were sitting on the front porch, reading the *New York Times*, which had come over on the ferry earlier, and Dino was having breakfast in the kitchen.

"When did Stanley get here?" Helga asked, giving him a kiss.

"Very late last night," Stone said.

"Were you expecting him?"

"I was not, but he came anyway. Is he up?"

"Yes, he and his friend are 'patrolling the perimeter,' as he put it."

"It's not much of a perimeter. It's only a couple of acres. Were they armed?"

"To the teeth."

"Oh, shit. I hope the neighbors haven't spotted them." He went in search of them and found Stanley marching along the property at the road.

"Good morning, Mr. Barrington."

"Good morning, Stanley. Do you remember what I told you last night?"

"Yes, sir."

"Then why are you parading around here armed and dressed like a refugee from a SWAT team?"

Stanley blushed to the top of his scalp. "I'm sorry, sir."

"I think a handgun will suffice, and get into some civvies, will you?"

"I'm wearing them under the armor."

"That will make it convenient. And hunt down Lewis, too, and give him the same message." Stone walked back to the house and joined Dino at the kitchen table.

"I ordered for you," Dino said.

Mary set down a platter of scrambled eggs and bacon. "Good morning, Mr. Barrington."

"Good morning, Mary, and thank you." He dug in. "I'm surprised to see you up so early," Stone said.

"I don't need all that much sleep."

"I'm sorry Viv isn't here to keep you entertained."

"It's her new job," Dino said. "I'm having trouble getting used to it. It's just as well she's not here—she'd be going on about the new apartment, and I'm trying to back her out of the deal. Turns out there's a ten-day cancellation clause in the contract."

"Dino, relax and let the woman take care of you—you'll be a happier man for it."

"I'm happy enough."

"You want to play golf? There's a nice nine-hole course here."

"Sure, but don't let Helga join us. I can't afford it."

"I don't think I can stop her," Stone said.

An hour later, the four of them got out of the old Ford station wagon at the little golf course, and Stanley and Lewis pulled in behind them. Stone rented three golf carts; he and Marcel took one, Helga and Dino another, and Stanley and Lewis drove slowly behind, their weapons stuffed into a couple of golf bags.

Marcel hit his drive straight and fairly long. "I don't think I've ever been guarded by armed men on a golf course," he said.

"That makes two of us," Stone replied.

"Stone, I think I'll be off to Paris when we get back to New York. My work here is done, and I'm having too good a time. I might get lazy."

"Can you delay your departure until Tuesday morning?" Stone told him why.

Marcel grinned. "For that I can delay. Do you want me to offer Helga a ride back to Stockholm? My lawyers left town yesterday, so if she's looking for a private ride, I'm the only game in town."

"I hate to lose her, but I think she's ready to go. I'll ask her tonight."

Each time they got to a green, Stanley and Lewis took up posts on opposite sides and watched the woods like hawks. Stone was glad there weren't many people on the golf course; most of the summer crowd seemed already to have departed for points south and west.

For dinner, Mary had apparently mugged a lobster fisherman, because an enormous platter was piled high with the steaming shellfish.

Helga produced a bottle of aquavit that she had smuggled to Maine and hidden in Mary's freezer, and it went down very well with the lobsters. By nine o'clock they were all fairly drunk. They were just getting up from the table when there was a short burst of automatic weapons fire somewhere outside.

Stone and Dino grabbed their weapons and ran outside, then warily started to cover the property, looking for Stanley and Lewis. They finally found Stanley at the edge of the woods, looking down at someone at his feet.

"Oh, shit," Stone said. "This is going to mean calling in the Maine state police."

"I hope he didn't shoot a neighbor," Dino said.

They walked over to where Stanley stood, while Lewis covered the area around them. "What have you done, Stanley?" Stone asked.

Stanley pointed down. "I only got a glimpse of him but I connected with the first burst." He switched on a small flashlight and illuminated a good-sized deer at his feet.

"I hope you know how to field dress it," Stone said.

"I haven't a clue."

"Go get Seth, and tell him to bring that little utility vehicle of his and some rope."

Stanley left in search of Seth, and Stone and Dino started back to the house. They had walked perhaps a dozen yards when they heard two *pffft* sounds and the noise of bullets slapping into a tree. They hit the dirt.

"Maybe Stanley isn't crazy," Dino whispered.

"Stanley!" Stone yelled.

A voice came back. "It's Lewis, sir. I'm sorry I didn't ID you properly before I fired, but they were just warning shots." Lewis stepped up and offered them a hand to their feet.

"Lewis, go inside, get rid of the MAC-10, then get out of your body armor. If you and Stanley *must* patrol, do it in civvies and with well-concealed handguns, got it?"

"Yessir." Lewis vanished into the darkness.

"You know," Dino said, "I'm surprised you've still got any neighbors in New York who are still alive."

52

On Monday morning, Seth drove Stanley and Lewis to Rockland to meet their helicopter. Stone and the others stayed through lunch, then headed back to the Islesboro landing strip.

Dino was ever the harbinger of doom. "I'm not sure you can make it out of this strip with four of us and our luggage aboard."

"What? You want to stay on, rent a car and drive back?"

"Will we make it?"

"Since we've burned off half our fuel getting here, probably," Stone said.

"*Probably?*"

Stone shoved him onto the airplane. Helga was

already in the copilot's seat, so Dino joined Marcel in the rear.

Stone ran through his checklist, explaining the items to Helga. He noted that the wind was brisk, favoring a northerly departure, so he taxied to the southerly end of the runway, checked for traffic, announced his intentions on the common radio frequency, and lined up as close to the end of the runway as possible. He went through his final take-off checklist, then, while firmly holding the brakes, pushed the throttles all the way forward and waited a few seconds for the engines to spool all the way up. With the engines whining in protest, he released the brakes and began his takeoff roll.

Helga watched as the end of the runway loomed. "I want to fly now," she said.

Stone obliged her by easing back the yoke and allowing the bird to take wing. Just above the treetops he leveled and let the airspeed build, then he began his climb and called Boston Center for his clearance.

"I didn't think we would make it," Helga said.

"I've made it at least a dozen times," Stone said. "The airplane is built to do it. I wouldn't want to try it with full fuel, though. I've tried to talk the locals into adding another few hundred feet to the runway, but nobody wants to encourage larger aircraft to land. I don't think they want to pay for it, either."

When they landed at Teterboro and taxied to Jet Aviation, the big Mercedes van pulled up, with Stanley aboard, and they were away in no time. Stone noticed that, as they drove through the security gate, two other vehicles joined them, one ahead and one behind.

They reached Stone's house without incident. "Are you going back to the office?" he asked Dino.

"Nah, everybody will be gone by now anyway. I've got nothing on that won't keep until tomorrow. I'll just get a cab home—never mind the van. Somebody might take a shot at it."

Stone got his guests and their luggage inside and upstairs.

"We need to change for a party," he said to Helga.

"Oh, good. What party?"

"You'll see. Marcel is flying home tomorrow and has offered to drop you in Stockholm. I'd like it if you'd stay on for a while."

She put her arms around him and kissed him. "Oh, thank you, Stone, but it's time for me to go home to Sweden. Being in Maine made me miss my island."

"I understand," Stone said. "I'll let Lance know your plans, and someone will meet you. You'll be home for dinner tomorrow night."

Dino arrived at his apartment building and went up in the elevator. He wasn't expecting Viv back from her business trip until the following evening, so he thought he'd order his dinner delivered: Chinese, maybe.

He let himself into his apartment, dropped his bag, and switched on the lights, then looked around. He was in the wrong apartment; how had he managed that? This one was unfurnished; he must be on the wrong floor. Then he saw an envelope with his name on it taped to the phone, which rested on the bare floor. He opened the envelope; inside was a handsome, engraved invitation:

> *Chief & Mrs. Dino Bacchetti*
> *request the pleasure of your company*
> *at a housewarming in their new home,*
> *600 Park Avenue, Apt. 12A*
> *7:00 PM, Drinks and dinner*

He walked slowly around the apartment; everything was gone: his clothes, his books, everything. The place looked absolutely forlorn.

Stone, Helga, and Marcel rang the bell at number 12A, and the door was opened by a uniformed butler, supplied by the caterers. They were led into the living room, where they were met by the sound of jazz music from a piano and bass fiddle. The place was packed, and everybody had a drink in his hand. Stone spotted the police commissioner and his wife and the mayor and his girlfriend. Half of police headquarters seemed to be there, too, and some of the old regulars from Elaine's.

A waiter took their drinks order, then Viv broke away from a group and joined them. "Thank you so much for getting Dino out of the way for the weekend," she said, kissing Stone. "He would have been impossible if he had been here!"

"How did he take it?" Stone asked.

"He walked in, took one look around, and said, '*I* live *here?*' He couldn't believe it! He had never seen the rugs, the curtains, the piano, and half the furniture. His clothes were unpacked and in his dressing room; his books were in the library, and the booze was in the bar. He was just flabbergasted!"

"It was exactly the right way to handle it," Stone said, "and I'm delighted you pulled it off."

"I wish I could have seen his face when he walked into his old apartment and found everything gone and an invitation to the housewarming waiting for him," Viv said.

Dino wandered over, beaming, a large scotch in his hand. "Welcome to our home," he said, waving a hand. "We've got a Steinway grand piano—can you believe it?"

"I can believe it," Stone said.

"Come on, let me show you the place." Dino led them through the whole apartment: all the bedrooms—one of them now Viv's study—the huge kitchen, and the library. He was so proud Stone thought he might pop a button. "And Viv promises me we can afford it!"

"Congratulations, Dino," Stone said. "You deserve this place and the woman who made you move into it."

"I think the co-op board liked the idea of having a cop in the building," he confided.

"I'm sure they all feel safer," Stone said.

"Come on back to the bar for a refresher, then dinner will be served. It's a buffet."

They all followed Dino back to the living room.

"Stone," Helga said, "I left my handbag in the van. I'll be right back."

"I can call Stanley to bring it to you," Stone said.

"No, it'll only take me a moment."

She left and headed for the elevator. Stone was in the middle of dinner before he realized she had not returned.

53

Stone set down his plate and stood up. "Excuse me for a minute," he said to Marcel, who was deep in conversation with an attractive female police detective. He caught Dino's eye.

Dino came over. "What's up?" he asked.

Stone steered him toward the front door. "Helga went down to get her handbag a few minutes ago and hasn't returned."

Dino went to a hall closet, unlocked his gun safe, and clipped the holster to his belt. "Let's go."

They were grimly silent on the way down. When they reached the lobby, Dino asked the doorman, "Did you see a large, beautiful blond lady leave the building?"

"Yessir, a few minutes ago," the man replied.

Stone was already out the door, looking for the van, but it was nowhere in sight.

Dino brushed past him. "Over here," he said. He led the way a few yards down the street where, between two parked cars, a man's hand could be seen. They both rushed to him and found Stanley unconscious.

"Is he alive?" Stone asked.

"He has a pulse," Dino said, "strong and steady." He lifted Stanley and rolled him onto his side; there was a large gash in the back of his head.

Dino phoned the 19th Precinct, his old house, and ordered an ambulance and every available officer. "We're looking for a large black Mercedes van," he said. "Start at Park and Sixty-fourth and work outward in all directions. If it's spotted, approach with caution, but don't let it drive away."

Stone stood up. "I'm going to have a look up and down Madison," he said. "I'll call you if I see anything."

"I'll join you as soon as the ambulance gets here." As Stone started down the block, he called Mike Freeman, who was at the party.

"Yes?"

Stone could hear the jazz and conversation behind him. "Mike, it's Stone. Dino and I are

downstairs. Stanley has been rendered unconscious, your van is gone, and so is Helga."

"Any sign of my other men?"

"No, and there are three of them and the driver."

"I'm on it." He broke the connection.

Stone reached the corner of Madison, stopped
and looked both ways for the van. No sign of it.
He went back to where he had left Dino, who was
sitting on a car bumper, holding a handkerchief to
the back of Stanley's head.

Mike Freeman came out of the building, his
phone to his ear. "My guys are over on Lexington,
having dinner. They're on their way back."

"So is the entire Nineteenth Precinct," Dino
said.

The ambulance arrived, followed by more than
a dozen cops, in and out of uniform, who fanned
out and began a methodical search.

Stone's phone made a musical noise, and he
dug it out of his pocket. A message was on the
screen. *We'll be in touch*, it read.

Stone pressed his FAVORITES button and called
Holly, who was upstairs at Dino's party.

"Holly Barker."

"It's Stone. Dino, Mike, and I are downstairs.
Stanley is being put into an ambulance as we speak,
unconscious but alive. Your van and its driver are

gone, and so is Helga. She has an Agency iPhone." He gave her the number. "Can you locate it?"

"Yes," she said. "And I can do more than that. I'll call you back."

Stone watched the ambulance drive away, with one of Dino's cops inside with Stanley. Holly came out of the building, her phone in her hand. "Got it," she said, showing them the map. "FDR Drive, headed south, doing at least eighty."

Dino called it in and asked for an intercept.

"Turning onto the Brooklyn Bridge," Holly said. "Not slowing down."

Dino transferred the information to the dispatcher.

"Off the bridge," Holly said, "on the Brooklyn-Queens Expressway. Wait, it's turning off onto Atlantic Avenue."

The three men watched with her, while Dino kept talking to the dispatcher. "We've got an APB for all of Brooklyn," Dino said.

Holly's phone rang, and she answered it, pressing the SPEAKER button so she could keep the map.

"Yes, ma'am?" a female voice said.

"Give me the view from the phone," Holly said.

The map closed, and the screen went dark. "The phone must still be in her handbag," Holly said to the group. "All right, keep an eye on the phone and be careful of the battery life. Call me when you've got a view. Also, switch on the van's camera." She switched back to the map.

"It's gone," Stone said. "It's not on the map anymore."

"They're indoors," Holly said, "probably a garage."

"Probably switching cars," Stone added.

"Oh, shit," Dino said. "We're going to lose her."

The image on-screen changed.

"This is the view from the van's camera," she said, "looking forward through the front passenger window."

The view was of a row of parked cars.

"They've left the van," Holly said.

Then something flashed by on the screen.

"Another van! Hang on!" She reversed the footage, frame by frame, then stopped it. "Gray, maybe a Ford."

"Can you view the plate?"

"No, it's below our van's dashboard."

"Let's hope they took Helga's handbag with them," Dino said.

They all stood helplessly and watched the map for signs of movement.

"You know where they're going?" Stone said.

"No," Dino replied, "enlighten us."

"Brighton Beach," Stone said.

"Oh, shit."

54

Dino pressed a button on his iPhone. "Captain Andrew Shirah, please," he said into the instrument. "Chief Bacchetti calling. Stone, have you got a picture of Helga?"

Stone went to the photo page on his phone and found a shot he had taken in Paris. "Here you are," he said, showing it to Dino.

"E-mail it to me," Dino said. "Andy? Dino Bacchetti. I'm about to e-mail you a picture of a missing woman. Hang on." Dino switched screens and e-mailed Helga's picture, then went back to the phone. "Her name is Helga Becker, she's Swedish, six feet one or two, a hundred and fifty pounds, give or take. She's been kidnaped by a Russian gang, and I think they're on the way to your precinct with her. I want you to turn out in force, flood the area with plainclothes people, but no uniforms or marked cars, and no lights or sirens. If the locals see us coming, they'll clam up. Show the picture around and tell them she's a Russian girl who's been kidnapped. They may have her in a Ford van, gray, and they're probably going to take the van indoors to a garage or other building. Got it? Keep me posted on my cell. Thanks, Andy." Dino hung up. "Andy Shirah is one of the best cops on the force, and he'll do everything that can be done in Brighton Beach."

An ambulance pulled up to the curb; Stanley had regained consciousness and was sitting up. "I heard that," he said to Dino. "You need me for this. I know the territory and a lot of the people."

"You shut up and lie down," Dino said. "You're going to the hospital and get patched up and x-rayed."

But Stanley was struggling to his feet. "You," he said to an approaching EMT. "Get my head bandaged right here. I'm not going with you."

Dino shrugged and nodded at the EMT. "Do it."

The EMT looked at the back of Stanley's head and got a compress on it. "He's going to need stitches."

"Tape it shut," Stanley said, "and don't argue with me."

The EMT made him sit on the fender of a car while he applied a dozen butterfly bandages to the wound. "That will hold it, if you don't move around too much."

"Stanley," Dino said, "go sit in the front passenger seat of my car and don't move. All you're going to do is talk, nothing else. You got that?"

"Yes, Chief," Stanley said, then did as he was told.

Stone turned to Mike and handed him the keys to the Bentley. "Send one of your guys to get my car, and the other two upstairs to keep an eye on Marcel until the car comes. When he's ready to leave, have them take him to my house and lock it down."

Mike grabbed his returning men and gave them their instructions.

"Okay," Dino said, "Stone, Holly, come with me. Mike, you do whatever you can do. We're going to Brighton Beach."

The three of them got into the rear seat of Dino's department Lincoln. "All right, Paddy, we're going to Brighton Beach: Brooklyn Bridge, Brooklyn-Queens Expressway, et cetera, et cetera. That's Stanley in the front seat. When we get there, he'll tell you where to go. Use your lights and siren as necessary, but not after we get there."

Dino settled back in the seat, and the car rocketed forward, lights flashing, siren on.

"Holly," Stone said, "what are the chances of picking up Helga's cell phone again?"

"Slim," Holly said. "The tracer will work even with the phone shut down completely, but it's gotta see the satellite now and then or get a good cell or Wi-Fi connection. Let's hope to God they took her handbag with her when they changed cars. Dino, can you get somebody to the last location of the Mercedes van and look for her phone or handbag in it?"

Dino got on the phone and gave the orders. "Ten minutes," he said, "maybe less."

Five grim minutes later, he got a call. He listened, then hung up. "No phone, no handbag," he said.

"That's a relief," Holly said. "Now we've got a chance." She checked the map page of her phone again. "Nothing yet."

Stanley spoke up from the front seat. "Something you need to know," he said. "They're going to try to negotiate—probably to get their hands on you, Mr. Barrington—but if they think negotiations will fail, their attitude will be, if she's not an asset to them, then she's a liability. They'll kill her. They won't be dissuaded with thoughts of getting caught or the death penalty—it's how they do things."

Nobody said anything.

"We're a couple of miles out," the driver finally said. "I'm killing the siren and lights." He switched them off.

"Stanley," Dino said, "what's your best guess?"

"They'll avoid the beach area," Stanley said. "They'll be inland a few blocks, heading for a garage or factory—something they can drive into."

"Tell the sergeant where to go. We're in your hands."

Stone's phone chimed, and he checked the screen. "We've got a text," he said. "It says: 'You for the girl.'"

"Tell them yes," Stanley said. "Don't threaten them."

Stone texted back: *Agreed. Where and when?*

Holly spoke up. "We've got a hit on the phone. It's moving." She held the phone where Stanley could see it.

"Hang a left," Stanley said to the driver.

55

Helga sat in a cane-seated chair, her hands tied behind her and her feet tied to the chair. She had been working on freeing her hands since her arrival in this place, and she was nearly there. Her ankles, however, were another problem. She strained against the cord binding them, hoping to stretch it a bit, as she had done with her wrists. She knew that her guard had a switchblade knife, and she decided that she must have it, if she wished to be free again.

She tried very, very hard and managed to slip the cord binding her wrists over one hand, at the expense of some skin. The man was too far away, though, for her to reach his knife, which was tucked into his belt. She renewed her efforts to stretch the cord binding her ankles.

She was making progress when one of the other men walked into the officelike space where she had been put. He was a nasty piece of work, and he kept his weapon, a silenced pistol, in his hand at all times. He walked over and ripped the tape from her mouth.

"That's better," he said. "Now you can suck my cock."

"Yes, yes, give it to me," she said, "and I'll bite it off for you and send it to you at Christmastime, gift-wrapped."

He backhanded her with his free hand, toppling both her and the chair. Helga struggled to right herself, kicking off her shoes and renewing her efforts to free her ankles. She managed to keep her hands, now free, behind her, holding tight to one wrist with the other hand.

He walked over, grabbed the chair and pulled it upright. "Jesus," he said, "you weigh a lot." Helga stood up, grabbed the silencer, held on to it, then struck him flush in the nose with a hard right. She felt it break, and blood began to stream down his face. She wrenched at the pistol, trying to dislodge it from his grasp, but he was a strong man, and he wouldn't let go. This time she aimed a fist at his throat, but he lowered his chin and caught the punch there.

Her guard suddenly came alive and simply pushed her to the floor, her ankles still bound. The man with the pistol approached now, his body language indicating a kick to her head.

"Stop it!" Majorov screamed from the doorway.

The man froze.

"I told you she is not to be harmed. Not yet, anyway."

The big man backed away, and her guard got busy retying her hands.

"I have never dealt with such incompetents," Majorov said. "I leave you alone for a few minutes and return to find that she has freed herself and broken your nose. What an idiot!" He turned to Helga. "Miss Becker, I will have no more of this nonsense. I am prepared to release you when my business is done, but if you give me further trouble, when we are done I will allow this gorilla to have his way with you, then shoot you."

"Hah!" Helga responded. "Free me, and I will hand you his head!"

"We will leave his head where it is for the time being," Majorov said. "It is time for us to go and meet Mr. Barrington."

"He will not meet you," Helga said. "He is too smart for that."

"You are quite wrong," Majorov said. "He will

meet me, give me what I want, and then I will free the both of you."

"I'll believe that when I see it," Helga said.

"You two," Majorov said, "put her in the van. We are wasting time."

The two men cut her feet loose, and Helga slipped into her shoes again. Then they put her in the van.

56

Paddy, Dino's driver, followed Stanley's directions, whipping around corners and dodging pedestrians.

"We've lost Helga's phone again," Holly said, "but it had stopped moving."

"We'll continue to the last fix," Stanley said. "Hang a right, Paddy, then pull over on the right."

Paddy put the big car into a four-wheel drift, then slammed on the brakes.

"Here," Stanley said.

The building took up half the block; no signs or numbers, and the windows were painted over. There were two steel garage doors, and one of them had a smaller entry door next to it.

"Okay," Dino said. "Stone, you're unarmed—you stay in the car, you hear me?"

"Oh, all right," Stone said.

"Paddy, you're with us. As I recall, you have some lockpicking skills, right?"

"Yessir."

Everybody got out, except Stone and Stanley.

"Fuck this," Stanley said, half to himself, then got out of the car, reaching for his pistol.

Stone continued to behave himself.

Dino stood over Paddy, willing him to hurry with the lock. Three minutes, and they were in. He looked over his shoulder to see if Stone was staying put. He was.

"Everybody behind me," Dino said. He opened the door and looked inside. The group flooded in behind him. A gray Ford van was the only object visible in the empty building. They surrounded it, then opened the doors. Paddy reached inside and came up with an iPhone.

"Cell right here," he said.

"Then we're fucked," Holly said. "We have no means of tracking them. We don't even know what they're driving."

"Then we'll just have to take to the streets like everybody else," Dino said. "Let's go."

They hurried back to the door and stepped into the street.

"What the fuck?" Dino yelled.

The Lincoln was gone.

"Stone got himself taken! Paddy, get on the radio and put an APB out for my car, and get us another couple of vehicles, pronto!"

"Dino," Holly said, "this is the best thing that could have happened."

"What are you talking about?" Dino demanded.

"Stone has the same cell phone as Helga—one of ours. We can track it." She called her base and gave the instructions.

Stone sat between the two large Russians, one of whom had a pistol with a silencer jammed uncomfortably in his ribs. He was in the rear seat of a tan van, and Helga was in the seat ahead of him. He had tried to talk to her, but every time he opened his mouth, the big Russian next to him stuck his pistol into it. They had searched him perfunctorily for a gun, and not finding one had gone no further. They hadn't bothered with his cell phone, and he figured that was the best chance he and Helga had. They had taken the Lincoln, which followed behind, stranding Dino and Holly.

They had driven only a few blocks when the driver turned into a parking garage. They drove up the spiral ramp five stories, tires squealing, and emerged onto a rooftop, where a black Mercedes

S-class sedan awaited. It was dark, but the rooftop was dotted here and there with lights. Yuri Majorov was leaning on the Mercedes, holding a briefcase and talking on his cell phone.

First Helga, then Stone were hustled out of the van and presented to the big Russian. Majorov first glared at Stone, then smiled a little.

"Well, Mr. Barrington," he said, putting away his phone, "you have given me quite a chase."

"Fun, wasn't it?" Stone asked. The man behind him with the pistol rapped him sharply on the head. "You know," Stone said, "unless you take these apes in hand, you're just going to slow down the process."

"What process is that?" Majorov asked.

"You must have something in mind, or we wouldn't all be here, would we?"

Majorov held up a hand before the man could hit Stone again. "All right, all right," he said. "Now to business."

"I thought you'd never get around to it," Stone said. "Your message said me for her. I'm here, let her go."

"First, we have some formalities to complete." He set his briefcase on the hood of the Mercedes and opened it.

"You don't need her for formalities," Stone said. "Let her go *now*."

"Mr. Barrington, you are hardly in a position to give me orders," Majorov said irritably.

Stone didn't bother to reply.

"Now," Majorov said, taking a sheaf of neatly printed documents from the briefcase, "I will need your signature in a dozen or so places."

"For what?" Stone asked.

"We are going to execute a transfer of your stock in The Arrington Corporation to a company that I own in Paris, then a sum of money will be transferred to whatever bank account you wish. Miss Becker will witness your signature." He nodded to the man standing next to Helga; he produced a switchblade knife and cut the bonds that held her hands behind her back.

She held up her limp hands. "My hands are numb," she said to Majorov. "I can't hold a pen."

Majorov sighed and spoke to the man with the switchblade. "Massage her wrists."

The man closed the knife and tucked it into his belt, then did as he was told.

While they were occupied with Helga's circulation, Stone took a moment to look around. At one end of the building, perhaps thirty feet away, was the top end of a steel ladder, hooked across the building's parapet. Fire escape—the only way down, except for the ramp they had driven up. He looked at Helga; she had spotted it, too.

Stone looked around them for weapons. The man behind him still had the silenced pistol, and the man massaging Helga's wrists had the switchblade, but those were the only weapons in evidence. He had no doubt, though, that the others were well armed. If he could get his hands on the silenced pistol, he might get off three or four shots before anybody could get ahold of a weapon and fire back, but he was going to need some sort of distraction.

Helga, thoughtfully, provided that. Her guard had stopped massaging and pulled out the switchblade again. She lifted a leg and drove the six-inch spike heel of her shoe through his shoe and foot. He screamed and let go of the knife, which Helga caught before it hit the ground. She grabbed him by the hair, jerked him around, and stood behind him, the knife to his throat. "Now, please, everyone will throw the guns over the edge of the building."

Majorov turned to the man with the silenced pistol and jerked his head toward the man with the knife to his throat. The man raised his pistol and shot his colleague in the chest. Helga held him on his feet for protection.

Stone seized the moment, grabbed the pistol by the silencer, and wrenched it from the man's hand. Then things began to happen very fast.

57

Stone shot the man whose gun he had taken, because he liked him the least, though he wasn't very fond of the others, either. That left only Majorov and one other man, who was clawing at his clothing, trying in his nervous condition to come up with a weapon. Majorov just stared with an expression of mild surprise at the change in his fortunes.

Stone trained the pistol on the other man, who stopped groping himself and put his hands on top of his head.

Helga dropped the dead man she had been holding by the neck for cover, went to the surrendered man, and frisked him expertly, coming up with a .45 automatic, then she began striding toward Majorov.

"Now, Miss Becker," Majorov said, backing away from her.

She raked his face with the barrel of the .45, then, when he leaned back against the Mercedes, kicked him in the knee.

Majorov fell to the concrete deck, yelling—no doubt swearing—in Russian. A gust of wind came up and scattered the papers that had been stacked on the hood of the Mercedes.

"Nicely done," Stone said, starting to embrace her, but she was going over Majorov's fallen form with care, tossing two guns and a knife onto the deck.

When she had finished, Stone gave her a hug and a kiss, but not before she had kicked Majorov in the ribs. She seemed to appreciate the affection but then became businesslike. "Now we must decide how we must dispose of these two," she said.

"Dispose?" Stone asked.

"If we let them be taken by the police, then there will be only a big mess, with lawyers and bail money, et cetera. I know these things. I have watched all the episodes of *Law & Order*, you see."

"I see," Stone said tonelessly.

Majorov's henchman, hearing this conversation

and seeing them momentarily distracted, made a dive for one of Majorov's pistols.

Helga turned and shot him with his own gun. "Good," she said, "now we have only to deal with Mr. Majorov."

Majorov had struggled into a sitting position and was leaning against the Mercedes, clutching his knee, while blood dribbled from his broken nose and off his chin. "Really, now, Mr. Barrington. Surely you are too civilized a gentleman to listen to such ill-considered talk from this woman."

"Oh, I don't know," Stone said, "I think she's making a lot of sense."

"Let me offer a more businesslike alternative—two alternatives, actually."

"Go on," Stone said.

"Why don't we just throw him off the building?" Helga asked. "We can say he ran, then fell."

"That's certainly a possibility," Stone said, "but I want to hear what his idea of business is."

"Very wise, Mr. Barrington," Majorov said. "There is a piece of luggage in the trunk of my car containing two million dollars in cash. My travel expense money. Why don't you take that—and the car, if you wish—and just go home? I'll clean up here, and the police need never know about these events."

Helga spoke up. "Why don't we throw him off the building, then take the money and the car?"

"You see," Stone said to Majorov, "she's really thinking very clearly."

"Yes, Mr. Barrington," Majorov said, "and I admire her acuity. However, then you would still be left with elaborate explanations to the police, and some risk to yourselves."

"He has a point," Stone said to Helga. "Neither of us really need the money, and I already have two cars, so why don't we just hog-tie him and wait for Dino to figure out where we are? In fact," he said, getting out his iPhone, "I can satisfy his curiosity right now."

"Really, Mr. Barrington," Majorov said, "there is no need for this pig-tying business. I have been crippled, you see, so I will not be fleeing. It is quite impossible in my condition."

"You're breaking my heart," Stone said.

"And you didn't listen to my second alternative," Majorov said.

"You're right, I didn't."

"The second alternative is to wait here for another minute or so, when this rooftop will be flooded with my associates, whom I have already asked to join me here. They will be heavily armed and not so inclined to be businesslike as I."

Stone had just pressed the speed-dial button for

Dino when, with a roar, two unmarked NYPD police cars shot onto the roof from the ramp and spilled out Dino, Holly, Paddy, and Stanley, each waving a weapon.

"It looks like you didn't need us," Dino said, surveying the rooftop carnage and the cringing Majorov.

"Well, Dino," Stone said, "if what Majorov has just told me is true, not only do we need you, but we may need reinforcements as well."

Then, from somewhere, came the beat of helicopter blades, and a large, evil-looking chopper rose from below the building's parapet and turned sideways, revealing a wide-open door and several men inside, bristling with automatic weapons.

58

Everyone stood transfixed, staring at the helicopter and its deadly cargo. Majorov used this moment to slither around the Mercedes and begin to hobble painfully toward the machine.

Then, as one man, Stone and his group dived behind the Mercedes as the firing began. The Mercedes, which seemed brand-new, began to disintegrate into small pieces of flying glass and metal, as did the two police cars behind it.

"Stay behind the engine," Stone yelled, and they all huddled more closely together.

"This car will be gone in a minute," Dino pointed out.

"Just stay behind the engine!" Stone yelled.

Then the firing, unaccountably, stopped. Instead

of automatic weapons fire, Stone could hear the sound of a second helicopter.

"I hope to God they don't have reinforcements coming," Dino said.

Stone took the opportunity to peep from behind the remains of the Mercedes and saw Majorov being assisted into the big helicopter, then the machine turning away from the building. "It's leaving," he said. Then another helicopter hove into view, and this one was a welcome sight.

"Dino," Stone said, "check this out. Is that a Black Hawk?"

"I believe it is," Dino said.

"And, Holly, is that Rick LaRose behind the machine gun in the firing bay?"

Holly popped up. "One and the same!"

Rick gave them a wave as his chopper turned in pursuit of Majorov's transport, which was beating its way at top speed toward the beach.

Stone stood up. "Is anybody hit?"

"Strangely enough, no," Holly said.

Helga, Stanley, and Paddy got to their feet.

They all turned and looked at the two police cars that had brought them there, which were in approximately the same condition as the Mercedes.

"Anybody seen my Lincoln?" Paddy asked.

"I think I saw it on a lower level as we came up," Holly said.

"Go find it, Paddy," Dino said, and Paddy trotted off toward the ramp.

They all turned and watched the progress of the two helicopters and found themselves witnessing a running air battle. The two machines were banking and swerving just off the beach, four or five blocks away, and the view from the five-story parking garage gave them a princely perch for watching.

"I don't think I've ever seen anything quite like this," Stone said as the two choppers continued to exchange bursts of fire, nearly at wave height, lit by the lights of Brighton Beach and Coney Island.

Then, as they watched, a small puff of black smoke erupted from the engine area of the Majorov machine, and it began to yaw and look less controllable. Then the chopper began a long, slow turn in toward the beach, and people began to spill from the helicopter into the sea, perhaps ten feet below. A moment later the machine vanished in a huge ball of fire as the fuel tank exploded.

Two police helicopters now converged from the edges of the conflict and began to pick up survivors. The Black Hawk climbed a few feet and turned back toward the garage. It hovered overhead and switched on some floodlights, illuminating the top deck of the garage, then it sank slowly until it touched down and its engines were brought to idle.

Rick LaRose hopped out of the machine and strode toward them, smiling broadly. "Everybody here okay?" he yelled.

"We've got three dead," Stone said, pointing toward Majorov's men, whose bodies had been further ripped by the fire from the helicopter. "All opposition."

"Was Majorov aboard the helicopter?" Rick asked.

"We saw him get aboard," Stone replied. "Has his body been recovered?"

"I haven't heard yet," Rick said, "but they were low enough when they abandoned ship that there should be survivors. Some of them were making for the beach when I last saw them."

"If they make it ashore," Dino said, "they'll disappear into the Russian population out here, and they'll be tough to find."

"Dino," Stone said, "in the unhappy event that Majorov made it ashore, he will be heading for an airport as we speak, probably to his own airplane."

"I'll take care of that," Holly said, reaching for her phone. "I can order a federal presence to every airport in the greater New York area. Inside an hour or two, nobody will exit the country that we don't want to leave." She pressed a button and began talking.

"Can I offer anyone a lift to the East Side Heliport?" Rick asked.

"You bet your ass you can," Stone said.

The Lincoln came up the ramp with Paddy at the wheel.

"I'll take my car," Dino said.

Stone herded Holly, Helga, and Stanley toward the waiting Black Hawk.

They were nearly there when Helga stopped. "Just a moment," she said. "I forgot my luggage."

She returned to the remains of the Mercedes, rummaged in what had been the trunk, and came up with a small, tattered alligator suitcase, then she returned to the Black Hawk and was helped aboard.

Everybody buckled in, the rotors began to spin noisily, and the big helicopter lifted off and turned toward the sea. As it turned again to follow the shoreline back to Manhattan, they could see the scattered fires and oily smoke that had been the Majorov chopper.

"My people have recovered the black Mercedes van," Holly said over the intercom. "I've asked them to meet us at the East Side Heliport."

"I hope this will be my last ride in that thing," Stone said.

It was after three in the morning before Stone and Helga made it to bed, too tired to molest each other.

59

They all met for breakfast in Stone's kitchen at around ten a.m. Stone was stiff and sore, and he expected that Helga was, too, though she seemed very happy.

"I've had news this morning," Marcel said, "that my newly armored Maybach will be at Le Bourget to meet me this evening. That will be a comfort, as will the presence of Mike Freeman's men."

"I hope you won't need them much longer," Stone said. "Even if Majorov survived the helicopter crash, I can't imagine that, after his experience, he would come after you or your business again."

"I hope you are right, Stone," Marcel replied, "but if he does, I will be ready."

They packed their luggage into the Mercedes

van for the trip to Teterboro. Stone noticed that the black alligator suitcase was missing and asked Helga about it.

"It had bullet holes," she said, "and I thought that might attract the attention of Swedish customs. So I'm making a gift of it to you."

"Thank you so much," Stone said. "A little legal advice—taking cash out of the country is not illegal, but not reporting it is. When you clear emigration on your way out, ask for a form to report cash aboard. List the amount, sign it, and turn it in."

"But they will tax me."

"I don't think so, but if they search your luggage, you're covered. Also, I hear that there are so many of those forms turned in that it takes them years to record them all, if they bother." He helped her into the van.

Marcel shook Stone's hand, then hugged him. "I have never been entertained in such a fashion," he said. "I will dine out on the stories for years."

"As will I," Stone said.

"I have sent you a small house gift to express my gratitude for your hospitality," Marcel said. "It will be delivered later today. And I want to thank you for the experience of your American wines. They were very interesting."

"Thank you, Marcel," Stone said. "And I look

forward to a long and happy experience with you in the hotel business."

Marcel got into the van, Stanley closed the door, and they were off.

Stone went back into the house through the office door, and Joan was at her desk, working. "Hi, there. Everybody get off all right?"

"They did."

"I got a call that we'll be getting a delivery late this afternoon. Something Marcel sent."

"Yes, he mentioned it—a house present, he said."

"I hope it's not another car. The garage is full."

"I doubt it."

"By the way, when I came into work this morning, I ran into a woman, a real estate agent, putting a 'for sale' sign on the little house next door, on the garage side."

"So we'll be getting new neighbors, eventually."

"She took me through the house," Joan said, "and it's charming. In perfect condition, ready to move into and mostly furnished. It has been very nicely turned into a duplex and three apartments, and there's an elevator. It's available, empty, with no lingering tenants."

"Well, I hope it attracts nice people on the downstairs floor, since their garden is just over the wall."

"I was thinking," Joan said, "Helene's lease is up in a couple of months, and she has to move, and

I could use more space myself. Why don't you buy the house and move us into it? There'd still be room for guests—maybe Peter and Hattie?"

"They're going to be living in L.A.," Stone said. "But how much are the owners asking for it?"

Joan told him. "The market is still depressed after the housing crisis. I think they might take a good deal less for a quick cash sale. Also, you could break through from the garage into their basement, making more room for the cars and a bigger wine cellar and a nicer exercise room for you."

Stone thought about that for a moment. "All right, make them an offer—negotiate, if you have to. I'll trust you to make the deal."

Joan jumped up and hugged him. "You're wonderful!"

"So are you and Helene," Stone replied.

He went to his desk and began sorting through the correspondence and phone messages. There was one from Mike Freeman, and he returned it.

"Exciting events last night, eh?" Mike asked cheerfully.

"A little too exciting," Stone said. "I'm still feeling the effects."

"My sources tell me that two survivors of the helicopter crash were picked up. Neither of them was Majorov. He's in the wind."

"As far as I'm concerned, he can stay there,"

Stone replied. "I should have shot him when I could have, or followed Helga's advice and dumped him off the building."

Mike laughed. "That Helga is a piece of work, isn't she?"

"She certainly is."

"I don't think we'll hear from Majorov again. I think he's found you to be too much trouble for the effort."

"I hope you're right," Stone said. They said good-bye and hung up.

The phone rang. "Hello?"

"It's Dino. I thought I'd bring you up to date."

"There were two survivors, but not Majorov?"

"Where do you get this stuff?"

"I have connections."

"You want to join me for dinner at Patroon tonight? Viv is still cleaning up after the party last night. Eight o'clock?"

"You're on. I'm glad you don't have to do the dishes."

Stone worked through the afternoon, then went upstairs to his study for a drink. Joan buzzed him. "Your package from Marcel has arrived," she said. "Shall I bring it up?"

"Sure," Stone said, and collapsed into his easy chair.

60

Stone sat, too worn out even to get up and get himself a drink. He closed his eyes for a moment, and when he opened them, a man was standing in the doorway. He hadn't heard him approach.

He was small, perhaps five-five or -six, and wiry, with short, thick gray hair. He looked to be fiftyish, and he was wearing a well-fitted, three-piece tweed suit.

"Good afternoon, Mr. Barrington," the man said. His accent was Cockney.

"Good afternoon," Stone replied. "Where did you come from?"

"Ms. Robertson escorted me from her office."

"Ah, you're here to deliver a gift from M'sieur duBois."

"That is correct, sir. My name is Frederick Flicker." He handed Stone a thick buff-colored envelope. "My credentials."

"Credentials?" Stone asked.

"My particulars, Mr. Barrington. I would be grateful if you would peruse them. If you have any questions, I would be pleased to answer them."

Stone opened the envelope and shook out a couple of sheets of paper and a binder holding many more pages.

"May I get you a glass of your bourbon while you're reading them, sir?" Flicker nodded toward the bar.

"Yes, thank you," Stone replied. "Fill a whiskey glass with ice, then fill it with bourbon."

Flicker did as instructed, selecting the Knob Creek without being told.

Stone took a sip. "How did you know which bourbon?"

"Your reputation precedes you, sir."

Stone set the papers in his lap. "Why don't you just tell me about yourself, Mr. Flicker? I'm too tired to digest all this. And please sit down. Fix yourself a drink first, if you like."

"Thank you, sir, but no," Flicker said. He sat down. "First, to business. I was born fifty years ago next month in London, the East End, within the sound of Bow Bells."

"Which makes you a genuine Cockney, does it not?"

"Just so, sir," Fred said in his genuine Cockney accent. "I was educated at the local grammar school but could not afford to attend university, so at seventeen I enlisted in the Royal Marines. I served thirty-two years in the Commando Brigade, retiring with the rank of regimental sergeant major. I fought in Northern Ireland, Iraq, and Afghanistan. And, since I understand you sometimes have security concerns, you should know I was twice the Royal Marines pistol champion."

"That is an impressive record, Mr. Flicker."

"I would be pleased, sir, if you would call me Fred."

"Certainly, Fred."

"After my retirement I was at loose ends, so I attended a renowned school for butlers in London, and after that, the Bentley chauffeurs' training course, plus a course in high-performance and defensive driving. Then I was employed for a year by M'sieur duBois at his Paris home and office as second butler. I regret to say that I found my character and nature incompatible with those of the head butler, whom I thought insufferably French, with a profound disrespect for anything English, so I tendered my resignation ten days ago, leaving with a resounding recommendation from M'sieur duBois, which you will find in my file."

"I see," Stone said, and he thought he was beginning to. "Fred, am I to understand that you are a gift to me from M'sieur duBois?"

"Quite right, Mr. Barrington. M'sieur duBois has given you one year of my service, paid in advance. After that, we will see if we may reach an accommodation regarding the future."

"Well," said Stone, "welcome to my household, Fred."

"Thank you, sir," Fred said. "Might I begin by asking Ms. Robertson to give me a tour of the house and kitchens and to introduce me to the cook?"

"What a good idea," Stone said.

"Oh, and I presume you have a wine cellar?"

"I do."

"Then perhaps I should immediately cellar the dozen cases of very fine French wines that M'sieur duBois has also sent you. After all, wine is a living thing." In Fred's Cockney accent, this came out as "Woyne is a wivving fing."

Stone laughed. "I don't think M'sieur duBois was as impressed with our American wines as he pretended to be."

"Perhaps not, sir. By the way, I am aware that my accent is impenetrable to many Americans. I can quite easily speak in BBC English or, if you wish, with more of an upper-class accent. Which would you prefer?"

"About halfway between your Cockney and your BBC, I should think."

"As you wish, sir."

Joan appeared at the door, apparently having been listening outside. "Fred, if you will come with me, we'll get started."

"Joan," Stone said, "you can put Fred in the room at the rear of the fourth floor, overlooking the garden. Assuming we successfully complete the purchase of the house next door, you can arrange an apartment for him there."

"What a good idea," Joan said, "since the seller has already accepted your offer, which was fifteen percent below the asking price. We close on the fifteenth."

"Very good," Stone said.

Fred stood up. "You may keep my credentials and read them at your leisure," he said to Stone, then he and Joan left the room.

Stone slowly finished his bourbon. "Dino," he said aloud, to himself, "you are not going to believe this one."

Then Joan appeared in the doorway, holding a package wrapped in brown paper, which seemed to be leaking. "Another gift arrived for you," she said.

"What on earth is that?" Stone asked.

"Fifteen pounds of moose meat."

AUTHOR'S NOTE

I am happy to hear from readers, but you should know that if you write to me in care of my publisher, three to six months will pass before I receive your letter, and when it finally arrives it will be one among many, and I will not be able to reply.

However, if you have access to the Internet, you may visit my Web site at www.stuartwoods.com, where there is a button for sending me e-mail. So far, I have been able to reply to all my e-mail, and I will continue to try to do so.

If you send me an e-mail and do not receive a reply, it is probably because you are among an alarming number of people who have entered their e-mail address incorrectly in their mail software. I have many of my replies returned as undeliverable.

Remember: e-mail, reply; snail mail, no reply.

When you e-mail, please do not send attachments, as I never open them. They can take twenty minutes to download, and they often contain viruses.

Please do not place me on your mailing lists for funny stories, prayers, political causes, charitable fund-raising, petitions, or sentimental claptrap. I get enough of that from people I already know. Generally speaking, when I get e-mail addressed to a large number of people, I immediately delete it without reading it.

Please do not send me your ideas for a book, as I have a policy of writing only what I myself invent. If you send me story ideas, I will immediately delete them without reading them. If you have a good idea for a book, write it yourself, but I will not be able to advise you on how to get it published. Buy a copy of *Writer's Market* at any bookstore; that will tell you how.

Anyone with a request concerning events or appearances may e-mail it to me or send it to: Publicity Department, Penguin Group (USA) Inc., 375 Hudson Street, New York, NY 10014.

Those ambitious folk who wish to buy film, dramatic, or television rights to my books should contact Matthew Snyder, Creative Artists Agency, 9830 Wilshire Boulevard, Beverly Hills, CA 98212-1825.

Those who wish to make offers for rights of

a literary nature should contact Anne Sibbald, Janklow & Nesbit, 445 Park Avenue, New York, NY 10022. (Note: This is not an invitation for you to send her your manuscript or to solicit her to be your agent.)

If you want to know if I will be signing books in your city, please visit my Web site, www.stuart woods.com, where the tour schedule will be published a month or so in advance. If you wish me to do a book signing in your locality, ask your favorite bookseller to contact his Penguin representative or the Penguin publicity department with the request.

If you find typographical or editorial errors in my book and feel an irresistible urge to tell someone, please write to Sara Minnich at Penguin's address above. Do not e-mail your discoveries to me, as I will already have learned about them from others.

A list of my published works appears in the front of this book and on my Web site. All the novels are still in print in paperback and can be found at or ordered from any bookstore. If you wish to obtain hardcover copies of earlier novels or of the two nonfiction books, a good used-book store or one of the online bookstores can help you find them. Otherwise, you will have to go to a great many garage sales.

New York Times bestselling
author Stuart Woods is back
with another thriller.
Read on for a preview of

STANDUP GUY

Available from Putnam
in January 2014 everywhere
books and e-books are sold

1

Stone Barrington made it from his bed to his desk by ten a.m., after something of a struggle with jet lag. Granted, the three-hour time change between Los Angeles and New York was not a killer, but it mattered. As soon as he sat down, his intercom buzzed.

"Yes?" he said to his secretary, Joan Robertson.

"You have a visitor," she said, "name of John Fratelli. Says he's a friend of Eduardo's."

"Send him in," Stone said. Any friend of Eduardo Bianci was a friend of his.

A vision of the mid-to-late twentieth century appeared in the doorway.

"Mr. Barrington? May I come in?"

"Of course," Stone said, rising to greet his

visitor, who was wearing a boxy light gray flannel suit, a starched white shirt, and what appeared to be a clip-on bow tie. He was carrying a salesman's suitcase and a porkpie hat and had a haircut that had probably been accomplished entirely with electric clippers—short sides and a Brylcreemed top. "Come in and have a seat, Mr. Fratelli."

"Thank you," the man replied. "It's nice of you to see me." This was delivered in what appeared to be an old-fashioned Brooklyn accent, the likes of which had not been heard for many years from a man as young as Fratelli, who appeared to be no older than fifty. He came in and took the proffered chair across the desk and set down the suitcase.

"How may I help you?" Stone said, hoping the man was not a salesman.

Fratelli stood again, reached into a pocket, and pulled out a wad of bills; he peeled off five hundreds and placed them carefully on Stone's desk.

"All right," Stone said, "you've paid for a consultation and bought yourself some attorney-client confidentiality."

"Good," Fratelli said, sitting down again.

"I should inform you, though, that if you confess to a crime and I end up representing you in court, I will not be able to call you to the stand to testify on your own behalf."

"Why not?" Fratelli inquired.

"Because I cannot call a witness to the stand who I know will lie under oath."

"I understand," Fratelli said. "That's reasonable, I guess."

"How is Mr. Bianci?" Stone asked, by way of getting the man to relax.

"Who?"

"Did you not tell my secretary that Eduardo had sent you to me?"

"Oh, I meant Eduardo Buono."

"Not Bianci?"

"No, Buono."

"I don't know anyone by that name," Stone said.

"Well, he knows you."

"How does he know me?"

"He read an article about you in a magazine— *Vanity Fair*."

That magazine had published an excerpt from a book about Stone's late wife, Arrington. "I'm afraid I—"

"Eduardo says you're a standup guy."

"Well, as kind a characterization as that may be—"

"Eduardo and I shared a living space for twenty-two years."

"I'm happy for you both, but that still doesn't—"

"Eduardo was a very smart man, even if he did get caught."

"Ahhhh," Stone said. Now he understood. "Where did you do your time, Mr. Fratelli?"

"Sing Sing."

"And when did you get out?"

"Yesterday afternoon."

"How long were you away?"

"Twenty-five years, to the day. I did my whole sentence, no parole."

"What was the rap?"

"Armed robbery. I did it—no excuses. That's why I didn't apply for parole."

"Then you, not I, are the standup guy, Mr. Fratelli."

Fratelli actually blushed. "Thank you," he said softly.

"Now, please tell me, how can I help you?"

"Eduardo left me two million dollars," he said. "And change."

"Congratulations, but if you're looking for investment advice, I'm not—"

"I'm looking for advice on how not to go back to prison," Fratelli said.

"That's fairly simple, Mr. Fratelli—don't commit another crime."

"Oh, sure, but—"

"Oh, I think I see. Did Mr. Buono acquire your inheritance by extralegal means?"

"Exactly."

"Did he rob somebody?"

"Exactly, but Eduardo said the statue was done."

That stopped Stone in his tracks for a moment, then he figured it out. "Do you mean the statute? The statute of limitations?"

"That's it!"

"Well, the statute of limitations for robbery is five years, so if you and Mr. Buono were cellmates for twenty-two years . . ."

"So it's mine, then?"

"I wouldn't go as far as that," Stone said. "It's problematical."

"I was afraid you'd say something like that."

"Mr. Fratelli, let me put this hypothetically, since you and I do not want to discuss a real crime."

"Okay, I get that."

"If prisoner A committed a crime, and the statute of limitations has run out, then he can mention prisoner B in his will."

"It wasn't exactly like that," Fratelli said. "There wasn't—I mean, in this story prisoner A didn't have a will, he had a safe-deposit box. He, hypothetically speaking, had a bank account, and every quarter for twenty-five years, the bank deducted the rental of the safe-deposit box from his account. From time to time, his lawyer deposited funds."

"And prisoner B has access to the box?"

"Prisoner A told me—ah, him—where to find the key."

"And has prisoner B visited the box?"

"You could say that."

"And he emptied the box?"

"About an hour ago," Fratelli said. "Just as soon as the bank opened, prisoner B was there with the key."

"Did anyone see what he removed from the box?"

"No, he was in a little closet, and he had brought a suitcase. He just walked out with the money."

"I see."

"His question is, what's he going to do with it?"

"Whatever he likes," Stone said. "As long as no one knows he has it."

"Does prisoner B have the money legally?"

"A better question might be, is anyone going to be looking for the money? A widow? A nephew? A bookie?"

"He didn't have any of those, and nobody knows about the money. Hypothetically."

"How about the lawyer who made the bank deposits?"

"He died three weeks ago."

"Then, Mr. Fratelli, prisoner B is laughing."

Fratelli laughed.

"His first move should be to go to a bank—a different bank—open a checking account with less than ten thousand dollars, then rent another safe-deposit box. After that, he could remove enough money periodically to support himself. Lashing out with large amounts could get him into trouble, as you might imagine. People will steal, after all."

"Yes, they will," Fratelli said.

"Ten thousand dollars is the magic number. If prisoner B banks that much, a form reporting it goes to the Internal Revenue Service, and, although they are said to have stacks of those forms, which they never read, it's not a good idea to generate such a form. After all, they may start reading faster, or they may teach a computer how to read them."

"That's good advice," Fratelli said.

"One other thing: if you should seek legal advice again, it might be in your interests to go to an attorney who has not heard this hypothetical story."

Fratelli stood up. "Thank you, Mr. Barrington," he said, offering his hand.

They shook, Fratelli left, and Stone opened a desk drawer and raked the little stack of hundreds into it.

Joan came in a moment later. "While you were talking to Mr. Fratelli, a secretary to the president of the United States called. You're invited to dinner tomorrow evening with President and Mrs. Lee at their apartment in the Carlyle."

Stone had not heard from the Lees in months. "Call back and say that I accept, with pleasure."

"You may bring a date."

Stone's current squeeze, the fashion designer Emma Tweed, had returned to her native London for a few weeks. "Say that I will come alone."

2

Stone wore a dark suit and a tie, because he didn't know who else was invited. He entered the Carlyle Hotel and got off the elevator at the penthouse level, where he was greeted by two Secret Service agents to whom he identified himself. That wasn't good enough; they went over him with the wand.

Katherine Rule Lee, now retired as director of Central Intelligence, answered the door. She was wearing tight jeans and a sweater, and she looked good in both. "Oh, Stone," she said, offering both cheeks to be kissed and giving him a hug, "nobody told you to dress down?"

"I didn't get that part of the message," Stone said, "but I'm not in the least uncomfortable."

"Will's watching the news. Knob Creek?"

"Perfect."

She pointed him at the living room, then went to the bar, while he continued.

Will Lee stood up and offered his hand. "Good to see you, Stone."

"And you, Mr. President."

"It's still Will."

"Good to see you, Will."

The president waved him to a chair, and Kate brought him his drink.

"They're showing excerpts from last night's Democratic campaign debate," Will said.

The three of them watched in silence until the program ended, then Will turned off the TV. "What did you think?" he asked Stone.

"I think there are at least three guys and one woman in that field who would make a good president."

"And?"

"And not one who could win against Taft Duncan," Stone said, referring to the Speaker of the House and presumptive Republican nominee.

"I'm afraid I agree," Will said. "What have you been up to, Stone?"

"I've just come back from Los Angeles, where my son, Peter, who recently graduated from Yale, has established himself on the Centurion Studios lot as a director. Dino's son, Ben, is his partner, and Peter's girlfriend, Hattie Patrick, writes the music for their films."

"I've met them all, last year at the opening of The Arrington," Will said. "Remember?"

"How could I forget?" Stone said.

They all shared a laugh.

"And what does the next year hold for you?"

"My year seems oddly empty, with Peter on the other side of the country, so I guess I'll have to think about practicing some law. Bill Eggers is making broad hints about my absences from the firm."

"Ah, yes, the partners won't want to share income with one of their number who is an absentee."

"Well, I have made a lot of rain," Stone said, "so I don't think I have to worry about them ganging up on me. What brings you to town?"

"Well, Kate is supposed to have an informal meeting with the board of Strategic Services tomorrow evening."

"Yes, I know. I'll be at the dinner." Kate had been invited to join the board of directors after Will left office.

"Our other reason for being here is to see you," Will said.

That puzzled Stone. "Oh?"

A man in a white jacket appeared and announced dinner, so they all went to a table with a spectacular view of the New York City skyline. Stone took a sip of his wine and waited for the president to finish his thought.

"Stone," Will said, "the day before yesterday I received a bundle of twenty letters, each of them written by a Democratic Party bigwig or a major campaign contributor, all individually composed but with the same subject. Can you guess what that subject was?"

"Well, it seems a little late in the game to get a constitutional amendment passed that would allow you to run for a third term."

"Thank God for that," Will said. "What they wanted was what they see as the next best thing." He sat silently and waited for the penny to drop.

It took Stone a moment. "Kate," he said finally. "They want Kate to run."

"Terrible idea, isn't it?" Kate said. She had been quiet until now.

"I think it's a terrific idea," Stone said. "But we're halfway through the primaries."

"My very point," Kate said, "but Will doesn't think that is an impediment."

"And I think Stone can figure out why," Will said.

"Because it looks like none of the candidates is going to have anything like a majority of the delegates going into the first ballot at the convention."

"Right you are."

"So, for the first time in I-don't-know-how-long, we'd have a brokered convention?"

"Since 1952," Will said, "when Adlai Stevenson got the nomination. We've had some close brushes since, but not the real thing. The primary process usually works to nominate a candidate."

Stone thought about that. "I was just thinking about Gore Vidal's play *The Best Man*, which dealt with that subject."

"Do you remember what each candidate needed to get the nomination?"

"Yes, the support of an earlier president, a Trumanesque figure."

"Right."

"Well, I don't think Kate would have any trouble getting the support of the sitting president, would she?"

"I'm trying to get him to withhold that support," Kate said.

"Actually, she doesn't have to try," Will said. "It would be politically impossible for me to support her."

"The Republicans would say you're trying to create a dynasty," Stone said.

"Not just the Republicans," Will replied. "A lot of Democrats, too, especially the three or four leading candidates."

"So you'd have to sit back, clam up, and wait for the convention to sort it out—after the first ballot."

"Exactly," Will said.

"You don't really think anybody's going to buy that, do you?" Stone asked.

"Of course not. All the commentators and not a few of the delegates will say I'm pulling all the strings."

"And how would you handle that?"

"By not pulling any strings."

"You mean you'd actually sit out the nomination without showing the slightest support for Kate?"

"Not so much as a nod or a wink," Will replied. "And not a word of advice to her or any of her supporters on obtaining the nomination. If she gets it, then I'll shoot my mouth off at every opportunity, of course, but after tonight, I won't say a word to her or anyone else on the subject, except 'no comment.'"

"You see how crazy this is?" Kate said.

"Kate," Stone said, "let me ask you a question: do you think you'd make a good president?"

"I think I'd make a sensational president," Kate said.

Stone turned to Will. "And, Will, do you think she can beat Taft Duncan?"

"In my last word on the subject, yes," Will said.

He looked at his watch. "I'd better hurry," he said. "I'm sneaking into the Blue Note to hear Chris Botti's last set."

"Can I come with you?" Stone asked. "I'm a big Chris Botti fan."

"No, you have a meeting to attend."

"What meeting is that?"

"In about an hour the twenty people who wrote me those letters are arriving here for a drink with Kate, so I can't be here. But you can."

Will got up and shook Stone's hand. "Hope to see you soon, Stone, but when I do, I don't want to hear a word about Kate's plans."

"Gotcha, Will." He and Kate watched him disappear out the door, two Secret Service agents close behind him.

"Well," Kate said, heaving a sigh, "now I have only you to help me greet the throng."

"What are you going to say to them?" Stone asked.

"I think it's better if you hear it at the same time they do," she said. "Now, if you'll excuse me, I have to get into something more presidential." She got up and left Stone to contemplate his dessert.